Anchored in Embo

by

Christine Campbell

Published in 2024 by FeedARead.com Publishing

First Edition

A CIP catalogue record for this title is available from the British Library.

Contents

For Gus My Best Friend

Thank you to all my loyal readers, whoever and wherever you are: thank you for choosing this book to read when there are so many out there to choose from. I deeply appreciate it.

A big thank you to Wendy Janes, who beta read, critiqued, advised, proofread and generally helped me in my writing, giving me of her time and energy so unstintingly to help me make my book better.

Thank you also to Claire Shankland for proofreading and to Aimee Campbell and Murdo MacKinnon for helping me with the artwork for the cover of this book.

As ever, very special thanks must go to Gus, my dear husband of more than fifty-five years, who has been a tremendous source of encouragement, support and brainstorming, as well as walking all the paths I was unable to walk in the name of research for this book.

Anchored in Embo

Eilidh

Blue sky thinking

'Blue sky thinking,' my Bill called it. He knew it was a bit of a cliché, but it worked for him.

Whenever I found him sitting somewhere, deep in thought, sitting perfectly still and composed, this was never the time for my usual chatter, not a time to ask what he wanted for dinner, or whether he wanted me to return his library books; not the time to talk about the trivia of ordinary life, the day to day.

No matter the weather, no matter his surroundings, if he had a problem to solve, or if he just wanted to allow his mind to reflect on something he'd found interesting, he sought out some solitude to ponder as deeply as he desired, and as far as he was concerned, there was a huge empty, deep blue sky overhead and he was thinking.

It seemed his thoughts were rarely jumbled and flitting about as mine tend to be, buzzing about like a busy swarm of bees.

Bill's were more like a murmuration of starlings. They swirled and swooped in his big, blue sky, always orderly, no matter how often they changed direction, and they only changed direction when he so directed them.

Or geese. Sometimes his thoughts resembled more the flight of geese. He brought them strictly under control and herded them into formation until his conclusion was reached.

I sigh.

I could never get my geese in a V, and my murmuration would inevitably disintegrate – with starlings flying here, there and everywhere, crashing into one another or falling from a grey sky.

Today, here in Embo, the sky is huge and truly is that beautiful deep blue. As I study the far horizon, that line between sky and sea hazy with heat, I find myself remembering Bill and finally, after forty years of marriage my memories are a murmuration – albeit not quite flying where I intended.

The children have brought me here, remembering holidays of their younger days, remembering the good times they'd had playing in the sand, jumping the waves, skiddling in rock pools looking for crabs and tiny prawns.

With Bill.

He'd run along the beach trailing a kite for them to chase, their joy and laughter lighting my world. Three pop bottles stuck in the sand made great wickets for a boisterous game of cricket – he always remembered to bring the bat. When they tired of that, he'd lead them into the cold North Sea to splash and swim and jump the waves – my signal to find the towels and put the kettle on for hot chocolate when they tumbled, laughing, into the caravan, racing to claim first shower.

For them, this seems a fitting way to remember their dad.

I wish I was at home where I could quietly whisper, 'Happy Anniversary,' to his memory.

Breathing

'Take three long, deep breaths,' Bill would say. 'Whenever life is overwhelming, whenever you find yourself not coping, stop, go to the open back door and breathe. Just remember to breathe,' he'd say. 'And remember, the long breath out is the important one. It's the calming, centring one. You'll automatically breathe the fresh air in again.'

So I breathe.

As I sit here on this amazing beach, I sit up straighter, wipe my face and breathe. I don't count the breaths – I forget to – but I take enough to steady myself, to steady my thinking.

To everyone else, I must seem an organiser, a coper, but that outward organisation was taught, learned from a young age. I think of myself as a 'scatterbrain', knowing myself as a dreamer who learned to stop dreaming.

I'm lost without Bill.

He was my anchor.

He grounded me.

Since he died three years ago, I have been adrift, lost at sea, so to say.

And here I am, in this gorgeous place, listening to the endless waves, blessed with a clear blue sky, space and solitude to ponder my future – and instead, I'm remembering the past.

My 'blue sky thinking', as endless as the sky and the sea, refusing to roll forward as the waves, but pulling me backwards as the receding tide.

Bill was my sounding board, my plumb line, and he's gone.

Deep breath, tears again, always tears, as endless as the waves and the sky.

My horizon misty.

Earlier, the heat of the late afternoon won and I removed my jacket, folded it neatly and placed it on the rocks as a comfortable, cushioned seat.

And here I sit, Queen Canute, endeavouring to hold back the relentless tide of memories that have rolled in since we arrived here earlier today.

More deep breaths.

I can do this.

I can marshal my thoughts, bring them into subjection and plan my future. I know I can.

'You need to focus first on something outside yourself,' Bill would say. 'Let the thoughts you seek creep quietly in behind whatever you're focusing on.'

'But I can't,' I'd wail.

'You can if you let yourself.' And he taught me to take my breaths, to roll my shoulders, straighten my back and look ahead. 'Into the distance or near at hand makes little difference,' he said. 'Just find something outside yourself to think about. You'll get there, Eilidh. I have faith you can do this.'

I close my eyes and thrill at the thought the man, my man, had faith in me.

I can do this.

So far, looking out into the distance led me where my thoughts have dwelt most of my waking moments for the past three years, so I look for something close at hand to study. And there it is, about five yards in front of me, a very old, encrusted anchor embedded in the sand.

I've seen the anchor before, on previous trips to Embo, but I'm sure it wasn't always so deeply embedded. I have memories of Bill and the children trying to dig it out – a fruitless exercise I'm certain many other families have embarked on – and it was in soft, dry sand. This year, the tides have been high, the winter winds fierce, the waves stronger, the sand stripped from further up the beach and the anchor's base further hidden by hard, wet sand.

Determined not to dwell on the past efforts of Bill and the girls, I study the anchor.

Where did it come from? What ship is it from? And why have I never bothered to ask these questions before?

Before – ah, before – I was always too busy to stop and wonder.

I would have been going to the shop almost as soon as we arrived, to buy buckets and spades, again – because each holiday, Bill liked to leave them for some other children to find 'as treasure' after we left for home.

Always too busy issuing an endless stream of instructions and platitudes, sorting out childhood scuffles, consoling weeping children, and wiping sand and tears from their eyes:

'Oh, don't do that, darling. Try not to throw the sand about. Look, Daddy's just emptying his spadeful to the side.'

'No, she didn't do it on purpose, Abigail. It was an accident.'

'Play nicely, Donna, or I'll have to take you up to the caravan for a nap.'

'Of course you can build sandcastles, if you'd rather.'

'No, Emily didn't stand on your sandcastle deliberately, darling. She didn't see it while she was working. Why don't you move over to the side, a bit further away here, and build another?'

'Well, why don't we go up to the caravan and start the lunch if that sandcastle is not the same?'

Busy checking from the caravan window that Bill was remembering he was an adult and in charge of the older two girls, not so engrossed in the task in hand he was unaware of them drifting away, off to paddle in the sea.

Too busy to think about the origins of a tatty old ship's anchor.

But the girls are full grown now and Bill's not here.

All I have is time.

Time to think.

I concentrate my focus again on the anchor.

Where did it come from? How did it get here? Was the ship driven onto the beach by the ferocity of the wind and the waves?

It could not have been by choice they anchored here, surely? No, the bay is far too wide, the stretch of sand far too long, though I doubt the crew would have seen much sand during the height of a storm. The tide would bring huge waves crashing onto the beach, the spume of them adding to the lack of visibility.

We were here during a storm, one year.

The waves were huge mountains of water, crashing into one another and onto the beach, the tide coming almost up to the stairs down from the caravan site. The rain came down in great, slanting torrents, thrown relentlessly at the caravan windows by a wind we felt rocking the sturdy, static caravan.

The girls were not often afraid of storms, delighting in the show put on by thunder and lightning, but they were afraid this time. They felt less safe when there was only a caravan shell between them and the elements.

When the worst of the storm had passed, Bill and I ventured onto the caravan balcony, holding tightly to one another not to be blown away, the girls clustering behind us just inside the French doors. It was, for all the world, as though we were peering into a ginormous glass of Guinness! The wind and the rain had caused the waves to stir the sand up into a thick, dark-beige, foamy head lying all the way along the beach, the water beyond it still unsettled with bubbles of foam rising through dark waters.

With a little coaxing, the girls also donned their anoraks, hoods up, holding tightly to one another and to us, to witness this phenomenon.

Hard to imagine the sea could ever become so treacherous, on a calm day, like today.

We used to walk along this beach, Bill and I, once the girls were a little older and settled in the caravan for the evening. We'd put one of their favourite DVDs on for them – after Bill solved the arguments over which one, by making a rota for the week's viewing, starting with Donna's choice, since she was the youngest, then Emily chose the next night and finally Abigail on the third. Rinse and repeat.

That way, we managed through the week's holiday comparatively squabble free in the evenings.

We'd see them settled, in their pyjamas, with popcorn and hot chocolate laid out on the little table in front of the telly – the popcorn evenly shared out, of course – and we'd head out for our evening walk along the beach, knowing they only had to holler on the walkie-talkie we left in Abigail's responsible care if they needed us – which they never did in all the years we holidayed here.

With each year, the routine was honed. If Donna fell asleep, the girls would gently settle her on the couch with a duvet and her rag-dog, for us to carry her to bed when we returned and, if they had not been much impressed with the wee one's choice, they would swap the video for another.

It became easier each year for me to relax and enjoy the evening perambulations, as Abigail showed herself more and more responsible.

This was the time Bill and I could chat about the day's activities and slip into deeper conversation after that was done, often about what he was reading once we went to bed – I usually fell asleep with whatever book I'd thought I might read lying open on my chest.

This stretch of beach was where Bill coached me about his type of 'blue sky thinking', which I've come to realise is too organised and further from the original definition than mine. I sigh and raise my eyes to look at the expanse of clear blue above me. Deep breath, try again! Concentrate on the anchor as a means of switching from the past, through the present and on to the future.

No more 'grey sky thinking' that goes nowhere, and in my case can very easily leave me in the doldrums.

Deep breathing and 'blue sky thinking'.

Memories and decisions

Thank goodness I'd just wiped my face of tears, blown my nose and taken three good, deep breaths before a gentleman passes in front of me on his way along the beach.

"Afternoon!" he says with a nod in my direction.

I must seem very rude because I don't return his greeting but quickly lower my head, afraid my face will still display the traces of the grief I succumbed to for some time before he appeared.

So much for 'blue sky thinking'. Thus far, the anchor has miserably failed to move my thinking forward. I must have practically used up all the available oxygen, I've resorted to so many of Bill's deep breaths. If only he was here for me to tell him his theory is rubbish. If only he was here.

Three years of grief and I am little further forward in living without him.

True, at home it's getting easier. Eighteen months ago, Abigail ruthlessly 'helped' me clear Bill's clothes out of his wardrobe and drawers. While she was taking the first of the bin sacks to her car to go to the charity shop, I raked through another of them, rescuing the things I'd begged her to let me keep, hiding them under the bed when she came back for the next two.

But I'm grateful to her for doing it – let's be honest, she did more than just 'help' me, she did it. If it wasn't for her, everything would still be there and I would still cry every time I opened one of his drawers or his wardrobe, before climbing into bed and pulling the duvet over my head.

The girls had unanimously agreed an intervention was called for. Abigail volunteered for that particular task, her being the most likely to achieve it without ending up under the duvet with me.

I still cry into the pullover I'd rescued of his. Whenever I think I might forget the smell of him, and the feel of his arms around me of an evening, I pull the jersey over my head, cuddle into it and climb into bed to wallow in self-pity – but not nearly so often now, now his smell has long since evaporated into the ether and the soft wool no longer reminds me how it felt with his form wearing it and him wrapping me in his arms.

Emily and Abigail took it upon themselves to arrange for his favourite armchair to be carted off to the dump – all it was fit for – and they rearranged the furniture to make it less obvious where it had sat for more years than I care to remember. They rearranged the furniture in the bedroom too, decorated the room and encouraged me to buy new bedding and curtains, which I did willingly enough, having never particularly liked the ones we'd had for years. Bill tended to have stronger likes and dislikes than I did, so I'd just fall in with whatever he pointed out to me. It never seemed to matter enough to squabble over. So, it was not difficult to watch the girls rip off the old wallpaper and make way for the new rolls of softer, plainer ones I was drawn to.

Truth to tell, it did all help and it has been getting easier.

I thought I'd be okay for this trip. I thought a walk down memory lane would be more pleasant than painful. Given time, perhaps it will. By the end of the week, perhaps I'll be able to appreciate the natural beauty of the area without always looking for Bill here, listening for the sound of his voice.

When I think about how much easier it's getting at home, how I have managed to stop looking for him sitting in his old chair of an evening now it's not there, how I've stopped wondering if there is anything of his needing a wash, stopped taking two plates out of the cupboard at meal times, setting the table for two, I realise I have, in fact begun to 'move on', as it's so often called.

So there, three years of grief and I *am* further forward in living without him.

I'll never stop loving him, but perhaps, through time, I'll stop missing him when I go somewhere he used to go with me. Perhaps.

Meantime, I need to make some decisions about my future – and this is why and where I need to focus my mind.

This is why I came down to the beach while Abigail and Trevor went back to Tain for the supermarket shopping. They asked if I wanted to go, but really, I was tired enough after four hours sitting in the car.

Bill and I always used to pack the car with enough food to last us for the first few days because neither of us relished the straight turn around back to Tain, or the trawl round a supermarket before we'd had a walk along the beach, no matter what time we arrived here.

Trevor, of course, didn't want to delay getting here, so he picked me up from the house. 'Ten o'clock, sharp!' he'd insisted. 'That will give us four hours for the drive with time to stop for a quick picnic lunch in the car and a toilet stop, if necessary, and still be there to have early access to the caravan. Let's face it, they're sure to have it cleaned and ready before the four o'clock official entry time.'

As it happened, we had to wait for another hour after we arrived for the caravan to be ready. I didn't say anything, but I'd rather have had a cuppa somewhere to break the journey, but that was not in Trevor's plan. It had been, 'Right, back in the car,' after we'd all been toileted in Aviemore. My back-seat companion, Forrest, seemed used being ordered about: he climbed in the car without a murmur and plugged in his earphones for the remainder of the trip. In all his eleven years, I don't know if I've ever managed much conversation with my grandson after he grew out of the baby talk chatter.

I sigh.

That sort of regimented journey would have driven Bill crazy. He liked the travelling to be part of the holiday, with frequent stops wherever we chose and for whatever reason we requested them. 'A toilet stop, if necessary,' Trevor had said. *If* necessary. Toilet stops were frequent when the girls were young, and Bill took delight in finding off-road villages or tearooms where we could make them. He made any slight detour a fun part of the journey.

Ah, Bill. Bill.

Today – perhaps it was weariness from the journey – as we turned into the narrow road down to the caravan park, instead of that glorious moment of joy, an overwhelming feeling of loss arose in me, landed on my chest and stole my breath.

The bright yellow flowers of the gorse, which I always loved when we came in springtime, are no longer in flower, it being early August, and the bareness of the roadside bushes matches my mood.

It took a Herculean effort not to give vent to my anguish at the memories of Bill's victorious whoops of delight as we entered the reception car park. His joyous, 'We made it! We're here, girls!' rang in my ears as Abigail silently made her way into the building to get the caravan keys.

I thought of walking down to the sea front while we waited for the caravan to be ready for us, but found myself overcome by a terrible inertia, so stayed there in the car with the family, while Trevor silently sulked, Abigail dozed in the front seat, with Forrest not so much as looking up from his device.

An hour later, after my bags were brought in from the car, I unpacked my things and found places in the cupboards for the different items, making the tiny bedroom as homely and comfortable as I could, all the time promising myself a late afternoon walk on the beach before dinner time, a chance to stretch my legs after the journey and a chance to examine and make sense of my feelings of overwhelm.

I shiver, only partly because the wind is getting up and clouds are hiding the sun. There is still plenty of blue sky. Worth waiting until the sun warms me up again. I'm not ready to go back in yet.

Giving myself a shake and sitting up straighter, I try again for the 'blue sky thinking'.

The girls think the house is now too big for me – for just one. They tell me they're looking ahead. 'Let's face it, Mum,' Abigail said – ever the direct, practical one of my daughters – 'You're not getting any younger. The time will come when it's harder to go up and down the stairs, harder to vacuum them, harder to keep everywhere clean.'

I hated to admit to her I don't often vacuum or dust – only when I notice it really needs doing – however, she's right, it is getting harder to vacuum the stairs. I've been putting it down to lack of energy because I'm still grieving, but I have noticed.

But it's my home!

It's been my home for forty years. We moved in right after our honeymoon. Can they really expect me to give it up? With all its memories? It doesn't matter that it's too big, that the empty rooms echo with loss, that the house needs more care than I feel I can give it. It would feel like I was leaving Bill behind, and that's too much to ask. Can't they see that?

It was our home.

It's still our home.

I can't imagine living without the echoes.

And where would I go? Into some plain little flat in a characterless newly built row of buildings? With no garden, no view, nothing familiar to hang my memories on?

No. No. No!

I try to stand up to dust off my joggers, in a gesture of decisiveness, but the effort of unkinking my hips proves too difficult, so I pat my knees instead. Decision made.

I'm not selling my home.

There. That was easy. Didn't require 'blue sky thinking', or much of any thinking, in the event. Perhaps I needed to be away from home to see things clearly, to put things in perspective.

I feel quite satisfied with myself. I achieved what I set out to do. Made a decision about my future.

I'm not going to be persuaded into selling the house, no matter how impractical the decision, it is finally made.

I'm staying put.

Making a new friend

Having dispensed with the need for further concentrated thinking, I stretch and shake my shoulders, as my mind drifts in its comfortable, aimless way.

Looking beyond the anchor, way out across the sea, I wonder, if I could sail in a straight line, how far till I could land on the opposite beach, and where would that be? We're pretty far north, up here, so, Norway, perhaps? I wonder how many times I'd have to raise and lower the sails to catch the wind. How many miles I'd have to row when the sails had nothing to catch. Surely, altogether, several hundred miles.

Closing my eyes, I try to imagine that little sailboat when it's becalmed and the sails hang lifeless. Imagine myself rowing, rowing, rowing for days. I'd need to sleep, I'd need to eat, go to the toilet. I'd need a good supply of fresh water. I shiver. It would be cold, terribly cold.

Opening my eyes. Looking at the enormous expanse of water, I shiver again.

It would be incredibly lonely out there. Frightening. People really do things like that. I search inside myself, knowing I couldn't do it. To save my life? Hmmm, maybe, but I don't know.

I'm aware I'm losing myself in imagining the scenario. I feel tired, my arms are sore. But what will happen if I stop rowing? Endless sea, endless sky, would I go mad? Am I going mad? Losing my reason?

I can't stop thinking about that long, arduous journey and I can't stop identifying with the loneliness.

I've been so incredibly lonely as I've endured a real, long, arduous journey these past three years; through rough waters, with short periods of calm before I hit rough water again.

I wonder if I'd meet anyone on such a journey across the North Sea? Ships that pass in the night, perhaps.

It's been like that, since Bill died, people coming and going in my life, they might pop in for a cuppa and what they intend as an encouraging chat, but as soon as I wave them off, I'm alone again, navigating an endless sea of mourning.

While I sit in peaceful contemplation of my imagined journey across the vast sea, the wind drops to a soft breeze and the waves still to gently lapping against my boat.

Gradually, the line twixt sea and sky becomes so blended as to make indistinguishable the one from the other, the fading light making it simple to imagine celestial clarity slipping into the bounty set below it. And a longing rises within me, to put my thoughts on paper, poetry enticing images to come forward from the deep recesses in my soul, until at last I find what I know can only be a temporary peace.

Back here, on the beach, the late afternoon sun has hidden behind the gathering clouds and I'm beginning to shiver. While deep in thoughts, memories and imaginings, it was getting cooler, and now I need to move. It's even beginning to drizzle and there's a rainbow further to my right.

Dragging myself back to reality I realise I probably need to warm up in the caravan. I shiver again, this time, not only with being cold. Oh dear! How am I going to survive a week in Trevor and Abigail's caravan? Maybe I should invest in a pair of headphones to plug into my phone too. Perhaps Forrest's idea is not such a bad one, after all. A bit anti-social, true, but not a bad idea.

It's not that they argue all the time, because they don't; not even that I don't love them both, because I do; it's just that Trevor finds it hard to engage in conversation and Abigail insists on trying to encourage him to do so. It's painful to be part of the struggle and I understand why Forrest prefers his headphones so no one will try to chat with him.

I sigh again and look at how far the sun has moved and work out they could all be back by now and the shopping put away, so at least I might have avoided that bit of supreme organising by Trevor.

With a long, last look at the North Sea, enjoying its calmness and the last warming rays of the emerging sun, I imagine the rowing being easier now. Perhaps it would be okay to rest for a bit, to indulge my mind as it slips in and out of reality. I sit back for a while, allowing myself the sheer luxury of drifting with the tide, not thinking, not worrying, just *being*.

Dreamy stillness envelops me.

"Are you okay?" A kind, concerned voice draws me back from that fanciful, dreamlike place my mind had wandered into, back to cold reality.

I see the same legs that greeted me before. Well, it wasn't really his legs that made the greeting, but it was all I'd seen after the 'Afternoon!' greeting, with my head quickly lowered the first time he passed.

"I only ask because you've been sitting here for quite some time and it's getting cold. Plus you seemed rather distressed when I first passed."

This time, when I look up, I see the face matches the voice; a pleasant face and a pleasant voice. Kindly, concerned. I try to reply, but it seems my voice has disappeared with my tears. I cough, clear my throat and try again. "Thank you, yes, I'm okay, thank you," I say as I make the first, unsuccessful, attempt to get up.

"I don't wish to intrude, but I'll just wait till I see you're able to get off that rock, if that's okay with you."

Second attempt aborted. My hips are totally seized and my muscles have atrophied it seems. “Ah, yes. I think I might have sat too long.”

The gentleman looks at his watch. “Well, it’s a good bit more than two hours since I passed the first time, even longer since I first noticed you, so yes, I’m guessing it has been too long sitting on a low, cold rock.” He grimaces comically, making me laugh. “If you don’t think it too presumptuous …” He offers his arm.

Polite, unassuming. He really is a gentleman.

“Thank you. I’d be grateful for your help.” I take the proffered arm and he helps me to my feet, then shakes out my jacket and helps me put it on.

Definitely a gentleman.

“Is your caravan far along the beach?” He looks up at the row of holiday homes. “Assuming you are holidaying here.”

I look too. “Hmm! I don’t think so. To be honest, I don’t remember. We only arrived earlier this afternoon.” I pull a face. “I haven’t had time to get my bearings yet.”

He chuckles.

A gentleman with a lovely smile and a lovely chuckle.

“In which case, if you can remember in which direction you approached the anchor, I could escort you to the nearest set of stairs up from the beach and send you on your way?”

As we walk, I realise the nearest set is not the stairs I came down. “I’m afraid the steps are further along the beach by quite a distance,” I say.

“That’s okay. I’m going that way myself. If you prefer, I can walk along behind you or I can have the pleasure of your company as we walk. But, one way or the other, I feel duty bound to see you safely off the beach and on the way to your caravan.”

“Thank you. I do appreciate it. I’m not actually feeling so good, having sat so long, and I should probably have brought a bottle of water.”

He takes a water bottle from the pocket of his walking jacket. "I'm so sorry. I had the last of mine a wee bittie ago."

"A refillable water bottle. A good idea. Saves plastic."

"That was my thinking too. Look, I have another at home." He holds this one out to me. "Please. You have this one. A good wash and it'll be good as new, then you'll have it for your next walk."

"Oh, I couldn't …"

"Sure you could. Go on. That could be my good deed for the day." He smiles.

Such a kind smile.

Such kind eyes.

I find myself wanting to hold their gaze.

"Thank you." I take the bottle. It feels good in my hand, with comfortable ridges for my fingers, another for my thumb. A good colour too. Deep blue.

The colour of the evening sky.

When I look up to admire it, I find there is a wash of pink appearing. Blue and pink, beautiful together. Looking up, rather than at my feet, which I have been doing, feeling uncertain of my steps, I see the sun is getting low in the sky at the far end of the beach.

As we walk along in that direction, the colours deepen and change, going through shades I'd love to mix on my palette – if I had one. I used to have one. A very long time ago. I used to paint. Watercolours. I'd forgotten I used to paint.

Something is happening to me since I stepped onto this beach.

I feel different.

As well as the memories of Bill, of when we used to come here, there are memories going way, way back, before Bill. "Poetry, painting, dancing, singing, things I used to enjoy. I'd forgotten." Realising I'd spoken my thoughts aloud, I look at him in alarm. "Oops! Didn't mean to say that out loud. Do you think I'm losing it?"

He smiles. “No, I think you’re finding it. Finding the you, you used to be, by the sound of it.”

“It’s this place. The sea is so vast and beautiful, the sky so big, the air so fresh, it gives this amazing sense of freedom. Freedom to be the someone I’d forgotten I was.” Again I look to make sure he hears me. “Please don’t misunderstand, I had a great life with Bill.”

“Your husband?”

"Yes, my husband. We’d been married for what would have been forty years this week. We were happy, brought up three beautiful, talented daughters, had a nice home, plenty of friends, a good life. But he’s no longer here – he died three years ago – and life feels very empty.”

We stopped walking and I can see that, not only has he heard me, he’s also understood. Two very different things.

“I feel as though the show is over, but I’ve been sitting staring at an empty, bare stage. Seeing the scenery for what it is, a passing illusion. All I’m left with is a pleasant feeling that I enjoyed the show.”

He nods, his brow furrowed in thought.

“I’ve been sitting in an empty theatre for three years.” I sigh.

We walk a few more steps in silence. I’m thinking about what I’ve said aloud, something I hadn’t even thought before, but describes what I’ve been doing this past three years very well. “I wonder what I’m waiting for.”

“Three years, in one way is no time at all, but in another way, perhaps it’s time enough.” He looks back at me with earnest concern in his expression. “Perhaps what you’re feeling is that it’s time for the next act, or a new show?”

Now, there’s a thought! “Yes, I do believe you might be right.” Quite a thought. Quite a new thought.

We walk on for a while, until we reach where I think the wooden beach stairs I came down are hidden behind the scrub growing around them. “Thank you so much for listening to this silly, dehydrated, old lady and for seeing me home." I indicate this is where I need to go up to the caravans.

"Do you need any help to climb the steps?"

"Oh, thank you, but I'm sure I'll be fine now." I wave him away. "Once I got walking, I soon loosened up."

"Well, if you're sure. But just for the record, you are not silly and not old. You may have become a little dehydrated, and you are certainly a lady, and I have taken great pleasure in your company."

I feel heat rising up my neck.

Such a lovely thing for a stranger to say to me.

He clearly intends to hang around until he sees I'm true to my word, so I start walking towards where I suspect the stairs I came down might be hidden, and I try not to grunt and groan with the effort of climbing them. When I reach the top, I turn around and my gentleman is continuing on his way and is already too far along the beach for me to call my thanks.

Not an Abbie

While I am searching my mind for which caravan number is ours, Abigail appears round the corner of one I'm approaching. "Mum! Where have you been? I was getting worried!"

"I didn't mean to be gone so long. I was walking on the beach."

"Well I can see that! But you left at the same time as we went shopping. The shopping's all put away, and the dinner's been ready for a while. I was getting really anxious."

"You said."

"Forrest and Trevor have gone looking for you up at the reception area in case you were up there."

"Sorry. I wasn't." As I hang my head like the naughty child she's making me feel, I give myself a shake and lift it again, squaring my shoulders. No! This is all wrong, I'm not ready to be an old lady to be looked after and restricted by my children. Perhaps the time will come, but it isn't yet. I walk past her into the caravan, get myself a glass and take a long drink of water.

"And you left your phone! I kept trying your number, thinking you just weren't answering, then Forrest heard it ringing in your room."

I give my newly acquired water bottle a thorough rinsing with hot then cold water. "Sorry, I forgot to put it in my pocket." Leaving the bottle on the draining board to dry, I turn to go to my room, via the toilet.

Abigail softens when she looks closely at me. "Oh, Mum, you look terrible! You're grey and drawn and look exhausted. Please try to remember to take your phone. You need to be able to reach us if you feel unwell or anything happens to you."

"I'm sorry. I'll make sure I take it in future."

"Thank you, Mum." She draws me in for a hug. "I was genuinely afraid perhaps you'd had an accident somewhere, twisted your ankle or something like that. We wouldn't have known where to look."

"You're right, of course. Sorry, love." I kiss her on the cheek as she releases me. "I'll go and wash up for dinner, shall I?"

I take my time in the bathroom, reminding myself that Abigail is right. I was inconsiderate. But she was not always so sharp. I know she misses her father terribly. She doesn't show it by weeping and wailing, but during the past two or three years, I've watched her become more and more unhappy and discontent. Losing Bill may not be all it's about, but I feel sure it hasn't helped.

When I've tried to ask if everything's okay, she snaps back at me that it's fine, but I'm far from convinced, and I'd love to gain back the close relationship we once had. This could be one advantage of being on holiday together, where there's more chance of getting her to myself, perhaps on the beach, when she's not rushing to do something else. I've already had a genuine hug from her. That has to bode well for the week we're housed here together.

I'm realising Embo is a great place to be when you've thinking to do, even if you have trouble keeping your thoughts in any way orderly. There's certainly plenty of blue sky. It seems to stretch forever, uninterrupted. And, down on the beach, there's little distraction. I'm sure it would be a good place for a confidential talk.

Perhaps, if I don't ask what's wrong, but simply start a light, casual conversation that becomes companionable and easy, she might open her heart to me like she used to before she married, before she had someone else to confide in. Sometimes you need another woman's ear. Sometimes, you need your mum, or so I'm told.

"Dishing out!" comes the call.

Dinner is a silent affair, with only the sound of the waves outside to accompany the scrape and chink of cutlery. Forrest can hardly wait to be excused to get back to his room and his games screen, Trevor sits himself in front of the television, while I help Abigail clear the table and wash the dishes.

"D'you fancy a wee walk on the beach?" I ask when the dishes are all put away.

"Are you not too tired, Mum? You're hardly back from the last one?"

"True, but I'm happy to join you if you'd enjoy a walk."

"Thanks, Mum, but I think I'm too bushed. It was such an early start this morning and what with all the travelling and shopping and everything, I think I'd rather sit and have a cuppa, then go to bed and read my book." She looks at me, her expression softening. "Maybe tomorrow? Before Emily and the kids get here?"

"That would be nice, love." I'm not really disappointed because I'm pretty tired myself. The idea of bed with a book, after a wee cup of tea, is quite inviting. The offer was made genuinely, as a start to the 'Abigail project', as I've called it in my mind, and at least it's opened up the possibility of tomorrow.

Abigail. It's funny, Bill and I always thought we'd shorten her name to Abbie, and we did when she was little, but, when she started school, she intimated she wanted to be called by her 'proper' name. So, Abigail she was from then on, and, truth be told, she is much more an Abigail than an Abbie.

Morning shock

Abigail takes the opportunity after breakfast to badger me about selling the house again. When I tell her I'm not sure I'm going to, she looks over at Trevor and raises an eyebrow.

"We were assuming you were finding the house too big and were sure you would sell," he says. "Only, you see we were hoping you might want to exchange houses with us."

This has caught me completely by surprise and, to my shame, without engaging anything resembling sensitivity, I retort, "With you? Why on earth would I want to exchange houses with you?"

"Well," he says, having the grace to look a little abashed. "Yours has three bedrooms where ours only has two ..."

"But I don't even like your house! The rooms are smaller and darker."

"But it's all on one level. You wouldn't have the stairs," Abigail says. "There's a clean, well-maintained lift up to the flat."

"And that's about all it has going for it. I'm sorry, but it has no garden, no outlook, and I don't know anyone else in the area."

"You'd soon make friends, Mum."

"That may be, but the answer is unequivocally, no! Even if I did want to sell, which I don't think I do, it would not be to buy your flat. I'm sorry." In order to curb my tongue, I leave them in the living area and go through to my tiny bedroom.

I'm stunned. Is that what all the months of persuasion were about? It wasn't truly about helping me look ahead to prepare for when I couldn't manage the house. It was about them getting their hands on it!

If there was more than two steps I could take in the caravan bedroom, I'd be pacing. As it is I'm smoothing and re-smoothing my duvet cover, thumping the pillows into shape, and looking for what else I can shake up.

There's a tap on the door. Without waiting for an answer, Abigail pushes it open. "I'm sorry, Mum, we didn't mean to upset you. Trevor thought he was being helpful, suggesting the idea. I said he could always ask, but I didn't think you'd be interested."

"And I'm not!"

"I see that, Mum." She sits on one of the beds. "I'm afraid Trevor didn't waste time on niceties, he just went in for the kill, tact and sensibility not being his strong points."

I'm aware of that and usually I would have handled his tactlessness better, but I was taken totally off-guard – and it was my home he was tactlessly talking about. "Is that what you're hoping too? That I'll hand the family home over to you?"

She shakes her head. "No, not at all. I'd hate to live in our family house without you and Dad in it. It would feel empty and awful. But I do think you should think about moving somewhere smaller. Somewhere of your own choosing." She waits, and when I say nothing, she says, "Promise me you'll at least consider it a bit more. Please?"

I can see this matters to her. I can see the worry and pain on her face. Trevor is not known for his sensitivity and diplomacy and I see she regrets the whole earlier episode, so I relent. "Promise," I say, opening my arms for a hug.

It seems my decision that I'm not going to sell up and move house is not as firm as it felt last night, even before this latest episode was added into the mix. Having had a night where sleep in the little, single caravan bed was hard won, I tossed about a fair bit, thinking and rethinking my decision.

The conversation I'd had with the gentleman I'd met on the beach really set me off. Was it time for, not only a new act, as in learning to go on as before but without Bill, but time for a whole new play? A complete change of setting in a complete change of story?

As it turns out, Abigail and I don't manage a walk together because Forrest and Trevor are keen for everyone to go to the pool for a swim. They had booked the session yesterday evening before teatime, when they went up to the centre to see if I was there. Abigail hadn't realised they'd booked it until they said this morning.

I'm afraid, I decline to join them, swimming not really appealing to me. In fact, I haven't owned a swimming costume for years, not since Bill died. He and I used to go to our local pool every Thursday evening with a group of friends. We all used to go for a light supper together afterwards. It was all couples and, since I was so brutally 'uncoupled', I've had no desire to join the group or to swim, no matter how they tried to assure me I'd be welcome. My swimming costume was getting old anyway, so I threw it in the bucket so the others would stop pestering me. Three years later and I still have no desire to swim without him.

After the family head up to the pool, I fill my lovely new water bottle with deliciously cold water from the tap, gather a cushion to take to the beach with me, because the wind is a little chill and I'm going to need my jacket on, rather than under my derrière.

As soon as I step out of the caravan, I feel myself unclench. Taking one of Bill's recommended deep breaths, I feel the fresh, sea air revive me, and find my way to the nearest stairs to head down to the beach for another good think.

At least Abigail and I connected again. That was nice. And I do believe her that she has no interest in taking over the family home. I'm happy about that because I would find it almost impossible to visit her there if she did. Her ideas and mine of home decor and usage are very different. Not that the decor in my home is really mine, as I realised yesterday when deep in thought further along the beach.

I stop half-way down the wooden steps.

Why had that not mattered before, but it does now?

It's strange that I am only now realising Bill had very definite ideas about what he liked and didn't like and, since I wasn't sure what I wanted, I went along with his taste until I thought it was mine too.

I really did.

I thought it was mine too!

Starting to descend again, I am halted after two more steps. What else had I just gone along with that I don't have to any more?

Hmm! I continue to the bottom of the flight. Something else to think about.

New scene, new act, new play – perhaps it's time to paint my own scenery too.

Hurting for the anchor

Because I'm having an earlier walk today, I don't expect to see my kind gentleman, but I find myself looking around for him all the same. I'd like to meet him again sometime, just to say a proper thank you – though I have to say, I did find him pleasant company for that short while yesterday and wouldn't mind having his company again.

My rock seat, looking out on the anchor, is occupied by a young couple watching their children play around the anchor. They aren't trying to dig it up, but they're hitting it with their spades. Anger rises in me, unbidden. "Oh, don't do that," I find myself saying, as I hurry forward. "That poor anchor has gone through many, many storms. We need to look after it. It's very old."

The children stare at me a moment, then continue their attack.

I look to the parents and they shrug. It shocks me that they see no harm in what their children are doing. I daresay it possibly stops them from taking lumps out of one another, but I am aghast at the destructive attitude these young children are displaying.

Not knowing what else I can do, I walk on along the beach with a very heavy heart, surprising myself that I have taken it so personally, wondering if I would have, had I not already weathered a bit of a shock with Trevor's declared intention.

I find another flattish rock further along and further back, claim it with the cushion I'd had the foresight to bring, and lower myself onto it, the thought occurring to me that this rock is considerably lower than the one I had so much trouble getting myself up from yesterday.

It's while I'm sitting there, a little while later, listening to Mozart's Clarinet Concerto on my phone – which I assured Abigail this morning was in my pocket – when my kind gentleman comes along again. Lost in the music, I have my eyes closed, so, once again, I am taken by surprise by his, "Good morning!"

Fumbling quickly to grab my phone, trying to find how to turn the music off, I look up and smile.

"No, please don't turn it off. I love this piece," he says, indicating he would like to sit beside me on a nearby rock.

I nod, and give up the attempt to find where to click, and we listen to the rest of the track together.

"A beautiful piece," he says. "Mozart's Clarinet Concerto, if I'm not mistaken."

"You're right, of course. A favourite of mine."

"Mine too, as it happens. It was a rare treat to hear it as I came along the beach."

"Oh, dear, was I playing it too loudly?"

"Not at all! Though it did seem to scare off the anchor vandals."

I look back along the beach and, sure enough, the family are packing up and walking back to the stairs up to the caravans.

Putting my hand to my mouth, I can't contain the delighted giggle that escapes.

Glancing over, I see he sports a broad grin.

"Did you see what they were doing?" I ask.

"I did, and no ancient monument should have to suffer such treatment. Had I been closer, I would have tried to dissuade them from their exercise, but I was pleased to see you try."

"Thank you, but to no avail, I'm afraid."

"At least they've stopped, and, as far as I can see from here, the anchor seems unscathed."

"I do worry, someday soon, someone will manage to break the top off. The neck of the curve seems to have corroded so much it's worn quite thin."

"While that is undeniably true, I think, since it's coped with a century and a half of abuse, it has a good chance of coping for a while yet."

"Oh, is that how long you think it's been there?"

"Well, it's reckoned the anchor probably came from the Prussian Barque, *Vesta,* which was wrecked in December 1876, in the early morning hours."

"Oh, that does make it almost 150 years old, as you say. Do you know how it got there?"

"I believe it came ashore in a fierce storm, some 300 yards north of the village."

"Is there any record of what happened to the passengers and crew? I hate to imagine them all drowning in a sea so angry it caused the wreckage of their boat."

"Well, fortunately, it being a coal-carrying barge, there were no passengers aboard and it is reported the Embo fishermen rescued all eleven crew. That's my understanding, anyway. Perhaps you could look it up somewhere and find out more and even check if the story was true, if you wanted."

"No, I'll take your word for it. You sound to have investigated it already." I laugh. "I'm happy to believe no lives were lost."

"So the story goes, anyway. Apparently she foundered in a particularly bad storm. In fact, the records show there was another wreck off Dornoch beach that same night. Sadly it seems only one of that crew was rescued."

"Oh, that's terribly sad. You say the Embo fishermen rescued them off the Prussian ship, I didn't realise Embo used to be a fishing village. I suppose I never thought about it."

"Yes, back then, fishing was a mainstay in Embo, but they still didn't have a proper harbour or much of a pier.

You can't help wondering, if there'd been a harbour, maybe the *Vesta* could have made it to shelter."

"So, did they just fish off the beach?"

"Herring fishing was a major industry all up and down the east coast here, going through a bit of a boom starting in the mid-19th century, so the Embo fishermen would have been keen to profit from that. Without a proper harbour and not much of a pier, the Embo fishing boats would have had to be small and light enough for the men to drag up and down the beach, and apparently, once they were dragged down the beach and launched into the sea each morning, the fishwives used to carry the men out to the boats to keep their feet dry."

"Wow, that's devotion."

"Aye, the men would have been wearing thick, woollen socks to keep their feet warm. You being a housewife and mother would know yourself, once wool gets a soaking, it takes a while to dry. So the fishwives would be keen to make sure their men survived the fishing and not freeze to death in the effort to catch their livelihood."

I nod, imagining the woman knitting the socks and being happy to help them stay dry when worn, seeing with my mind's eye the interesting spectacle of the willing piggyback rides down to the boats.

Frowning, I ask, "Is it just my imagination or rose-tinted memories, but did there not used to be a lot more sand on this beach, years ago?"

"You're right, there was. Sadly, due to one thing or another, Embo beach has lost four or five feet of sand over the past few decades."

"I thought so. There seems to be so many more rocky areas exposed – and I mean *so* many more. Although there are still large areas of sand, I used to think of more or less the whole beach as deep, dry sand with a few rock pools thrown in to make it more interesting and exciting for the children. Now it seems more rock than sand."

"It does. I agree."

"Still beautiful, still glorious, just different."

"Yes."

"It was thinking about the fishermen dragging their boats up above the high tide mark that brought it to my mind. I'm sure that task would have been so much easier on deep sand than bumping over slippery seaweed-covered rocks."

"I've no doubt it would have been. Plus, nowadays the tide travels far further up the beach than it used to, even in the ten years I've lived here."

"Can we blame it on climate change, do you think?"

"Why not? They tell us tides are rising and coastal land is being eroded. Embo beach would seem to bear that out."

I look out across the water. "Were the fishermen out there with fishing lines or nets, do you think?"

He nods. "Mainly fishing lines in the old days, I believe. Another of the women's responsibilities, back then, was digging for bait, lugworms and the like, and baiting long lines of hooks with that and some shellfish. The men would string the lines out behind or sometimes between the boats. The fishwives would also prepare and salt some of the fish the men caught, carrying them to market in large baskets, called creels, slung on their backs."

"Goodness. A woman's life must have been hard back then, with no washing machines, tumble driers, modern fabrics and the like, never mind digging for bait – not a job I've tried or ever fancied. As for carrying my husband, he was a good six or seven inches taller than I am and built to play rugby, so no, I don't think so."

We laugh then sit quietly for a while.

I've no way of knowing what my new-found friend is thinking, but I'm thinking about what it must have been like to live in this little village on the edge of the beach, living off what could be gleaned from it and the fishing out in the bay.

"Thank you for explaining all that to me."
"My pleasure."
"I've holidayed up here so many times in the past, and I'd never thought to attempt finding out about this village that has such a dear place in my heart." I look at him. "D'you know, I'm coming to realise I've never thought enough about enough."
"Many people don't."
"Most of my life, I just 'did'. Working, caring for Bill and the three girls, back to work part-time after Donna started school. I went through life without being interested or curious enough about other things to find out about them."
"Three children." He shrugs. "You have had a busy life."
"I've lived a small life."
A tiny life, I realise now. Slavishly following the same self-imposed routine, day in and day out, never stopping for long enough to remember I had interests, hobbies, passions even, as I was growing up. Why didn't I incorporate some of them into my life? I'm sure I could have, if I'd thought of it.
For so many years, Bill and the girls were the focal point of my life. I took it hard when, one-by-one the girls grew up and left home, making my life shrink even more.
Why didn't I listen to the well-meaning advice of the magazines I read when at the hairdresser's, or in the dentist's waiting room? They all spoke of what they called 'empty nesters', spoke of the need for them to find new interests, take up a new hobby, even if it's only gardening or going for long walks. Why didn't I even try to turn my attention to what I needed to make my life larger?
In fairness to myself I did go regularly to a yoga class, which I quite enjoyed, though it only aided my need for routine, it being more or less the same, week after week. I used to hear the music from the dance class along the corridor as I passed before and after my class, and

longed to dance with the class inside. But I never did. That seemed too frivolous a use of my time when I had to get home to make the dinner. So I kept to the routine I had established, but my heart wanted to dance. Looking back, it seems sad I chose to ignore it. But I realised joining would mean meeting a whole class-full of people, people who would want to become new friends and I didn't really have time to make new friends.

Oh, why didn't I look outwards, instead of inwards?

When there was only Bill left to care for at home, instead of enriching my own life, I concentrated on his. What Bill needed, what would please him, what he wanted to do when he retired. Nothing wrong with that, I was a dutiful wife, a good wife, I think. I suppose the only thing that was really mine at that time, was the yoga class I went to, because I was told it was good for me.

I stand up, only vaguely aware the gentleman has joined me and we're standing there, me staring out to sea and him waiting to see I'm okay.

"But now?" Without thought, I speak aloud, following my own line of thought. "Well, now I'm lost." I put my hands out, palms up. "I don't really know who I am without Bill."

He starts to speak as he places my cushion in my outstretched hands. I take it and turn and walk away, deep in troubled thought.

It's only later I realise how rude I was, and that I don't even know this new friend's name.

The family next door

A little after four o'clock, we hear a car, then noises from the caravan next door, heralding the arrival of Emily, Bryan and their three.

Before we can decide whether to leave them to unpack or pop in to say 'Hello!', the children are tumbling in the door, their excitement palpable.

"We here!" announces Chiara. "And I'm neawy five!" She launches herself into my arms, smothering me in kisses, for all the world as though I hadn't seen her for far longer than the few days it's been.

"Hi, Gran," Mario says, giving me a more sedate peck on the cheek – the one not being devotedly pressed by Chiara's sweet wee face.

"Is it okay if we visit here while Mum and Dad do most of the unpacking?" Francesca asks as she takes her turn to kiss my cheek.

I look to Abigail.

"Of course you can, love. Probably a good idea to let them get on with it," she says.

"Mum said she'll give us a shout when we have to go sort out our own rooms," Francesca says. "Which is okay because then I can choose which bed I want."

Chiara bounces up and down. "I'm going to be sharing a woom in the cawavan with Fwannie," she says with a huge grin, her eyes wide with excitement.

I smile at the look of resignation on her sister's face. Just like her Aunt Abigail, Francesca insists her name is not to be shortened, but she is yet to win that battle with the baby of the family.

"Is Forrest in his room?" Mario asks. "Can I go through to let him know we've arrived?"

"Of course." Abigail shows him through. "That's probably the last we'll see of either of them for a while," she says when she returns. "Forrest has his Game Boy, or whatever you call the latest contraption, all set up."

"It's probably a Nintendo, or something, Auntie Abigail," Francesca says, her slight amusement at her aunt's faux pas hard to hide.

"Whatever it is, they seem happily talking about it. Now, have you had your lunch and, if so, do you two want a wee drink and a biscuit?"

"I'm okay, thanks, but I'm sure Chiara won't refuse. She didn't eat much at lunch because she was too excited."

I look at my oldest grandchild with fond pride. She seems so grown up for her fifteen years and is always such a lovely, polite child. She, like her mum and dad, is very musical and, at the start of the academic year, is hoping to get into St Mary's Music School – like her mother before her. A career in music beckons her and I hope with all my heart she gets accepted. It was the making of her mother.

"How did your dad's concert go last night?" I ask her now. Bryan was the soloist for Mozart's Clarinet Concerto at an orchestral concert in Inverness last night, which is why I was listening to the piece on my phone this morning. I'd have loved to be able to attend but Bryan only managed to get tickets for his immediate family, and I didn't manage to procure one for myself in time.

"It was good," she says. "He played very well and got a huge round of applause afterwards."

"Good." I nod. "That's lovely. And as it should be. He's an excellent clarinetist."

"Yes," she says, her face showing her daughterly pride.

"Have you heard anything from the music school?"

"You know I've had the interview and the audition?"
"Yes."
"Well, I'm still waiting to hear the results of that." She sighs. "I'm hoping 'no news is good news'. Mum says there were a lot of applicants for a very few places, and they go through a sort of process of elimination. She says they might call me again, to go through another round of auditions."
"Yes, they did that when your mum applied."
"She said. So I've brought my violin and my clarinet to practice here."
"Thank goodness you'll not be in our caravan," Abigail says, with a grin.
Francesca bumps arms with her. "Cheek. You're supposed to encourage me." But she's laughing, enjoying the teasing with her aunt.
Chiara is getting bored with the conversation, since she is not part of it and has finished her drink and biscuits. She starts a chant, "I want to go to the beach! I want to go to the beach!" She was not born the last time we were all up here – in fact, even the boys, Forrest and Mario were only little – but she can see it from the balcony and she's eager to be there. "I want to pway in the sand! I want to pway in the sand!"
I laugh. "Come on then." I hold my hand out. "Let's go ask Mum if it's okay for you and me to go build sandcastles."
She takes my outstretched hand, pulls me through the open French doors onto the balcony, and has me fair running round the side of the caravan, down its stairs, round her caravan, up its stairs and, before I can even knock, she flings the door open and tells her mum she and I are going to the seaside.
Emily laughs. "Hi, Mum." She gives me a hug and a kiss on the cheek.
"Sorry I can't stop to chat." I laugh with her. "It seems I have somewhere to be – urgently."

"Yes. Do you think you could wait two seconds till I dig out your bucket and spade?" she asks Chiara, lifting the car keys. "They're still in the boot."

Bucket and spade in one hand and a tremendously excited little girl in the other, I am dragged to the nearest set of stairs to the beach, having to slow her down a little so neither of us take a tumble.

We're soon on the beach and she runs straight towards the water. Fortunately, her mum also made her wait at the boot of the car long enough to get her jelly beach sandals on.

"Come on, Gwan! It's lovely." The letter 'r' has proved slower to join Chiara's library of sounds, though she now seems to have allowed it occasional entry in her vocabulary.

I hang back, shaking my head. "You didn't give me time to get my jellies on," I say. Not that I have jellies. But now I look down, I realise I have been dragged out with my house slippers still on. I laugh. "I'll come in next time."

"But I want you to come in now. Come in the watta!" she chants. "In the watta, scawdy cat." And she splashes me.

Laughing, taking off my slippers and leaving them further up the beach, I roll up my jogging trousers and put my feet in the water. It's freezing, but my pride forbids me to make a fuss about it and I join with her in a splashing game.

Being only four years old – still ten months till she'll be five, no matter she can't wait to start school – she soon tires of that and wants to make sand pies so runs off up the beach to where I left the bucket and spade with the slippers.

I take the time to unroll the legs of my joggers and use them to rub my cold legs dry a little before walking up the beach to join her. When I see what she's happily engaged in doing, I start to run. "No! No!"

Too late. The little monkey is busy filling my slippers with wet sand and seaweed, even topping off one of them with a dead crab, laughing like the proverbial drain.

"Oh, no." Rescuing the slippers, I pretend I'm going to catch her and she runs off with the bucket and spade.

Too tired and out of breath to keep up the chase, I sit on the rock that looks out to the anchor. 'Oh, Bill,' I whisper. 'How did you do all this for so many years?'

Thankfully, sensing that game is finished, Chiara comes to make her sand pies a little in front of me. Thankfully again, that seems to occupy her for long enough for me to do my best to clean out my slippers – not enough to be sand-free, but enough to put my already sandy feet in when it's time to move on to another game.

There's a bunch of seaweed a little further along and Chiara selects a suitable bit that she can make trails in the sand with as we walk – no, as I walk and she runs. Where do young children get all that energy?

In the distance, I see my gentleman walker coming towards us. I really hope he doesn't notice my slippers.

He does, of course, and smiles widely.

"Dragged out too quickly to change them," I say, by way of explanation.

"I guess this is one of yours." He nods in Chiara's direction.

"Second daughter's third child, my youngest grandchild, Chiara, spelt with an 'h' and an "i' in it, but pronounced plain Cara." I shrug and spread my hands.

I know I'm not one to quibble over fancy spellings of names, Eilidh being a difficult one for people to pronounce and spell, but I didn't choose it. At least my three girls have easier names to pronounce from their straight-forward spelling.

Chiara is busy filling her bucket with seaweed and carrying it down to the water, returning for another bucketful, after watching the previous one float away.

"Quite a handful, by the looks of it," my gentleman observes.

"I'm exhausted," I confess.

He laughs. "Hardly your usual sedate stroll along the beach."

"No, but it looks as though rescue is at hand. I see her dad is on his way, either to join us or to coax Chiara to the caravan for a nap. I can't help admitting I'm hoping for the latter."

We both laugh, and laugh the more when Bryan tries to round up his daughter, who leads him a merry chase along the beach before he snatches her up and carries her, squirming, protesting, all the way up the nearest stairs, leaving me to round up the bucket and spade she dropped, before joining them – realising once more I didn't say goodbye and I still don't know my new friend's name.

Emily opens her heart

There is a lot of to-ing and fro-ing between the caravans for the rest of the afternoon, then everything quietens down for dinner and the evening, especially once Chiara is tucked up in bed.

I am requested for the reading of bedtime stories, in my role as 'Gwan', which I do willingly, expecting it to be a long process and many stories. As it happens, the sea air seems to have worked its magic and my youngest grandchild is out for the count half-way through the first one. However, instead of leaving her in the 'sandman's' tender care, I find myself reclining on the other single bed, watching her sleep.

She's a pretty wee thing, with reddish-blonde curls, blue eyes and long dark lashes, like her dad. No wonder she effortlessly 'winds everyone round her little finger', as the saying goes. Even I have fallen under her spell and tend to over-indulge her a little.

Thinking back, she's a lot like her mother was, apart from Emily's almost black, curly hair. She was also a very engaging child. Not quite so 'full-on' as her daughter, though. She was always a more studious child, more like Francesca and Mario in that. Where she and Francesca are very musical, Mario has proved more academic, quite the mathematician. He may only be eleven years old, but since my Bill passed on, he's the one I always ask to help translate the gobbledegook of utility notices and things.

I sigh.

How Bill would be enchanted by Chiara's energy. How I wish he had lived to get to know her and find she has more of his personality than anyone else's. She and Mario may have Bryan's reddish-blonde hair, but I see so much of my Bill in her.

There is a light tap on the door and Emily opens it cautiously. When she sees Chiara is asleep, she beckons me out. I follow her to the living room, where Bryan is slumped in front of the television and Francesca is reading a book.

"Neither of these two fancy an evening stroll, but I wondered if you might." She looks at me carefully. "Unless you're too tired."

I am tired. It's been an exhausting day, but I so seldom have Emily's company without the children, I jump at the chance of a beach walk with her.

This time, I already have a pair of deck shoes on. My slippers are still on the radiator, recovering from the scrubbing I gave their insides earlier. I had to scrub so hard to have any chance of getting all the sand and the smell of dead crab and seaweed out of them. Poor things. They may never recover.

Going through next door to pick up my coat, I escape, unheeded, back out and down to the beach with my beautiful middle daughter, disregarded by the boys, who are completely absorbed in a complicated-looking board game of some sort up at the table.

It's a beautiful early evening; hardly a breath of wind, tide going out and an empty beach. What more could you wish for?

Walking in silence for a while, I begin to sense Emily has something on her mind. She keeps looking like she's about to speak, then deciding against it. I wait, knowing my girl needs time to make sense of what she's wrestling with within, before she'll be ready to share it.

We're well along the beach before she asks me if I'd ever doubted her dad's faithfulness.

"Hmmm! Not really," I answer. "From time to time, I'd notice this one or that one from his office was making eyes at him. You know, at office parties and the like. But, to be honest, he never seemed to notice and was always very attentive to me. And I never got the feeling his eye was wandering in response to their flirting." Another few steps further on. "Why do you ask, love?"

A huge sigh from her is all I get at first. A few steps later, she stops walking and turns to me. "It's Bryan, Mum, I think 'his eye is wandering', as you would say."

"What makes you think so?" I lead her to some rocks and we seek out somewhere flattish to sit.

"There's this younger woman in the orchestra, a flautist. She obviously likes him. He says it's nothing more than a silly crush, but I'm not so sure. Whenever I go backstage after one of their concerts, he's always talking to her, never anyone else. Just always her. 'See you later,' he mutters to her when he sees me approach. And she gives me this weird look as she slinks off."

"What kind of look?"

"You know, as though she knows something I don't know."

"Have you tackled Bryan about it?"

"He says I'm being paranoid, imagining things because I'm jealous of him still having a career."

"Are you jealous of him?"

"Not really ... well ... perhaps a tiny bit. I'm very conscious I gave up performing because I wanted to put family first, after I started having the kids, and I do sometimes wish I was still part of that world he inhabits. He always makes me feel terribly excluded."

"Oh, I'm sure he doesn't mean to."

The rock is cold to sit on and, without saying anything, we both stand up and resume walking.

"I'm not so sure. He rarely invites me to his performances when he's playing somewhere I could get to. I only manage to catch the concerts if he bothers to get us tickets. I've taken to checking where the orchestra is scheduled to be all season, so I can apply early to anywhere a reasonable distance from Edinburgh. It's ridiculous! As you know, he spends a lot of time away from home, as we both did before the children. You'd think he'd want to see more of us, not less."

"And that worries you, him being away so much?"

"Darn tootin' it does! Because I was part of that closed-off world, I remember what it feels like. Family, friends, everyone who is not part of the elite world of the orchestra seems apart, less important – almost not worth bothering about."

"Oh, is it really as bad as that?"

She digs the toes of her deck shoes into the sand. "Oh, probably not. I'm probably remembering when Bryan and I started only wanting to be with one another, only wanted 'us' and the music. I think I'm frightened it's now 'them' and the music."

"But he did come up here to be with the family."

"It felt as though he was coming because he felt he should. He didn't seem to be looking forward to it, though that might have been because he was preoccupied with the concert in Inverness."

"Of course. It's natural he would be. Having that wonderful solo was so important."

"He only got us tickets because it was in Inverness last night and we were travelling the extra hour from there up to Embo today." She picks up a stone and tosses it ineffectually in the general direction of the water, though we're quite some way off from it. "I've hardly seen him these past few months. He's always rehearsing for some performance or other. I don't remember the last time we went out to dinner, just the two of us. Date nights disappeared eons ago."

She looks so bereft, I put my arms around her and hold her close. "Oh, my darling, precious girl, I hope with all my heart you're wrong."

"But how can I know?" she wails. "How can I be sure he's not playing away in that sense too?"

"How about I do a bit of child-minding this week and you and Bryan book a special dinner for two somewhere nice in Dornoch or somewhere one evening?" Memory strikes, suddenly, coming from who knows where. "Oh, isn't there a rather posh seafood restaurant in Portmahomack, out near the lighthouse? Do you remember, your dad took us once for a treat? Before you were all married and had kids of your own. I know that was a long time ago, and perhaps it's not still there, But if it is, that might be a nice, romantic place to go."

She looks at me as though I'm an alien. "Mum! It's a seafood restaurant. Bryan is allergic to shellfish."

"Ooops! I forgot."

"But it is a nice idea and a nice offer to go somewhere just the two of us. I'll look into it." She pulls a face. "And see if he's up for it – this time. Thank you."

We hug again, and wordlessly both turn and head back along the beach.

When we reach the wooden beach stairs, she stops and turns to me. "Thanks, Mum. You're right, perhaps there's nothing to worry about."

"I hope not, love, but it's certainly worth fighting for your marriage. Not giving up without a lot more evidence."

She hugs me. "You're right. Of course, you're right."

In the distance, I see my gentleman friend coming along the beach from his evening walk.

"Would you mind terribly," I say, "if I stay out a few minutes longer to sit over there." I point to the rocks overlooking the anchor, a little further back along the beach. "I'd love to watch the colours of the sky change as the sun sets behind the caravans. I find this a soothing place to sit with my memories."

"Of course, Mum, but please don't stay down here too long. It'll get cold once the sun's gone. In fact, here." She takes off her warm jacket and hands it to me. "You can always throw that round your shoulders if you start getting cool."

"Aw, thank you, love. That's really thoughtful. I'll be up in a bit. But you go inside before it's you who gets cold."

One last hug and she's gone, leaving me smiling to see her perkier steps as she goes. 'Oh, please, God, let her be wrong,' I silently pray.

Getting to know you

It's true, I do find this a place where I can remember Bill. At home, I feel I've almost lost him. The girls have helped me so much to 'move on' that my daily life without him has become much easier to bear, but harder to remember what I want to remember of a long time shared.

This is also the place where I am making a pleasant new friend, and I'm reluctant to miss him when I see he's here on the beach, so I wander slowly to what I've come to think of as 'my' rock seat and wait for him to find me.

I'm already smiling my welcome when he stops in front of me.

He steps forward and extends his hand. "Ruairidh MacRae," he introduces himself.

I laugh. "Eilidh Crawford." I return the handshake. "When I saw you were on the beach, I held back to ask your name. How did you know I wanted to know it?"

He laughs too. "Great minds think alike, to use an old phrase from my school days." The increase in his laughter is music to my ears. I love the mellowness of it: how it makes me laugh too; how it makes me feel happy.

He hums a snatch of a tune.

"Oh, that's pretty. What is it?"

"It's a Gaelic song called Eilidh."

"Goodness, a song called after me." I laugh again. "Though I rather suspect it's the other way round. It was probably written first."

He grins at me, stands back a little, looking set for a performance. "If you'll bear with me, I'll give you my introduction when I play and sing it at the ceilidhs." He clears his throat and adopts an important stance. "'Eilidh' is a Gaelic song composed by John Bannerman, Lord Kildonan, who lived from 1901 to 1969, a Liberal politician, Gaelic activist, Scottish rugby internationalist, and singer and composer of Gaelic songs. *Eilidh* is Gaelic for Helen, and the song is set on the Isle of Harris." He closes his eyes and begins to sing, softly and clearly, just loud enough for me to hear.

"Tha slighe dhoirbh gu beanntan àrd ar n-eilein,
Tha 'n dìreadh garbh tron mhòintich is tron fhraoch,
Ach shil do dheòir nuair thug mi pòg dhut, Eilidh,
'S ar cuimhn' air lagan glas an taobh a' chaoil."

Hanging his head, he stops and shuffles a few steps away. "There's a bit more, but I'll not bore you with it. However, it was written for a girl called Eilidh." He blushes.

"Oh, it sounds lovely. I'd love to hear more."

"Aye, well, if you ever manage to get to one of the ceilidhs I'm playing at, I'll play and sing it just for you." He blushes even more.

"What do the words mean in English?"

"Och, lass, I'd have to know you a lot better before I'd sing it to you in a tongue you understand. I was embarrassed enough singing it to you in Gaelic. Next time, I'll play it for you on the wee box."

"The wee box?"

"Aye, I play the accordion, both piano and button accordions. I play that one on the wee button box or the fiddle."

"Goodness, you remind me of my Emily. She plays a variety of instruments too."

"Nice to have a musically accomplished daughter in the family."

"Francesca, Emily's eldest, plays several instruments too. It's a great thing to be able to do."

"How many children does Emily have?"

"She has three: Francesca who is fifteen, Mario, eleven, and Chiara, who you've met and who's only recently turned four, though she'll tell you she's nearly five."

"Oh, all Italian names. Did your daughter marry an Italian?"

I laugh. "Bryan couldn't be more Scottish if he tried. Born and bred in Edinburgh, like Emily herself. Possibly of Irish extraction. Certainly not in the least Italian."

"But the names …"

"Emily and Bryan are both very musical. It's how they met, playing in the same orchestra. They both studied for a while in Italy and love everything Italian: Italian food, the language, Italian names."

"I get it." He chuckles softly.

"They have a new kitten, Bianca."

We both laugh. "Of course," he says.

"It's so sweet. I'm not really a cat person, or wasn't, but it's a cute wee thing and wants cuddled all the time." I look up at him. "I found it a comfort while I was trying to get back on my feet after …" Closing my eyes, deciding not to go there, I sit up straighter and continue, "Backtracking a little, you said you play at ceilidhs. Will you be playing anywhere soon?"

"Aye, I have a few on the horizon. It's coming to that time of year when lots of folk like to get married, so I'll be playing at a few weddings and the likes, I've one coming up in Bonar Bridge, another in Inverness the week after. And there's one or two coming up that are just for the fun of a ceilidh."

"Nothing this week?"

"I'm afraid not."

"I'd have loved to hear you."

He shrugs. "Another time."

"But there, I've had a wee private taster show. Thank you."

"My pleasure." He takes a bow, the glow still upon his cheeks. Coming to rest beside me on the rock, after checking I don't mind, he says after a beat or two, "Eilidh, eh? I'll lay odds you've had almost as many amusing mispronunciations of that, as I have of Ruairidh."

I laugh. "Oh, yes. It sounds such a simple name when you say it, 'Ay-lee', but the Gaelic spelling makes it look much more complicated and folks often try to sound it out as it's spelled."

"Aye, same with Rhairidh." He spells it out for me. "I'll tell them it's pronounced 'Rury' but same thing, they try to sound it out as it's spelled and I get called all sorts. I remember once, at a wedding in Inverness, I was introduced as 'Ray Red MacRae'. The lads in the band could hardly play for laughing."

"Oh, you win." I laugh again. "Your name has even more amusing variations than mine. Sorry, Ruairidh, I really must go up before the kids send out a search party for me, but I truly enjoy your company. Do you mind if I watch out for you tomorrow morning? It would have to be fairly early, though – before daughter number three arrives on the scene and I'll be completely swallowed up by the family for a few days. That's if you're still going to be here?"

"Och, lass, I'll be here alright. I live up in the village." He nods beyond the caravans. "And I take a stroll along the beach most mornings and evenings, part because it passes the time and part because these are the times the dolphins often visit to fish a wee bittie off-shore. Early suits me just fine. So, yes, I'd be honoured to make that assignation with you."

"Lovely. And you can tell me more about the dolphins. I haven't seen them yet this trip, but I remember seeing them on previous ones." I hold out my hand and he helps me up from the cold rock seat. “I’ll look forward to that, Ruairidh MacRae.”

Ruairidh bows over my hand before releasing it. “It will be my pleasure. But first, let me see you safely home.” And he walks me back along the beach and watches as I climb the wooden stairs.

It has been a very long time since I’ve been treated like such a fine lady, and I have to say, I rather like it.

Dolphins in the morning

Determined to get my morning walk before everything kicks off in the caravans, I sneak out when I hear Abigail go into the bathroom – feeling slightly ridiculous to be 'sneaking out' but, to be honest, I am just not ready yet to take the interrogation and interference.

My daughters are wonderful, caring girls, but they seem to think since Bill died I'm incapable of looking after myself or making rational decisions. I did try to point out that up to then, I was the one who paid all the bills, decided what was for tea, and ran the household for the two of us.

I know after the terrible shock of Bill's death, I fell apart and was incapable of looking after myself for quite some time. They were marvellous, how they stepped in to do everything for me, even deciding what I would attempt to eat every day. They tried to tempt me with all sorts of delicacies and comfort foods, until, at last my appetite returned and the inertia departed.

But that was a good eighteen months ago and they haven't stopped 'mothering' me.

So I sneak out.

Ruairidh is there before me, waiting for me by the foot of the beach steps, with two folding picnic seats beside him. "If you're up for it," he says, "I thought we could walk first then decide on somewhere to sit in comfort for a while, if you've time."

"Oh, that would be perfect." I feel a huge desire to clap my hands in delight, the way Chiara would.

“So, do you have a preference for which direction we walk in?” he asks, as he lifts the folded chairs, neatly encased in canvas pouches with long handles, which he slips over his shoulder.

I smile with pleasure at his forethought and his gentlemanliness. “Well, I usually go to my right from here, so what about heading the usual way?”

“Good choice.” He nods approvingly. “Better chance of seeing the dolphins this early. There’s often a nice wee shoal of fish over near the old tumble-down pier.”

Then I remember.

I stumble a little and Ruairidh’s hand goes out ready to support me should I need it.

That was where Bill and I saw the dolphins once before.

We had walked away a bit from the girls because we were rowing and never liked to do so in front of them. With great restraint, we kept our voices low as we disagreed about his method of keeping the peace when the girls were fighting over who should get first choice of which coloured kite they each should have.

When they couldn’t sort it out peacefully without the tantrums and squabbling they were engaged in, I took all three kites and handed them to Bill, saying they didn’t deserve to have them at all, they were being such wee horrors.

While I walked on with the girls, telling them their dad was returning the kites because they were causing such disagreement – which is what I thought he was doing – Bill had gone all the way back to the shop and exchanged the kites for three exactly the same – and bought them lollipops the same colour too. I walked away crossly and marched further along the path towards the pier, trying to cool the anger that was rising in me.

He was rewarding bad behaviour!

And …

I had specifically said no to them about the lollipops when we were all in the shop, reasoning they had already had ice-lollies and it was close to lunchtime.

He had made a fool of me!

Once again, he had turned me into the bad one.

Good old Dad, always the hero.

Then Bill saw the dolphins and it was all forgotten, brushed away as of no import, while we all stood to see the creatures jump and dive, putting on a fine show for us.

Bill put his arm round my shoulders and gave me a squeeze to show we were friends again, argument forgiven and forgotten, so there seemed nothing I could do without making a scene but let it go – again.

Now, I quicken my pace as we walk, probably walking out the remembered hurt and anger.

Ruairidh matches his pace to mine without questioning the sudden hurry. I take a deep breath and let the anger go on its exhalation. It's pointless to be angry about the incident since the man I'm angry with is beyond reach of feeling its heat.

It's funny I had not remembered the arguments and hurts till now. In three years I'd remembered only the good times, missing them, missing Bill. It feels better, more fair, somehow, to remember things were not always perfect. Until I stepped onto this beach this week, my grief had blinded me to the realities of forty years married to a man who so often made me feel undervalued.

I stopped in my tracks. Wow! What a huge realisation. Earth-shattering and more than a little sad. Could it be freeing too?

I walk on, almost forgetting I am not walking alone.

If Ruairidh feels shut out, he doesn't show it. He seems to be giving me space to go through what I'm going through without interference.

He looks at me after we've walked in silence for a while. "Oh, lass, I still see the sadness in your eyes. Do you want to share what you were distressed about when I first saw you? What still troubles you so much now?" He spreads his hands wide. "Unless, of course it is too personal and you feel it's none of my business, being a total stranger."

I look at him, realising he has been kind and patient and possibly almost deserves some explanation for my vacillating pace and mood as we've been walking.

"Here I am, to all intents and purposes a stranger, and sometimes it helps to talk it out with someone." He looks at me, the invitation and the question written on his face. "You could treat me as a therapist, someone who will listen carefully and non-judgementally. Only, unlike a therapist, I'll offer no words of wisdom. I'll only let you get what's troubling you off your chest." He looks at me with a cheeky grin. "And it'll only cost you the pleasure of my company."

I swallow hard. Perhaps, just perhaps, I can unburden myself of the crushing weight I've been carrying for so long. It gradually seemed lighter when I was at home, but this beautiful place is chock-full of memories. Mostly happy memories, others reminding me life was not always as happy as we pretended. These memories come in huge waves that I could so easily drown in. Meeting Ruairidh is like being thrown a lifebelt that my fingertips keep touching. Dare I reach out and grasp it more fully?

Ruairidh is right: he's virtually a stranger. I'm only here for a week in all, then I may never see him again.

I shiver at the thought of such a bleak outlook. I feel so at home up here. I'm loving the feeling of freedom it gives and, with a jolt, I realise I'm not going to want to go home.

I look at Ruairidh and summoning all my courage, I reach out for that lifebelt.

"I think you'll have gathered from the little bits and pieces I've said, that I'm recently widowed." I laugh. "It's funny, I was thinking three years was quite a long time, but sometimes when I'm sitting on the rocks, I feel as though it was only yesterday. Memories have a nasty habit of invalidating the work done through the years."

He nods empathetically. Later I might ask him who he still grieves, but right now, I need that lifebelt far too much to risk it being drawn out of reach again.

"I'm sorry. I want to take you up on your offer, I think it's something that would really help me, but I'm not sure I can speak out loud what weighs heaviest on me. It's pretty awful. At least, it is to me."

"Well, I am here, if you should wish to try."

Can I? Dare I say out loud what has tormented me for three years now? Dare I share it with someone else? I had the opportunity with my doctor but found I couldn't take it. The words were locked away securely in the deep vault of my regret. Can I take this opportunity, this encouragement to unlock it?

As we walk, I surreptitiously study this gentle, kind man walking beside me. He isn't pushing me to share. He's offering an opportunity and the certainty grows in me with every step – the certainty that he will listen without judgement or censure.

I take a deep breath, remembering the saying 'a burden shared is a burden halved', and yes, it's time to let someone help. It will still be my load but, hopefully won't feel so heavy.

A burden shared

"Bill's death was a terrible shock. He died beside me in the bed. He was first to put his book down and his light off. As he reached out for the light switch he made a really strange sound, a sort of guttural, throaty sound. I looked over and realised he was dead." My voice breaks and I stop walking, my hand to my chest, unable to go on for a while.

Ruairidh waits patiently, silently. After a few moments, we resume walking slowly along the beach.

I take a breath. "Lying there, just as he fell back, arm outstretched ... eyes open wide in alarm, but unseeing ... mouth open but unbreathing ..." Wiping the inevitable tears from my face. "And the stink. He had soiled the bed ... was soiling the bed ..." Taking a breath. "I've never said that out loud before." I close my eyes.

Again I stop walking.

"It was too, too horrible, grotesque even, to tell the girls. To see him lying there, totally colourless, lifeless, with his mouth hanging open and his tongue lolling to the side. It's a picture I've found hard to erase from my mind and I never want my girls to have it in theirs. An aneurysm, apparently, according to the post mortem." I look to Ruairidh. "They always have one for a sudden death, you know, a post mortem, I mean."

Another few silent steps.

"And I didn't tell the girls, or anyone else, that his life ended on a bad note, huffing because I was grumpy with him. In fact, far more than grumpy. I was furious. We'd had a disagreement over the fact he'd acted on his plans for retirement without consulting me, without caring to know what I thought of his plans before he set them in motion. Our final goodnights to one another were far from gentle and loving. Huffy on his side, positively angry on mine. I said some terrible things to him, even telling him I could see no place for me in any future he planned, and no place for him in any future I wanted." I turn to Ruairidh, my eyes pleading to be understood and forgiven by someone, anyone. Knowing there is no one's forgiveness that will absolve me from the burden of my guilt. That, I must carry alone.

"I didn't attend the inquest. The girls went, well, except for Donna, my youngest. She stayed with me. We were both still in shock. She stayed with me that first week, slept holding on to me every night. I don't know if it was to comfort me or herself. I hardly noticed she was there. Hardly noticed anything. The doctor gave me sleeping tablets. He came in every day, they tell me, probably afraid to give me the whole prescription in one go in case I took them all at once." Again, I wipe the tears away with my hand. "He had come when I called. I hadn't touched Bill. Had only slipped out of bed and sat staring at him from the chair across the room, willing it to be a spasm or something that would pass. Knowing it wasn't. So the doctor saw what I saw and was not at all surprised to have to treat me for shock – even without knowing the worst part for me was that we parted so badly and I was sure I caused his death."

Ruairidh hands me a clean, white, ironed gentleman's handkerchief with an intertwining 'RM' embroidered in the corner. I stare at it for a moment, amazed I can notice such things as a monogram at such a moment, marvelling too that here I am in my mid-sixties and a gentleman has never offered me his handkerchief before. When I use it, it's comfortingly soft, and I hold it to my face for a while until I'm ready to speak again, enabled by the comfort.

"I didn't cry at that time. Just lay in the bed in the spare room, sleeping or awake, doing nothing, feeling nothing. The girls made me drink, mostly water, I had no taste for anything else. I don't remember eating, but I believe they eventually gave me protein drinks, meal replacements because I refused to chew, or rather, I couldn't chew. I'd forgotten how to. If they put solid food in my mouth, there it stayed, uneaten until I coughed it out."

I have stopped walking, immobilised by the memory as I was immobilised at the time.

"They told me later, the doctor was for taking me into hospital, but they persuaded him they could care better for me at home. And they could. It's funny the things I remember about that time. I have no memory of being helped to shower and wash my hair, but I do remember lying there quietly humming to myself one day. It was the song, 'Just my Bill'. You know the one?"

I look at Ruairidh and he's smiling and nodding. And I feel better. Another deep breath and I find I can lift my head up and start walking again. "It seemed to take a long time to get over the shock, then I felt completely numb. Didn't want to do anything, go anywhere. No interest in anything. The girls thought it was because of my intense grief. I knew that grief was liberally laced with guilt."

Again, I look at Ruairidh, but there is no censure, no judgement on his face. Only compassion.

"Do you mind if I say something here?" he asks.

"Go for it," I reply, stopping, wondering what is coming.

"Correct me if I'm wrong, but I think you said your husband died from an aneurysm?"

"That's right."

"Then, I don't think you could have caused his death, because an aneurysm doesn't build to the point of bursting within a few, short minutes. I believe it grows over a period of time until it ruptures, often symptom free up to that crucial time."

"Oh!"

"You say he was huffy, was that his usual response to being criticised?"

"Absolutely! It used to frustrate me because he wouldn't argue with me about what was making me angry. He'd just go sulky, sometimes walking out the room, leaving me to fume on my own. He'd wait till I calmed down and then do whatever he wanted anyway. It was his way of allowing me to get over it when he did or said something he knew he was in the wrong about. I know that because when *I* was in the wrong, he'd stay and help me realise that I was. He was a consummate huffer when he was in the wrong."

"A huff is hardly the same as an outburst of anger, I think you'll agree. So, I doubt his blood pressure was anywhere near as high as yours when you said goodnight. A silent huff could hardly have pushed his blood pressure to the point where it could cause an aneurysm to rupture."

"Of course!" I look at him, stunned into silence for a moment. "Good grief! I hadn't thought of that."

"You were probably not thinking at all. You were in shock."

I put my hands to the sides of my head. "I was so sure his death was all my fault, my acceptance of guilt blinded me to the facts – and continued to blind me, because I worked so hard to forget that night, not to keep re-examining it."

Yet again, I start walking, poor Ruairidh having to keep adjusting to such a stop-and-start 'walk'.

"Bill was so health conscious, kept a close eye on things like blood pressure, did nothing to raise it inappropriately. Even when he exercised, he'd always wear a blood pressure monitor." I turn to look at my walking companion, not really registering it is Ruairidh, a virtual stranger I'm pouring all this out to. "I used to think he was obsessed with his health. All those check-ups, the close watch on his blood pressure, the health obsession. Did he know he had that threat hanging over him? If so, why on earth did he not tell me? Why did he not share it with me? I was his wife! He should have let me share something so important. He should have warned me if he knew it could happen."

Once more, as we walk on, my pace slower as I work through what these recent revelations mean to me, I almost forget I'm not walking alone.

"But, then again, if he had told me, would that have been years of shared fear, of watchful, fearful care? Would I have spent forty years nagging him to be careful when he was running about, playing with the children? To be careful every time he played squash or tennis? Every time we ran to catch a train?" I shudder at the terrible secret he may have decided never to share.

"Perhaps Bill knew best," Ruairidh says. "If he did know, he might have wanted to spare you all those years of worry and fear."

I look at him, hearing his soft voice, his words helping to calm me, helping me know I would not have been able to decide what to do if the secret had been mine.

What do you do in the winter?

We had walked this way, in the hopes of catching a glimpse of dolphins, and there they are, but we almost miss them, so engrossed are we in conversation – or, more accurately, so intent was I on unburdening myself as invited.

"Oh, look," I squeal, shaking off the sombre mood. "There they are!" I point to a little group of dolphins arcing out of the water not too far from the shore, all the time wondering where this new-found childish delight in things comes from.

Ruairidh opens out the camping chairs and we sit to watch the dolphin display for a while.

"They're such amazing creatures," I say in quiet awe. "I know next to nothing about them. I remember taking the girls to a Sea World exhibition once, but I don't remember all the wonderful information. What I do remember is I was too busy trying to keep Donna in her seat, terrified she was going to make a lunge for the low wall surrounding the pool area, get soaked, or worse, fall in the water. Bill did point out she was far too small to lean over the wall and fall in, but it didn't stop me fussing." I close my eyes and sigh. "How many, many times I've looked back on their childhood and wished I'd fussed less, cared less about keeping them and the house clean and tidy, and just *been there* with them. Played more with them. I suspect all their fun memories are with Bill. I was only ever the bystander, the audience, the coat holder."

There is a long silence, during which my regrets overwhelm me and I would be unable to speak if called upon to do so.

"I'm sorry you feel like that, though I wonder how common it is for mothers to have those sorts of regrets. I watch my great-niece with her wee one. She spends much of her time doing the mundane, necessary chores of family life, I wonder if she'll later wish she'd spent more time playing with the wee one."

"Probably," I say with a sigh, staring out at the dolphins happily at play. "I used to say to the girls, 'Work first, then play.' Do you think the dolphins have done their work first, filling their bellies with their catch before leaping about like that?"

Ruairidh smiles. "Nice thought. I can tell you that the best time to catch sight of dolphins near the shore is this sort of time or in the evening, when the tide is beginning to rise again, bringing the fish closer too, so a bit after low tide. There are many dolphins resident in Scotland though, like the fish, they are wild animals and come and go as they please, which is why you can never be guaranteed to see them."

"Ah, that explains why we were often disappointed when we were on the lookout for them – often in the middle of the day."

"The reason you sometimes do see them when they are around, is that dolphins have to breathe every two or three minutes. They don't always do more than come briefly to the surface as they swim along, but sometimes they just like to jump and play and do acrobatic spins in the air for the sheer fun of it."

"They seem such joyful, happy creatures."

"They do, don't they."

"Something Donna once asked me when she was a wee girl, and I've wondered since about all sorts of animals, including dolphins, is whether they ever sleep and where do they go to sleep? I suppose I should have looked it up somewhere, but I'm afraid I never did."

"I don't know about many other animals, but I believe dolphins often sleep on the surface of the water, or, if they lie lower, they will automatically rise to the surface regularly to take in oxygen."

"Goodness. I had no idea. I really must try to remember to tell Donna that – though I suspect she will have gone and looked it up. She's always had a lot more curiosity about things than I've had."

"It's something I looked up when I was a lad, because, like your daughter, I had a great curiosity about things like that, and dolphins, in particular intrigued me. I always loved when I was out on my father's boat, how they would sometimes surf waves when we were near the beach, even following the wake of the boat, or come alongside as though to race us."

We watch them for a while more until they start to move off, swimming further out to sea.

I think Ruairidh imagines I'll be happy to start walking back now they're gone, and he starts to get up, but I sit for a while longer, happy to be here, in this beautiful place, looking across the North Sea, next stop Norway.

"I don't want you to cause your family to worry," he says. "I think we should start back." And he folds his chair and feeds it into its pouch.

"Thank you, yes, probably time." But I'm preoccupied, wondering what it's like to live up here. I decide to ask someone who knows. "Have you enjoyed living here?"

"Very much so."

"Even in the winter?"

"Even in the winter. It's a good healthy place to be, and because of its situation, tucked into the bay here, it seems to have its own wee weather system which is often kinder than elsewhere."

"So, apart from coorying down in front of the fire in the winter, what else is there to do?"

"The weather is often reasonable enough to go on great winter walks, and I personally love the forests in winter. Winter is my busy time for ceilidhs, and not just private wedding ceilidhs. When the tourists are gone, it becomes party time up here. But it's also when I like to read more. There are lots of things I ought to be doing around the house but it's been a while since I've had the inclination, I have to admit. Winter can be a relaxing, lazy time if you don't push yourself out of the chair."

"If you don't mind me asking, how long have you lived in Embo?"

"Ten years. I came to care for my older sister after she had a series of strokes. She'd been a widow for many years and could no longer care for herself, so I retired from the sea and became her full-time carer, until she died nearly two years ago. I was the youngest of eleven kids, she was the oldest, so there was a considerable difference in our ages. She had always been more like a mother to me, than a sister. Especially when my mother died when I was only about ten."

"So really, you kind of lost your mother twice."

"That's exactly how it felt when Catriona died. She was my link to my mother, my past. She was my champion and my friend as well as my sister. I know it isn't the same as losing a spouse, but I still miss her and find it hard to be motivated to do much that I don't have to do."

For the first time, I see a different Ruairidh, he looks so terribly sad and lost. "I'm sorry." I wish I knew him well enough to put my arms around him. It's hard not to give him the hug we both need.

"Aye, lass, we're not so different in our present circumstances, I suppose."

"You said you retired from the sea to come to live in Embo. Where were you before?" I ask as I fold my chair.

He helps me feed the folded chair into its pouch. "Further up the coast," he says. "Helmsdale."

“Oh, I visited Helmsdale once. It has a gorgeous wee harbour.”

“That’s right.”

“So after your sister died, did you ever think of moving back up there?”

“I did.” He looks at me, his head to the side as he seeks the right words. “But by that time, Embo had become my home. I love my family but there really is no place for me up there now. I’m no longer a fisherman and have long since lost the desire to live that life, if I ever really had it, so I’d be no use to my brothers and the family business.” He looks immeasurably lost again.

I thought it was only me who needs the warmth and comfort of another human to share my troubles with. But, here, for one reason or another is a stranger in a similar plight.

“I love Embo. It’s just …”

I try to give him the space and patience he so recently afforded me.

“It’s just that the house feels empty without Catriona. She seemed to take the light out of it when she died.”

I nod, knowing the feeling.

“I’m not quite sure yet how to turn it back on, so I spend a lot of time outside.” He spreads his hands in a gesture of surrender. “Hence all the regular beach walks. I made a start on changing things in the house in an attempt to make it seem more my house than Catriona’s, but I really haven’t got that far yet.” He sighs. “Time, I suppose. It’s simply going to take time.”

“So, were your family always fishermen from Helmsdale?” I ask after we’ve been walking for quite a while.

He takes a breath and seems to feel on more solid ground. I’ve noticed he is a fount of knowledge, probably a bit of a history boffin, and so feels safer answering this question.

"For a long time, yes. But, before that, generations before, they were crofters further inland in Sutherland, in the Strath of Kildonan, and that's where my family consider we came from. When they were herded like animals to the coast, there was not much of what is now the village of Helmsdale, the village being a product of the Highland Clearances, planned to provide accommodation and employment for those evicted from their lands to make way for sheep."

"Oh, I've heard of the Highland Clearances."

"That doesn't surprise me if you visited Helmsdale."

"Such a wicked thing to do. And all for what? Nowadays, few people eat much meat of any kind. I was reading an article about how much the percentages have changed over the years, and there is now a high percentage of vegetarians around. Sorry to seem flippant about something so serious, but I doubt many will cook a leg of lamb for Sunday dinner these days."

"True, but back then, the Duke and Duchess of Sutherland were assured that raising sheep was the more profitable use of their land, so without giving notice of their intentions, they evicted all their tenants. The clearances which took place throughout Sutherland are remembered as the most notorious of all the clearances throughout the Highlands."

I stop walking and turn to look at him. "You say that with enough passion to convince me there are many hard stories in your family history."

"There are indeed."

"It's such a terrible, but important part of the history of Scotland, isn't it? I have so many questions to ask about Embo and this area."

"Oh, Embo was never a clearance village, it had been a fishing village way before that time."

"There, you see? So much for me to learn." I shake my head in growing awareness of how little I know. "Everything I've missed out on all these years – most of my life. I don't know when I stopped being curious about people, places, things. I was as a child, but I truly regret losing that curiosity, that interest in life outside my own little world. Being here, looking at the anchor, at long last being curious about its history, it has awakened me to the joy of finding out new things. Oh, Ruairidh, it's not too late to learn new things, is it?"

"No," he assures me, his hand on my arm. "It's never too late."

He quickly removes his hand, but not before I feel the thrill of its touch. Through all the layers I'm wearing, there is something that stirs me. Perhaps the touch of a kind gentleman showing me attention after the barren three years of my widowhood. It's strange, but when I stop and think about it, no man has comforted me with a simple touch during those years. Not relatives or friends. My daughters and my grandchildren do with hugs and kisses, and for that I'll be eternally grateful. But there has never been that comforting, companionable feel of a strong, sympathetic hand on my arm.

It's very companionable to walk together, even without touching or talking. It's lovely to be with someone who doesn't mind silence.

I'm afraid Bill often used to feel the need to fill any silence that fell naturally as we walked along this beach.

As we come close to the steps I must take to be reunited with reality, I find myself sighing. "Bless them," I say. "Once the family are all gathered, there's to be a special dinner for my 40th wedding anniversary to a man who can no longer share it with me. It feels empty to me, but it is what my daughters think will be a fitting way to mark the date." I sigh again and shake my head.

As we reach the steps, I feel it already, the knowledge I'll be swallowed up by them all. They're intent on taking over my life, taking my new-found independence, organising me. I know they mean well, but I'm not ready to be submerged in their lives. I want my own.

I turn to Ruairidh and put my hand on his arm. “Please, Ruairidh. It has been an awesome thing you helped me do today, to unburden myself like I have. You might have started out as almost a stranger, but I now feel you are a friend, one of the closest I’ve ever had. One who knows my deepest, darkest secrets.” I close my eyes for a moment and take a breath. “I don’t want you to be a stranger I never have to meet again, I hope you’ll be a friend I see often.”

“I’d like that. You know today has been a two-way thing. I felt comfortable enough to share my feelings too.”

I feel warm inside and find myself smiling. “There is not going to be much opportunity for walks on the beach, for our conversations, for me to learn from you, for all that I find myself now wanting. Not now Donna will have arrived and my family will be all gathered. They’ll take over the next few days. But I shall look out for you and join you any chance I get.”

“Aye, lass. And I’ll be here, taking my daily walks, all the time watching out for you. I’ve enjoyed our talks, I’ve enjoyed our walks and I’m sure there will be more in the days to come.”

“I’ll do my best to make it happen.”

“Now go to your family, Eilidh Crawford, and I’m sure we’ll catch one another again. And, Eilidh.” He grasps my hand. “Try to enjoy what they have so kindly, even though mistakenly, prepared especially for you.”

Holding his hand tightly, I’m afraid to let it go. Something in me knows for certain that I don’t want this to be over. Something inside me tells me, this could be someone I need in my life, someone special to me.

Dancing with Donna

Daughter number three and her hubby arrive, travelling up from Devon in their battered old Land Rover with caravan attached, and I'm guessing they'll be parked on a pitch round the site a bit.

Sure enough, I've no sooner swallowed the lump that came to my throat as Ruairidh let go of my hand, when I hear joyful sounds leaking from the caravan windows.

I don't understand what's happening to me. I'm here, ostensibly to celebrate forty years of a happy marriage, but instead, I'm already missing a brand new friendship.

"Mum!" Donna sees me appear at the top of the steps, comes careening out of the French windows, vaults over the balcony and runs to me. "Mum!" She envelopes me in her arms. "Oh, Devon was amazing but I missed you all the time. I kept thinking how much you'd love it." She spins me round and around, dancing me until I can no longer walk straight.

"Hold on tight to me." I find the breath to tell her. "You've made me dizzy." I laugh. It's hard to believe I saw her no more than a few weeks ago and I've had umpteen video calls, phone calls and texts since then. "Oh, Donna." I hold her close. "It's great to see you too."

She belongs to this place, she's such a breath of fresh air, making me feel alive in a way that the two older girls have never quite managed. I love all three of my girls, but the one whose company revitalises me is still dancing me about on the grass.

"Donna, put Mum down before you exhaust her," Abigail scolds from the balcony.

Donna looks up at her, looks at my laughing face, then dances me all the way round the side of the caravan to the steps leading up to the door, where she gently hugs me and leads me into the caravan.

I feel so alive.

What with the joy of finding an exciting new friendship still close to the surface, and the joy of my bouncy youngest daughter, I feel alive. This is the time to live, not to go back to dwelling in the darkness of grief and unmerited guilt.

Owen, Donna's other half, is already there and he greets me with a warm hug, the only one of my sons-in-law who ever does – but, then, he is married to Donna, one of the most exuberant, affectionate people I know.

"Right," Donna says. "Let's get to it." And she takes the large bag Owen is standing guard over, turns it upside down and shakes out all sorts of brightly coloured decorations, including miles of fairy lights. "Forrest, my sweet boy, we need your help."

Forrest looks up from his plate of cereal. "But I haven't finished my breakfast."

Donna takes the plate, hands it to Owen who finishes off the last couple of spoonfuls, and pulls Forrest up from the table, gives him a huge bear hug – she is the only person who gets away with hugging him – plants a big, slobbery kiss on his cheek and says, "Right, we need more helpers, so off you go next door and get the rest of the gang." She laughs. "And you know what to do if they haven't finished breakfast."

Forrest laughs and leaps to it, probably hoping to get finishing Marco's warm Italian, chocolate-spread-filled cornetto.

Within moments, he is back, with Marco, Francesca and Chiara, all rushing through the door behind him and into their favourite auntie's arms. It's a noisy business with lots of whooping and delighted squeals as Donna hugs and kisses each – wetly and noisily.

Even Abigail has to smile, and gives in to a chuckle. She's already been subjected to the Donna treatment and the immediate lifting of her mood with her sister's entrance is quite remarkable.

Donna and Owen allot everyone a task and in next to no time, the interior of the caravan looks like a bright, colourful, magical cave, and is ready for a party.

Trevor comes through from his hiding place in the bedroom – Donna is way too much for him at the best of times, and this, in his view, is not the best of times. "I thought this was to be a sombre occasion," he moans.

"Whatever gave you that idea, brother-in-law?" Donna chases him onto the balcony and, despite his brave resistance he gets a hug and a kiss too. "There!"

Abigail laughs and tells him, "You really should know by now, there is no hiding from your loving sister-in-law. She always gets you in the end."

"To get back to your question, dear Trevor," Donna says. "Did you ever meet my dad?"

"Of course I met your dad," he says, wiping off Donna's kiss, probably hoping his blush isn't showing, which, of course, it is.

"In which case, you will know he always loved a party, the more colourful, the better. There were never too many sparkly lights for him. This should not be a sombre, sad occasion. Mum doesn't need sombre and sad. She needs to remember the fun, the joy of her marriage, not the last three years of her grief." She turns to me. "Am I right, Mum, or am I right?"

"Oh, Donna, you are so, so right. I want to remember your dad, I want to remember his joy, his playfulness. I'll always love him, but I'm ready to live again. I'm immeasurably sad he can't be here to enjoy all this." I spread my arms to embrace this fairyland scene. "But he would have wanted us to be happy, to go on having fun, to live as he would have wanted to live."

“Well said, madre mia.” Emily applauds from the doorway of the caravan, where she has been standing, watching the scene. She spreads her arms wide, welcoming her younger sister, subjecting happily to her kisses and cuddles. “Let the party begin.”

From behind her, Bryan produces her violin, which she uses to play bright, pop/hip-hop tunes, getting everyone up and dancing, Donna twirling first one then another of them round and around, leading them about in the tiny space. It is ridiculous and wonderful.

When, one by one, the adults flop onto the long couch along the wall, and the children onto the floor, Abigail serves everyone soft drinks and ice cream, with Francesca, Donna and Emily helping her.

The party has begun – and it’s not even lunchtime yet.

‘Oh, wouldn’t Ruairidh love this,’ I catch myself thinking.

Lights!

After all yesterday's festivities, everyone else sleeps late, but I seem to have been energised, rather than tired out by everything, and I'm up before the sun today. Before getting dressed, I make myself a coffee and watch the sunrise set the water afire. Although the sun sets behind the caravans, it rises right out there in front of them, rising majestically and gloriously over the distant horizon, setting the sea aflame with reds and golds.

Waiting until the last of the beautiful, colourful display is over and the sun is a ball of fire in the sky, I get dressed and step out quietly to have my morning walk.

I've only been here a few days and already I know a week is not going to be enough for me. For the first time for a very long time, I feel as though my senses are waking up. Food tastes better, the air feels lighter. When I take a breath, I feel it power my body and my mind, helping me think, helping me feel.

Even before Bill died, I'd begun to feel old. I'd stopped wanting to do things, go places, see people. It was enough to cook and clean and sit of an evening watching television. I'd flick through the odd magazine in the hairdresser's to pass the time, rather than out of interest.

Already, in just a few days, I feel myself coming out of hibernation. I want to stretch my limbs, get them moving. I want to look around myself, notice flowers and trees, feel the wind on my skin and in my hair, watch how it bends the tall grass and whips up the waves.

Suddenly, sixty-three feels no age at all. I remember, before Bill died, how I dreaded turning sixty. The idea of picking up my 'old age pension', as I thought of the retirement pension I was going to be awarded in a few years from then, made me sink into the description.

Bill was different. At sixty-four, he saw his approaching retirement as something to look forward to. One of his colleagues who had recently retired was wanting him to take up tennis with him, another was pressuring him to join the golf club. Having always been an energetic man, he planned to do both. When I wondered how that would fit into our plans of being able to spend more time together, he assured me it would be wonderful. We could take holidays at the golf resort in Portugal where Harry and his wife went twice a year. While he and Harry golfed, Sandra and I could get to know one another. Right before he died, he had even started the process of buying a time-share apartment in the same building as Harry and Sandra. It wasn't what I had envisioned for our retirement, but I was not consulted. In fact, it was what I got angry about that dreadful night Bill died. I shudder and push the memory away, remembering his plan instead of his demise.

As it has turned out, instead of sitting back and relaxing on a golf club's verandah, sipping cocktails, living the life of a traditional golf widow, here I am, an actual real-life widow, sitting on a beach in the north of Scotland, sipping water from a water bottle gifted to me by a kind stranger. It may not have been what Bill planned, but this was not my original choice either.

At least, and at last, I have come to realise that, though I'm around retirement age, I am far from old. My hair is silvering, but that doesn't denote old age – my hair has been silvering since I was in my late thirties. I just covered it up for years with a hairdresser's expertise. After Bill died, there seemed no point in that expense any more. Who was there to notice? And in the three years since, I've become accustomed to seeing more and more silver emerge and I've grown used to it, even to like it.

When I looked in the mirror this morning, it was a lot like someone had turned the lights on, and I realised a decent cut and restyle could actually show the colour off to advantage – at least, that's what the magazines in the hairdresser's assured me – not that I've been in such an establishment for quite some time. Even that, I had stopped doing regularly.

But the invigorating air here, makes me want to walk taller, with my head up and my shoulders back. It makes me want to toss my head and feel the swing of well-cut hair, telling myself, 'I'm worth it.' It also makes me want to look better – not for Bill or anyone else – but for me. I want to look in the mirror with something akin to pleasure.

When we used to come to Embo years ago, I never took the time to take deep breaths of such a precious, life-giving commodity as fresh air. Now, I can't get enough of it, throwing the caravan's French doors open wide each morning, taking my morning coffee out onto the balcony, feeling the freshness bring my body alive. So I set my mind to wondering about selling up, as Abigail wants me to, and buying a wee cottage up here somewhere, which I doubt very much she'll want me to do.

Turning the spotlight on that thought, once more I am on the beach, looking out past the anchor with the blue of the miles and miles of North Sea merging into the big, blue sky. It's a bright sunny day, not a cloud to be seen, nothing between me and 'blue sky thinking', which is what I set out to do again today. Can I do that with a view to looking at cottages up here, available to buy? Or is that a step too far? Too soon? Should I try a few weeks more in a caravan to see if this is where I'd truly like to live? It would not be a popular choice, so not something I want to do on a whim.

Can I really book a smaller caravan and come back up here in a week or two? Which I find myself wanting to do, to be certain this is where I'd want to live permanently – so far from family and the city life I've always known. Would that be long enough to get a taste of life up here?

This would be an uncharacteristically impetuous decision. But the more I think about it, the more it appeals to me, and the more it reminds me of the dreamer I used to be, rather than the organised, careful planner I forced myself to become.

While I have quiet time to myself, I feel I really ought to make a solid decision and do something about it if that's what I want – before my common-sense daughters firmly decide against it and get in the way of that particular dream.

Oh, not Donna, of course – she would always encourage the dream. Ah, Donna. She thinks she takes after her dad, but she doesn't really because yes, he had a fun side, but, actually, even 'fun' was always meticulously planned by Bill. He didn't have Donna's spontaneity, nor was he anything like as exuberant. But I do know someone who once was. The same young girl who was also a great dreamer.

I sigh.

Donna brought the party to Embo – something she has the talent, the joie-de-vivre to bring to anywhere she happens to be.

She is the daughter of my three who grieved the most deeply, so much that, like me, she ceased to function for a while. We both missed the inquest, we both sleep-walked through the funeral, barely responding to handshakes and kind words. We both escaped early to my bed, using the duvet as a barrier between us and the world of pain that lay out there. She cried long and hard as we clung together.

And now, she is the daughter who best understands my grief has to end if I am to live.

Owen helped her to live again. He piled her into their old Land Rover, hooked their even older caravan on the back, and took her travelling.

Instead of making the rounds of auditions and accepting bit parts here and there in local theatres, they became travelling performers.

They stop somewhere on their travels, put out some signs advertising their performance, scheduled for a day or two hence, then they set up their auditorium wherever they can get permission to have it – on common ground, in parks and gardens, anywhere where people can bring their own chairs and rugs, picnics and children. Sometimes they put on a condensed take on a Shakespeare play, sometimes a poetry recital with songs and music, sometimes a children's book reading, sometimes they do face-painting and clown acts, often they sell charcoal portrait sketches, which many of those who had enjoyed the show sit for.

Always, they rely on voluntary contributions for the shows and, between that and the money they make from the sale of the portraits and the paintings they are commissioned to do after a show, and the ones they offer from the stock they keep replenishing in their caravan, they always earn enough to live on.

They love their travelling life.

When I close my eyes and remember my childhood dreams, those dreams look a lot like the life they live. I wonder – but only briefly – when my dream faded.

Camera!

When I think about it, turning the figurative camera lens on that time, which I don't often allow myself to do, I know exactly when the scene changed, when I had to change.

It was the day my father packed a suitcase and walked out on Mother and me.

Mother fell apart and took to her bed. I was heartbroken too – but someone had to keep us alive.

If mother and I were to survive this disaster, someone had to step up to the plate. Since mother showed no signs of doing so, the task fell to me. At only sixteen, I was forced to set aside that scatter-brained dreamer I was and train myself, by trial and error, to become an organised woman fielding the responsibilities of a household.

The life I'd cherished inside my head was far richer than the life I ended up living.

I learned, through bitter experience, when faced with something practical to be done it was best to square my shoulders, set to work and get it done sooner rather than later. If I didn't, no one else would. I learned the drawbacks of procrastination as the piles of dishes in the sink left me without anything to eat off of, and piles of dirty washing left me nothing to wear. Through time I discovered if I had something to organise, good planning enabled me to achieve the desired result.

So I became a reluctant organiser and a less-than-comfortable planner. I had to. There was no other choice open to me.

It didn't happen overnight, but I gradually developed a workable routine. I'd put washing in the machine before I went to school. I'd prep the veg for dinner when I rushed home at lunchtime to make a sandwich or a bowl of soup for Mum, to make sure she ate something, then I'd also hang the washing out, before rushing back to my classes. After school, I'd do the shopping on the way home, bring the washing in, make the dinner, take a tray up to Mother, eat my meal alone in the kitchen, do my homework, then the washing up, and fall into bed, exhausted and dreamless.

Mother did recover after a year or two and became, of all things, a party girl, always out, never home till late. And I still had everything to do. By the time I was leaving school at eighteen, Mother was leaving home, off to marry someone she'd met at a dance. He lived in Dagenham and she correctly assumed I wouldn't want to move all the way down there from Edinburgh when I'd already applied to go to Queen Margaret's College to study nursing – a choice I made when I doubted my mother would ever recover. I had visions of her becoming a helpless invalid I'd need to nurse for the duration, so I decided to be prepared.

Uncertain of the reliability of her dance partner, I did the training – on a daily basis expecting her to arrive home in a similarly helpless state to that from which she'd not so long ago emerged.

I'm not bitter about it. It was just the way it was. But it changed me. When I look at my Donna, I love that she still has a delightful childlike love of life and I envy her. I had to grow up very quickly and far too soon.

But, even now, when it comes to teasing out complex issues, things that require detailed and in-depth thought, my mind rebels and goes off in all directions, as it used to before that fateful day when my father left me to care for the wreck of a woman he had no further affection for.

I've never considered myself like my mother, in fact I think I deliberately tried not to be, but we reacted the same way to shock. And we each suffered a sudden, crushing shock.

'Ah,' I tell myself, somewhat smugly, 'but it isn't the same.'

My daughters, instead of being schoolgirls are all grown up, with families and/or careers already formed.

I was still at school, probably thinking I was grown up, but in reality was certainly not, when the first shock shook our world, Mother's and mine.

Both shocks, the one father dished out and the one Bill, without intention, delivered by his death, both happened totally without warning. There was no chance to discuss it, no chance to prepare.

But we both took to our beds. I didn't with the first shock, but mother did. I did with the second. It wasn't something either of us planned. It happened without our permission.

Again, with a smug uplift of my chin, I think, 'But it wasn't the same. My husband died. Hers only left her.'

My situation was far worse.

Or was it?

Where I am left with endless happy memories, she was left with nothing. Every photograph she looked at, she would wonder, was he happy that time? Every memory recalled, was he happy then? Was it real? Would she wonder, was he only pretending he loved her when he kissed her, when he made love to her in their marital bed? Or was that lust, the natural desire a man has to satisfy a need, rather than an act of love born out of a deep emotional longing to be one with your wife.

Oh, how could I compare her situation with mine?

She was so much worse off than I was.

For the first time since I was sixteen, I understand. When she took to her bed, she wasn't less traumatised than I was when I took to mine. Both events were brutally sudden, unexpected, final.

My poor mother. I feel terrible for the lack of insight and understanding I had for her pain all those years ago.

She left no forwarding address when she left, and I was too angry to ask her to. Sadly, it is too late to find her and apologise, tell her I did love her and I wish she'd kept in touch, because I received an invitation to her funeral years ago. I sent back a rather curt note: 'Thank you for letting me know, but sorry, I won't manage to attend.' It would have served no useful purpose, me turning up after all those years, knowing nothing and no one from her life for the past forty-odd years, and too late to make amends.

Looking back, I realise why she opted to change everything about her life. She needed to find who she was, what she wanted once everything she valued was cruelly snatched from her. To be honest, it hurt at the time to realise she didn't value me enough to phone or write when she was settled.

I don't want to go back to my old life, either.

True, I have a family who loves me and who I shall always love and value, and they'll remain part of my life. Part of my new life.

But they can't be all of it.

If I allow them to take over my life, I'll remain lost, never able to find me. Who I am as a person. Who I am as a widow rather than a wife. As an individual rather than a mother.

Bill was a very health-conscious man yet his life was snuffed out in a moment. If I've learned nothing else since, I have learned that life is too short and uncertain to stay stuck in a rut. Even before Bill died, I wasn't living life to the full.

I've decided it lies in my power to change that, starting today.

Action!

I had noticed Ruairidh walking along towards the pier earlier, but I knew I had thinking to do, decisions to make, so I didn't go after him, or wait for him to return. Having done my thinking and made my decision, I leave my rock seat and walk smartly up a set of stairs further along the beach, hoping not to be seen by my family and quizzed about where I'm going. Where I am going is up to the reception area to enquire about the availability of another caravan for the week after next. And the week after that, and maybe even the week after that. Maybe the rest of August and into September?

The schools will all be back in session, the caravan park will be quieter and the prices lower. Bill has left me more than comfortably off. His life insurance policies alone have given me more in the bank than seems decent to me, plus I am entitled to a very generous share of the work pension he'd paid into for most of his working life. That alone is sufficient for my day to day living. I can certainly afford to rent a caravan for a month or so.

Decision made.

Action being taken.

I decide not to just extend this week's stay after the others have gone home, because I'd like to bring up my own car, and I'd like to add to the few things I brought up to do me for this week. As I walk, I start making a list in my head of things I'll need for a longer stay.

By the time I reach the reception, I can hardly contain my excitement and anticipation – but I do, feeling sure the lady behind the desk doesn't need to hear about how good I'm feeling about myself right now.

There is an almost tangible sense of elation when I have succeeded in making the booking for the same caravan, having realised I enjoy the balcony too much to change to a smaller caravan as I had originally thought I might. So, I'll still be on the front, overlooking the beach, for four weeks, starting a week after I get home from this one.

Wow! I did it.

Drunk on the elation of it, I feel the bounce in my step as I return the way I came – again, hoping not to be spotted by my family, but keen to be spotted by my friend.

As soon as I reach the beach, I see him waiting near the anchor. He's gazing out to sea, probably deep in thought, but I know for certain he's waiting there on the off-chance I've managed to get away to meet him.

Running the rest of the way across the rocks and sand to him, it takes all of my self-control not to throw myself into his arms. I disguise that impulse by grinning like the proverbial Cheshire Cat and breathlessly telling him, "I've done it. I've booked it. I'll be back on the 11th for four whole weeks on my own."

He laughs, catching me as I almost fall into his arms, intended or not, because I have trouble stopping my forward motion. "Any chance you could take a breath or two and tell me that again."

So I do, and am rewarded with his gorgeous smile.

"Perhaps I'll be around to come to one of your ceilidhs!"

"You will, and it will be my pleasure to have you accompany me – though goodness only knows if I'll be able to overcome the subsequent nerves to find my voice and my fingers."

We laugh together and walk a way along the beach, with me feeling like a teenager on a first date, unsure whether it's too soon to take his hand.

Donna learns a secret

When we turn after a while, to come back and sit on the rocks opposite the anchor, we see a great hurricane of colour rolling towards us from some distance away.

"Oh-oh! I think we've been spotted by one of my daughters," I say, resigning myself to the inevitable discovery that I have a friend unknown to my family. It had to happen sometime, but I really hoped to have Ruairidh to myself for a little longer, there being a delicious pleasure in having a secret.

"Let me guess," he says. "From all you've told me of your three girls, this has to be the youngest, Donna."

"Ooh! You have paid attention."

"Of course."

Donna reaches us, gives me her usual greeting of throwing her arms around me, lifting me off my feet and swinging me round, finishing with a big, juicy kiss on the cheek.

Wiping my cheek with my sleeve, I introduce her to, "My friend, Ruairidh."

"Hi, Ruairidh. So you're the secret my mother has been keeping from us. We guessed she was up to something. She would go for a walk and come back with such a more-than-just-healthy glow on her cheeks. There had to be something, or someone, causing that. How delightful to meet that reason."

By the end of this short speech, Ruairidh and I are both blushing.

"You don't mind?" I ask.

"Of course I don't mind. I'm delighted. Time you met some new friends." She looks Ruairidh up and down. "And you look rather fun," she says to him. "You have a twinkle of mischief in your eyes and laughter lines in all the right places. I approve, and I look forward to getting to know you better." She holds out her hand. "I'm Donna, as my mum has said. The baby of the family and the fun one." She grins. "The other two are much better kept in ignorance for a day or two more because they'll have too much to say and too many questions to ask once they meet you, so your secret's safe with me, meantime."

Ruairidh makes quite a show of looking her up and down, taking her extended hand and using it to turn her round slowly as he looks. "Hmm! Yes, I see plenty fun and mischief in you too, and I think you and I will get on famously." He makes a courtly bow over her hand before releasing it. "Don't you?"

Curtsying in return, holding out her colourful layered skirt, she grins up at him. "Absolutely famously!" Turning to me, she says, "Well done, Mum, you seem to have found someone who will make an excellent new addition to the Shakespeare play Owen I have advertised for this Saturday down in Dornoch." Turning back to a laughing Ruairidh. "You do know a bit of Shakespeare, I'm imagining, with a voice like that? I see you as a seasoned fellow performer."

He laughs. "Well spotted. I'm a musician and singer, but I have to say, I've never in my life been in any sort of play, never mind Shakespeare."

"No problem," she declares. "We don't take the play too seriously and only give a taste of it. If you are capable of learning song lyrics, I'm sure you'll have no problem learning a few lines of Romeo and Juliet."

"And what part would you like me to play?"

"Oh, you don't have to do this, Ruairidh. They usually manage fine without an extra actor."

"Oh, but I'd love to do it," he says. "What fun, at my age, to embark on a new career."

Donna has been walking round Ruairidh and me, sizing us both up. "Since there isn't a lot of time for line learning, etc, what about if you, Ruairidh, play Friar Laurence, Romeo's confidant, and you, Mum, play Juliet's nurse?"

"I'm happy with that," says Ruairidh.

"Well, I am not happy to play the nurse. Apart from anything else, I'll be travelling home on Friday with Abigail and Trevor."

Donna dismisses my reaction with a wave of her hand. "Fiddlesticks to that, I say. What say you, sir?" She turns to Ruairidh.

"I say 'fiddlesticks' too."

"Owen and I shall look after you until a convenient day to drive you home in our jalopy."

"But ..."

"No buts, mother dear. You know, and I know, and Ruairidh here knows, we are going to have enormous fun on Saturday, as well as enormous fun dressing you up and rehearsing, which we can do along in our caravan right now, since the gang are all off to line the coffers of the Duke Of Sutherland's pockets by visiting his undeservedly beautiful and opulent Dunrobin Castle, Dad would be horrified to know." She puts her arm around my shoulders. "But Mother, here, bravely and wisely declined the trip, partly through loyalty to my dear old da, and partly, I'm guessing, because she hoped to 'bump into' you, down here on the beach. Am I right?"

What can I say to all of that?

Can I deny any of it?

On brief reflection, no, I can't. Once more, Donna's enthusiasm has bowled me over and I find myself tagging along with her and Ruairidh to rummage through her costume chest for suitable apparel to portray the part of Juliet's nurse on Saturday.

She's a whirlwind, but what a fun way to be swept off my feet. I find myself laughing as we walk along the beach to the last set of stairs and climb them to where Owen awaits us. A year ago, a month ago, I could not, in my wildest dreams, have imagined myself agreeing, and even looking forward to, such a crazy idea. I haven't been on any stage since I was sixteen, the night after my father left us.

I was due to be in a school production of Twelfth Night, playing the part of Viola. I had studied the part assiduously and knew my lines and actions intimately, which was just as well because I could not have got through the evening otherwise. It was not my best performance, by any means, given as it was, by some automaton that inhabited my shocked mind and body.

It had been a joyless experience for me and the last I participated in, despite the pleadings of the drama teacher, who had tried to coax me to go to drama college. I stayed on at school to get my qualifications but had no time, after that evening, for the frivolities of plays and musicals, pantomimes and poetry readings. And all these things have remained dormant in me ever since – until now.

Now, I am walking along the beach, smiling to myself, hardly believing this is happening.

I had thought I should rebel at my daughters' determination to take over my life but here I am, completely subjugating myself to Donna's enthusiasm and planning to re-learn lines I used to know well from other school performances; planning to make an utter fool of myself, donning enough of a costume to suggest the part I am about to play, and stepping out from behind a dilapidated old caravan to play it.

Unreal.

I look across to Ruairidh, walking beside me in animated conversation with Donna. I could hardly imagine having found a better friend to please my daughter.

And me? Does he please me?

I don't feel ready to think more about that. I just want to enjoy the here and now, without thinking too much about any future relationship. Enough that I have made plans to begin a new future for myself, by planning to practise living up here. Too early to make plans to share that future with anybody at all.

I stop walking, struck by the enormity of the realisation that, if I go through with this escapade, the next step I take will be the start of that future, ready for it or not, whether it includes Ruairidh, or not.

Starting right here, right now, my new life is truly beginning.

A new beginning

On Friday morning, at half-past ten, I wave two disapproving and doubtful daughters off as they set out on their journey home from Embo.

Both Abigail and Emily had protested that Donna and Owen were too unreliable to be depended upon to get me home safely. 'What if that dreadful old, four-wheeled heap falls apart and you're all stranded half-way down the A9?' Abigail said.

'Then I'll call the breakdown service,' I responded. 'My membership covers me for any car I'm in.'

'Where will you sleep tonight?' Emily asked. 'That old caravan is far too small for three of you to squeeze into beside all the junk they fill it with.'

'My bags are neatly stowed in the back seat of the four-by-four, and I've booked myself into a hotel in Dornoch.' I omitted to mention it was for several nights, until I'd had all the fun that could be had, performing here with Donna, Owen and Ruairidh.

True to her word, Donna had kept my friendship with Ruairidh secret, and so had I. Time enough for all their disapproval. As far as they were concerned, I just wanted to spend more time with their little sister, since I hadn't seen her for ages, and she wasn't ready yet for the hustle and bustle of Edinburgh.

They had so many more objections to the plan, but succumbed eventually when I held firm. I suspect they were surprised I had found enough new resolve to stand my ground against them, I'd been so long pliable to their wishes.

I suspect too, that it must have felt a lot like I felt when, one by one, I had to face the fact that my daughters had grown up and were ready to leave the family home. They looked a little shell-shocked and bewildered as they each waved their goodbyes and drove off today – much as I had been left shell-shocked and bewildered on the steps of said family home.

It always seemed impossible that these babies of mine could have grown up and become independent overnight; despite the fact I still needed them, they no longer needed me. My job was done.

It's now time for me to reassure them that their job of nursing me through my grief, of sheltering me and caring for me through the shock and bereavement of their father's untimely death, has come to a natural conclusion. From here on, I need to show them I can manage on my own. 'Job done.'

I explained to them, I can think here, I'm coming alive here. I know in myself that's true, but what is also true is that I want to get to know Ruairidh better. I want the real holiday – no, the real life – to start once they're all gone. I don't mean to be unkind, but…

After seeing them off, I tread the well-trodden path down to the beach to meet Ruairidh; to walk together to our next rehearsal of what is bound to be a great-fun, much abridged and distorted version of Shakespeare's tragedy, turning it into the triumph of sense over romantic stupidity that Donna always claimed *Romeo and Juliet* should be, and I always secretly wished it could be.

The fact that we'll be rewriting the Bard's centuries-old masterpiece, doesn't trouble any of us. After all, the posters only claim it is loosely based on the original play. Very loosely based, but so much more joyful.

It turns out to Owen's delight, Ruairidh also plays the tin whistle, relieving Owen of the dubious pleasure of playing the flute at each intermission. He'd always found it a bit of a rush since he was also responsible for changing the bits and pieces of scenery they use to denote each new location for the play as well as playing various parts in various scenes.

Truly it is a production intended to be a feast of fun, delight and joy. All miscues and unsteady scenery accepted as part and parcel of the entertainment. They had played Dornoch several times before, over the years, and many locals assured them they'd attend again to enjoy the 'sumptuous repast of theatrical conviviality' they advertise on the posters.

I can hardly contain my excitement as I stroll along the beach with my new friend.

A new life? Bring it on!

Saturday night

I'm sitting in my hotel room on Saturday evening after enjoying a delicious meal downstairs with Donna, Owen and Ruairidh, the cast of the afternoon's extravaganza. The meal is my way of saying a huge 'Thank you!' for having the faith and courage to entrust me with playing a part in it all. I enjoyed playing Juliet's nurse, the more so with the happy outcome of the play. It was so much fun.

Even more surprising, I enjoyed singing the little ditties Owen had written for each character to sing at the end of the play, putting into song how happy they were no one had to die in this joyful romance. Then I joined in the choruses we sang, accompanied by Ruairidh on the fiddle, Owen on the flute, and Donna and I playing tambourines.

It was such a merry and boisterous ending to the play. Conga-style, we wandered among the audience, a far bigger one than I thought might have attended, encouraging them to join in the dance we'd started.

It truly was an amazing, fantastic evening of entertainment for everyone, including the cast of the four of us. I could not have imagined I'd ever have the privilege and joy of being part of something so bohemian and off-beat.

And, to add to the joy, it had been a great success. The audience loved it and were extremely generous in their donations. Afterwards, there was a long queue of people waiting to have their portraits sketched or their children's faces painted, the latter of which Ruairidh and I had a great time helping with. The results may not have been as professionally face-painted as Donna and Owen might have accomplished, but, even if I say so myself, they were pretty good, and the kids were happy enough with them.

When Donna and Owen counted up before they joined us in the hotel's dining room, Donna declared they were, 'Well happy,' with their rewards. There were enough funds to keep them mobile for some time to come, even should they run into a lean spell.

Needless to say, it was a happy, raucous meal. Could it ever be anything else, with the adrenaline flowing more plentifully than the wine?

When we all said our goodnights, Owen and Donna climbed in their vehicle and trundled our theatre back to the caravan park, Ruairidh and I waving them off before he got into his car and I went back into the hotel – but not without a warm hug and a peck on the cheek.

My whole body tingles with the memory as I sit in bed, pretending I might read a chapter or two of my book.

Instead, I'm reviewing the unexpectedly wonderful week I've had.

Even my intentions to have a heart-to-heart with Abigail came to fruition. Instead of a walk on the beach, we sat in front of the electric fire with a cup of hot chocolate and some delicious pastries from the deli in Dornoch, while Trevor and Forrest went to play pool up at the entertainment centre one evening, and our conversation flowed with ease into what was bothering my precious daughter.

'I didn't give myself a chance to do anything with my life, other than being a wife and a mother, both roles I always wanted and still love, but don't feel totally fulfilling now Forrest is getting older. I know I'll still be needed as a mum for a while longer, since he's only eleven, hardly the finished article yet, but what then? I've nothing I can turn to for the fulfilment I feel is lacking. And, let's face it, being a check-out assistant in the supermarket down the road is really not cutting it.'

I listened quietly, knowing but with no intention of saying, 'I tried to tell you this when you left school too early, with no qualifications and no prospects.'

Abigail said it for me. 'I know, Mum. Everything you said all those years ago was spot on. It was good advice, but I couldn't hear it, wouldn't hear it. It wasn't what I wanted to hear. Even now, I don't regret leaving school when I did, or not going on to some form of higher education. I honestly was so done with all of that. Trouble is, it means I have no skills, no talents, no training.' She closed her eyes. 'I'm about to turn thirty-nine, Mum. Next year I'll be forty!'

'I know, love. Isn't that pretty awesome? To have so much to look forward to? You have your husband and your son, you have a lovely home and, when you turn forty, Forrest will be thirteen, well able to look after himself while you're at night school or something, depending what you choose to do.' I put a lot of emphasis on the word 'choose'.

'Oh, I hadn't thought of it like that.'

'Instead of dreading that big four-oh, why not view it as the start of finding a career for yourself.'

'You're right. It's not too late, is it?'

'Never. Many, many women start a new career far later than that. That's why there are so many courses available for mature students.'

She nodded, and I could see the penny poised, ready to drop.

'Why don't you start by taking some time out for yourself. Go somewhere where you can think, really think. Take a notebook and pen, and write down everything you enjoy doing. Everything you wish you had looked into but didn't take the time to consider before. Maybe go along to the library and look up the various prospectuses for local colleges or classes. Things like that. You have time on your side. You're not pushed to find a career or a job, so you can take as long as you need to find one that you *want.* That you really want.'

'Mum. You're brilliant. It sounds so obvious now you've said it. Yes, that's what I'm going to do.'

We ended our chat with many hugs and kisses and a glass of wine to celebrate. It was a lovely evening and I am so happy I could be of help.

It's funny, but often, the simplest things are the things we don't think of when we're grieving or upset over something else. I can't help but feel the fear of turning forty became a huge thing in Abigail's mind because her dad's life had ended so suddenly, making life seem a tenuous, short affair, giving her an awareness of time marching on for her and, when she looked at what she had done with the years she'd had already, it wasn't enough for her. She wanted more, and that 'more' is sitting so easily in reach now she's had her attention drawn to it.

I lie back against the pillow, feeling happier than I ever could have imagined after a week up here surrounded by memories of Bill, sharing a caravan with someone that wasn't him. Yes, it was my daughter and her family, but it wasn't Bill.

I thought I was losing sight of him, but up here, I find even with making a new gentleman friend, I haven't lost sight of Bill. He always said he'd want me to be happy if anything ever happened to him. That didn't use to mean anything to me. But now it does. It's as though he gave me advanced permission to make a new life after he was gone. It's taken three years and a lot of heartache, but I feel good about the fact I am doing exactly that now.

Donna drew my attention to a newish song by Celine Dion, called 'Love Again', from a film of the same name, and while it's far too early to think in terms of finding romantic love again, I'm certainly falling in love with life again.

A new life hovers in the wings

When Donna and Owen deliver me back to my front door in Edinburgh, a few days later, I realise this is not where I want to be. It's only been a matter of half a day since Ruairidh waved us off in Embo and already I miss him terribly.

Shaking my head, feeling a tad ridiculous for feeling as I do, I remind myself I am a mature woman – I so much prefer the adjective 'mature' than 'old', or even, 'middle-aged' – yet I feel like a teenager having her first crush, because surely, on such a short acquaintance, this must be a crush I have on Ruairidh, mustn't it? There hasn't been time for it to be anything more. Yet it feels so much more.

As I walk through my front door, instead of getting that nice-to-be-home feeling I always used to get after even the loveliest of holidays, I have an almost crushing feeling of loss. The loss of Bill, yes. But also the loss of my new-found friend, and the loss of the freedom I felt in Embo.

It would have been reasonable to assume that, having lived for a week in a caravan, the house would feel more spacious, but it doesn't. The walls seem to be closing in on me with every day. There's nowhere in this house to sit with my morning coffee and watch the sunrise because it rises behind the side wall where there are no windows. I try sitting out in the back garden on the patio, but the high hedge between this house and the neighbour's hides it from view again.

There's nowhere I can go to walk on the beach, without driving there. I feel trapped.

Over the next couple of days, that feeling only intensifies and I find so many things in my house I used to like are now meaningless to me. The ornaments, the furniture, the curtains and the cushions; the comfy bed, the pretty duvet cover, none of it comforts me anymore. This is not where I want to be. I'd had a taste of the new, I no longer feel 'at home' with the old.

I ask for a cardboard box when I'm in the supermarket and when I get home, before even unpacking the little bit of shopping I bought, I go round the house taking down the pictures and ornaments I have no affection for, realising why they are annoying me as I do. They are all things Bill saw or liked, or were given to him by his mother or his sister or friends at work. They never were my taste, but then, neither was the wallpaper, or the carpet.

To be fair, I didn't put up any other options, make any objections to what Bill chose, mainly because it didn't seem to matter to me.

I had lived for so long in my mother's house, with her taste in furniture, fixtures and decor, that by the time I married, I accepted the change to living with Bill's mother's taste, which Bill thought was his taste. He had been comfortable living at home with his mother for far longer than many men would have been and, all of a sudden, it's easy to see how he made our home an extension of hers.

So I went back to the supermarket to beg another couple of boxes in which to put the cushions, and anything else easily managed without, then I loaded the car with all the boxes and took them to the charity shop before anyone could suggest I shouldn't.

From having thought I could never leave this house, I now long to be away again, flying free up on the beach in Embo.

Not being silly, I know this could pass, this feeling of joy I had up in Embo, this delight in Ruairidh's company, so I do nothing rash. Despite the inclination to put my house on the market, I don't. Despite wanting to get rid of the furniture as well as the accessories, I don't. Despite the longing to talk about Ruairidh all the time, I don't.

I decide I will have my four more weeks up in Embo, as planned, and see if it still feels the same before making any hasty decisions. Apart from Donna and Owen, no one else knows about Ruairidh, so I decide to keep it that way. I also decide not to feel guilty about keeping it from the other two in order to find out for myself if this friendship might blossom into something more, without being told that 'of course it won't.'

When I announce I am extending my break away and have already booked the caravan for four more weeks, Abigail is somewhat aghast.

"What? On your own?"

"Yes."

"But, won't you be lonely?"

Curbing the desire to claim my new friend, I say instead, "I like I have time and space to think up there. When I'm here, I can't see the future without your dad, so I would never change, never sell up and move to a smaller house. Up there, I can see all sorts of possibilities, and I want to think about them."

"You mean, a bit like what I'm doing, Looking at college prospectuses and such?"

"A bit like that."

"You know, the more I'm finding out, the more exciting it is. There's so much open to me. To you, too. Mum. It turns out there are many women your age and older signing up for courses. I'll be by no means the oldest in any class."

"That's wonderful, love. It's great it excites you."

"Oh, it does, Mum, it really does."

"Then perhaps you can understand a little of my need to get out of the rut I find myself in."

She looks at me, concern and anxiety beginning to give way to understanding on her face. "I suppose I do. But are you sure you'll be okay on your own so far from home?"

I refrain from telling her this house no longer feels like 'home'. Instead, I say, "Of course I'll be okay. I appreciate all you girls did for me after your dad died, how you helped me to recover. And I have. I've been looking after myself for some time and I am quite capable of looking after myself wherever I am now."

"Yes. That's true. I know you can."

"So can you let me go without me feeling guilty?"

She hugs me. "Of course, Mum." Then says, "Do you need a hand with packing or anything?"

We look at one another and both laugh.

"Of course you don't. You always were a great holiday packer. When do you go?"

"Tomorrow morning. I should be at the caravan by late afternoon and I'll give you a buzz to let you know I've safely arrived."

We cuddle again and I get back in my car to drive the few miles to see Emily for virtually the same conversation. After she reaches the point when she can bear for me to go off on my own, even for four weeks, she also hugs me, and I feel better now they both see it's a good thing for me after all.

"By the way, Mum, after that dinner out you treated us to, up in Embo, Bryan and I have kept open the door of communication we broke through that evening. We've been talking a lot more frankly and it feels so much better."

"Oh, that's great to hear."

"It seems that young lady I was worried about was scaring the pants off Bryan – thankfully not literally."

We both laugh.

"He couldn't shake her off. He told me at first he was flattered. She's much younger than he is and she's very pretty, but he really and truly wasn't interested. Apparently, she bores him. She can only talk about fashion and make-up and who is in and who is out on social media. He says he doesn't want to be with her or anyone other than me and the children."

"So, has he decided what to do about it?"

"He has. We talked it through and he's going to make sure I'm around a lot more. My friend, Pam, from next door is going to keep an eye on the kids whenever Bryan's mum isn't able to. So whenever Bryan is playing anywhere not too far from home, I'll go with him and I'll be backstage before and after the performances. I'll also turn up at some of his rehearsals." Her face is glowing, her excitement palpable. "Who knows, in time, I might even be able to go back to orchestral work when the kids are older."

I smile to see the glow on her face as she talks about her dreams for the future.

"I've spoken to Bryan's mum and she'd love to babysit for me any time I need her."

"Well, that's great, love."

"And, since she only lives round the corner, sometimes she'll have the kids at hers, sometimes she'll stay at ours."

"Sounds like you've got it all well planned out."

"Oh, I have, Mum, and truly, it's all down to you. You helped me see all might not be as it seemed with Bryan and the flautist. And you encouraged us to talk about it. Isn't it strange how perverse we can be sometimes, always seeing the hopelessness and not the solution that is staring us in the face?"

"So true."

"When I stop and think about it, of course communication is the key. That's what you and Dad taught us by example. You guys always spent time together, talking, making sure you were on the same page."

"We did."

"And you did the same with us. We always knew we could talk about everything and anything with you both." Her face clouds. "Oh, I do miss Dad, Mum." She falls into my arms.

"I know you do, love, we all do, but we have so many wonderful memories to hold on to and, really, let's not go backwards. You have so much to look forward to."

She draws back to look at me. "Yes, you're right, and it's only fair you get a chance to think through what *your* future should look like now you're feeling up to it. And, if being in Embo helps you do that, then off you go. Only, do let us know, from time to time, that you're okay."

When I drive away from her, I feel a huge weight lifted from me. My three girls are okay with my plan, as far as they know it. I chuckle to myself. Let's hope they're still okay with it when they find out a new man may turn out to be part of that plan.

Back to the future

Driving so far on my own is a new experience for me and I find I love it. I stop wherever and whenever it pleases me, and I linger there for however long I want to linger, admiring pretty views, taking my time over lunch and afternoon tea.

Total luxury.

A great start to my new life.

By the time I reach Dornoch, it's time for dinner, so I stop again and order something in one of the hotel restaurants. It's a delicious feeling of power to defer the pleasure of seeing Ruairidh again. Being acutely sensitive to the power of freedom and the associated power of spontaneity, I'm trying to be in control, to not allow everything to run away from me. I need to know the relationship that is blossoming with Ruairidh is real, not just a passing infatuation.

We've spoken on the phone several times in the few days since I drove away from here with Donna and Owen, and he knows I want to enjoy my journey, not rush it. We've arranged to meet on the beach to watch the sunset, which, though it sets behind the caravans, we plan to watch by walking further along towards Golspie, to where there are no more caravans. We'll climb the dunes and set up our seats on the scrub at the top and we'll watch the sun go down. Always provided, of course, the weather plays fair with us.

Enjoying a light meal in Dornoch, I still should have plenty of time to get myself settled in the caravan and stroll down in the evening light for what we have agreed is our first proper date.

Shutting out all memories of past 'first dates', I am filled with delightful anticipation for this one. I've chosen a gorgeous, long summer dress, all pastel colours of the sunset we plan to share, with pretty sandals I can easily slip off and carry to walk barefoot on the sand and dip my toes in the water if I choose.

My hair was freshly washed this morning to show off the results of my visit to the hairdresser a couple of days ago, where a young woman who had never done my hair in the past excelled herself and my hair looks natural but well styled. It takes next to no care, but falls into shape with minimum help from me as it air dries. And the magazines were right, the new style shows off my silver to advantage, brings it to life, bringing light and movement to my hair and face.

I'm feeling good, all set for a romantic evening, all set for beginning a new chapter of my life.

I've driven hundreds of miles back up the road, potentially to find my future.

An unusual first date

Of course it pours with rain. From nowhere, while we are walking along the beach, enormous black clouds roll in, the wind becomes fierce and the clouds are split by bolts of lightning, noisily depositing a month's worth of rain on our heads as we run for cover to my caravan.

Giddy with laughing and running, I can hardly unlock the door and we pour ourselves in – that expression taking on a whole new meaning as the water runs from us. Within moments the kitchen floor is awash.

Snatching the towel and the dishtowel I had folded beside the cooker and grabbing more from the deep drawer where I'd neatly stowed weeks' worth of clean supplies, we do our best to stop the rivers of water from running off our clothes, our hair, our feet. Never, it seems to me, have two people been wetter without having swum in the sea, fully clothed.

I run to the bathroom and grab the large bath sheet I'd carefully hung there and hand it to Ruairidh to wrap around himself to stop his shivering, doing the same with the spare one I'd left on the bed in one of the bedrooms I'll not be sleeping in.

Making sure the heating is on, I throw the towels we are finished with on the floor to soak up the flood. I suggest to Ruairidh he's welcome to use one of the spare rooms in which to strip off his soaking wet clothes and wrap himself in the large bath sheet, toga style, while I rush to the bedroom to strip my pretty dress off and replace it with a pair of warm joggers, a thick jumper, and warm slippers instead of pretty, dainty sandals.

When we reconvene in the living room, I give him my bath towel to put round his shoulders and we hang his clothes over the radiators to dry. Poor Ruairidh, I have nothing that would fit him to replace his sodden clothes, but he claims they'll soon dry and, with my permission – gladly given – he's not going anywhere right now.

"Besides," he says. "I feel somewhat regal in my toga and cloak, quite Caesar-like." He strikes a pose. "What do you think?"

True to my nature, I burst out laughing, whereupon he adopts a crestfallen expression. "Et tu, Eilidh," he says in a strangled, choked voice as he sinks gracefully onto the couch clutching the towels round himself, dramatically accompanied by a flash of blinding lightning, immediately followed by the loudest clap of thunder.

"The storm must be right above the caravan, Caesar. You can't die now. I need you to keep me safe."

With a theatrical groan, he rises onto one elbow and assures me I will be unharmed. Then with a surfeit of over-acting, he chokes and dies.

"Oh, that's a pity," I say. "The storm looks rather exciting from this window."

"And, with one leap, he is freed from the chains of death and stands beside his lady."

Laughing, we watch from the French windows as the storm rages on.

Such an amazing sight: sheet lightning illuminating the whole scene, showing the rain being endlessly poured out from the bowl of the clouds. No 'gentle rain falling from heaven' as the poets talk about. This is a lusty waterfall from a black sky. And it seems never-ending.

Clap after clap of thunder follows flash after flash of lightning, which stays close above us for a while before slowly moving further towards Loch Fleet before heading out to sea.

It's beautiful and awe-inspiring to watch.

It seems to take forever to pass, by which time, the heating has helped us warm up and has dried Ruairidh's clothes sufficiently for him to go through again to the spare room and get dressed.

Saying a silent, 'Thank you' to my lovely hairdresser, I see with a glance in the mirror, the rough towel drying I gave my hair and the occasional journey of my fingers through it, have allowed it to dry quite nicely.

Now things outside have calmed down a bit, Ruairidh opens the picnic hamper he had deposited inside the door and proceeds to lay out the goodies within. Confessing he's had a trip to the deli in Dornoch, the table is spread with all sorts of tasty things, and a bottle of Champagne to mark our first date.

We're almost afraid to open the Champagne, since it has endured a lot of running and is bound to be almost as excited as I am to be picnicking in the cosy caravan.

Perhaps it's not the romantic first date we'd planned, but it's a memorable, super fun one, which I can't help but feel is better in its cosy, companionable way.

So, tell me ...

When we've picnicked sufficiently, we sit back with our Champagne glasses refilled, and play a game of 'so tell me', each of us taking it in turns to answer that question posed by the other.

We hadn't planned to play it but kind of fall into it when Ruairidh asks me how the girls responded when I told them I was coming back to Embo.

In turn, after sharing that story in all its detail, I say, "So, tell me about your family."

"Mine is not as interesting as yours because I have no children, in fact I never married, though I was engaged twice."

"So, how did you not end up married?"

"Well, the first time, I was in my mid-twenties and had been with Isla for two years. She made it plain she wanted a ring on her finger and a house on the hill, so we got engaged. But the life of a fisherman has never been easy and I was often away till late evening seven days a week, falling into bed in my brother's house after a bite to eat, too tired to go anywhere or do anything because we'd spent a tiring day chasing shoals of fish, hauling in near empty nets, laying lobster pots and all the rest."

He waves 'all the rest' away as of no interest to me. "Suffice it to say, after a further two years of engagement, I came ashore at the end of a long, wet week of long, wet days where we hardly caught enough for my share of the rent, never mind having something to save for getting married. After cleaning up and eating the meal prepared for me by my sister, I took a stroll down to the pub where

Isla worked, hoping for a welcome home cuddle and canoodle – to be met instead by a very grim, determined face behind the bar, and was handed back my ring. She had 'fallen' for the barman, and fallen pregnant by the barman, when I was away too much a few months earlier. They planned to marry at the registry office the next week and set up home together in the flat above the bar."

"Oh dear."

Ruairidh shook his head. "To be honest, I think the relationship had run its course and the biggest sorrow for me was having to change locals. I liked that pub. They did a good steak and ale pie."

"And the second time?"

"I was in my late thirties and believed I was madly in love with the singer in the ceilidh band we were both in at the time. I thought it was reciprocated when she accepted my marriage proposal and my ring. All was going well, until I found her wrapped in the arms of the drummer."

"Oh dear."

"Again, in retrospect, the worst of it was that I had to find another ceilidh band, though I have to confess I was pretty cut up about that one. We had even got the length of looking at houses and planning how many kids we'd have. I truly believed she was the one for me. I suppose the drummer felt that too."

I move closer to him and put my hand over his. "I'm so sorry, Ruairidh, it seems you haven't had a lot of joy in that department."

"Och, lass, dinna fash yersel. I've had my moments. There were other girls besides and I didn't want for company on a night out."

Despite his light tone and brave banter, I see pain. True it was a long time ago, but I can see the hurt by the clouds passing over his face even as he makes light of each story he tells.

Smiling, I pat his hand and move back to where I was on the short end of the L-shaped couch. "So, tell me about the rest of your family. You said you were the youngest of eleven."

"Yes, seven boys and four girls."

"I know the oldest was a girl, Catriona, but where did the others come?"

"Catriona was followed by the other three girls, and just when my dad was despairing of getting help on the boat, they were followed by the seven boys. All in the space of twenty-nine years."

"Does that mean there were twenty-nine years between you and Catriona?"

"That's the picture. My mother was glad of her being the eldest because she was a great help bringing up all the others."

"Wow! No wonder Catriona felt more like an auntie or a mother than a sister."

"Aye, she did that. And a fine fist she made of it too."

"I can see that," I say, blushing furiously as soon as the words left my mouth. "I mean ... I mean ... Oh, you know what I mean."

"I do," he says with a smile. "You're not so badly brought up yourself."

We laugh together and it feels good, companionable.

"So, what about you? Brothers or sisters?" he asks.

"None. I was an only child, which saved me the bother of trying to raise any others once my father walked out on us and my mother took to her bed."

"My turn to say, 'Oh dear'," he says.

I wave that story away for another day, declaring it boring. "The worst inconvenience of that was I had to grow up very quickly and suddenly, without any preparation, at the age of sixteen. That was when, I now realise, I lost who I was deep inside and became this adult who cared for everyone else, without actually knowing what I wanted or needed, even choosing a caring profession – nursing – instead of becoming the film and stage star of my girlhood dreams." I laugh.

"Well, you made a great start on the career of your dreams on Saturday."

"Oh, no." I wave my hands in the air. "That was very much a one-off, never-to-be-repeated, performance."

"Until the next time Donna ropes us both in with her enthusiasm." He raises an eyebrow. "I thought I made a rather good fist of playing Caesar earlier." He strikes a regal pose.

"Hmm! Perhaps you have received the call of the stage, but I'm afraid that voice long-since went silent for me. I daren't say never again, though it's what comes to mind, but I repeat, that was a one-off for me."

"Pity, I rather fancied us treading the boards together."

Looking at him askance as sufficient response to that, I ask him, "So, when did you realise you were a talented musician as well as a fisherman."

"Oh, that was when I was quite young. My father used to play and sing in the house between trips to sea. When I was a wee lad, I would join in with the Gaelic songs, and they all realised I had the best voice of the lot of us. Father procured a small melodeon for me to learn on, and it was discovered I had a natural gift for that too. Having watched his fingers move over the keys, I simply seemed to know how to play. Same with the fiddle and the tin whistle."

I laugh at his miming of playing each instrument in turn, getting one confused with another and ending in a delightful muddle.

"My mother decided I was a 'gifted' child and should not be put to sea with the rest of the boys, but, after she died when I was ten, my father liked me on the boat during the school holidays to play and sing to him when he was low. He loved all the sad traditional Gaelic songs, the ballads and the laments. Strangely enough, they seemed to cheer him. I think he drowned his personal sorrow in them."

"And after leaving school?"

"It seemed the thing to do, to join the family fishing business, though, truth be told, I was always a musician rather than a fisherman at heart."

"So, tell me, can you speak Gaelic? Not just sing it?"

"Och, aye, lass. Everyone in this part of the world used to speak Gaelic, until lowland and Sassenach schoolteachers tried to force it out of them. Long ago, the landowners declared it a heathen, barbaric language they had no inclination to learn, so they endeavoured to wipe it out among their tenants."

"How well did they succeed?"

"Better than they should have but not as well as they wished. Gaelic is my mother tongue. It's all my mother and father spoke and mostly what my brothers spoke, especially when we were at sea."

"But English at school?"

"Obligatory. The teachers refused to allow us to converse any other way. If we forgot ourselves and relapsed into the language of our ancestors, we were soundly beaten, thankfully a practice that has long since been frowned upon and eventually banned in schools."

"Oh, my word. How dreadful, to take such cruel measures to do away with an ancient language."

Ruairidh laughs. "Oh, that's not the half of the cruelty visited on the people of this poor beleaguered land."

"Yes, you promised to share some of the stories handed down through your family. The Highland Clearances, the Herring Boom and ..."

"The Gold Rush."

"The what? The Gold Rush? What, here in this area?"

"Oh, yes, up in the glen behind Helmsdale. You can still pan for gold up there, though it's been a long time since much was found." He looks at his watch. "But, my dear Eilidh, these are stories for another time. It's getting late, the rain has long since stopped, the storm abated, and it's time I wended my way home."

I yawn and, having checked the time on my watch, I really have to agree. "It's been a long and eventful day," I admit.

"Tomorrow?" he asks.

"Tomorrow." I smile.

Good companions

The sleep of the exhausted claimed me as soon as I fell into bed, postponed only by my bedtime routine, after I closed the door behind Ruairidh.

I looked forward to lying cosy in bed, thinking over the day and all the excitements it held. But, no, it seemed I had hardly pulled the duvet over my ears before I was pushing it back to greet the morning.

What luxury, to know I have the whole day to do as I wish, planning minimum housework and maximum pleasure.

I stretch luxuriously and lie a little longer, until the need to empty my bladder becomes too urgent to ignore. After showering and dressing, I stretch again and go through to open the French doors and step out onto the balcony to breathe in the storm-freshened sea air, though I've long since missed the sunrise.

We hadn't made a plan last night, agreeing only to see one another for our morning walk, and I am pleasantly surprised when Ruairidh knocks at the door of the caravan, clutching a bag of warm, buttered croissants and a flask of real coffee, both of which he'd prepared and carried down from his house, the nearness of which being easily deduced from the fact the croissants are still beautifully warm.

"Oh, good," he says. "You're up and about. I'd have felt a trifle silly having to carry these back home if my plan had been foiled by a sleepy-headed reception."

"Fortunately, not only am I up and about, but I haven't yet broken my fast." I laugh. "So you and what you carry are most welcome. In you come and sit yourself down."

The smell of his gift is intoxicating when the flask is unstoppered and the croissants plated, and we both set about enjoying them greedily at first, but soon, when the first gasp of morning hunger is assuaged, we sit back and savour them at a more leisurely pace.

"Oh, this is the life," I say on a long sigh. "This is a great way to start the day, rather than swallowing down my instant coffee while I unload the dishwasher, or put a few bits of washing in the machine."

He looks at me, a puzzled frown creasing his face. "Surely you don't still start the day like that of a morning, now there is just you to please?"

"Habit, I'm afraid. Once I was on my own, truly on my own, when Bill was gone and the shock had worn off sufficiently for the girls not to take it in turns sleeping over to look after me, I went back to the habits of a lifetime – habits formed when I was sixteen, I suppose."

"You do know you are permitted to break that unnecessary habit?"

"Then, during the next four weeks, you can have the privilege of helping me do that very thing." I hold up the last sip of my delicious, real coffee and grin triumphantly at him, knowing that, for four weeks, I'll be relieved of the dubious pleasure of throwing a spoonful of instant coffee grains in a cup of hot water and munching on a slice of toast as I go about the day's activities.

Luxury.

The few dishes take moments to wash and dry, with the two of us doing it together, and we set off on our walk. Without needing discussion, we automatically head towards the far end of the beach to see if the dolphins are coming out to play.

Walking without talking, revelling in the freshness of the morning breeze, the brightening of the sky as the sun takes its higher position, listening to the waves lapping the shore, idyllic!

Stopping for a moment, I close my eyes and take long, deep breaths. When I open them again, it's all still here and Ruairidh is still here beside me. The seagulls are still circling overhead, then diving into the water for their breakfast, snatching unwary fish from theirs. The sun is still slowly arcing through the sky, its movement imperceptible as its warmth increases. In this gloriously peaceful place, I am imbued with a serenity and contentment that has been eluding me for a very long time.

But I know this peaceful beach hadn't always been a holiday destination. It used to be a busy place, the sound of the water lapping the shore often drowned by the shouting of fishermen, one to another, fisherwomen shouting their entreaties to 'Take care!' or welcoming their menfolk home, the wheeling of the birds accompanied by a chorus of greedy cawing gulls deftly stealing an occasional unguarded fish from the nets and creels.

"So, tell me," I ask, "what would it have been like here a couple of hundred years ago?"

He looks at me. "Not the tranquil place it is now."

"I guessed that. I was trying to imagine it, but I think the imaginings of my mind are rather romanticised, even knowing the life of fisher folks was a hard one."

"Still is, in many ways," he says. "Now you have your car here, you should go up to Helmsdale one afternoon and you can see for yourself. You can watch the fishermen as they bring the boats in and unload the catch."

"Oh, I would like that. I'd like it very much."

"But, before that, you really should go to the Historylinks Museum in Dornoch, one afternoon. It's not over big, but it gives a great flavour of life in Embo and Dornoch in times gone past."

"Oh, that's a great idea. I'd love to do that too."

"Then you could widen out to take in what it was like further north when you go to Helmsdale."

"Perfect."

"If you're sure that's what you want to do with your few weeks here."

"Very much so. I have a hunger to broaden my mind, to learn about people and places and times and events I've never cared to learn about before. In particular, to get to know more about this area, this place, this village I'm becoming so very fond of." I stop and close my eyes a moment, knowing what I'm about to say might well be 'jumping the gun', but wanting to risk it anyway. If nothing else, it might help me discern if he is becoming as invested in this relationship as I am.

He stops, and waits to see why I stopped.

"Is it … well, is it presumptuous of me to ask …" I swallow hard and cross my fingers behind my back. "I mean, couldn't we do these things together? Please?"

He laughs. "That would give me more pleasure than you can imagine. But I didn't want to assume you would want that too."

"Then, perhaps it's time we each owned up to the fact we're wanting to spend more time together, lots more time. Then we could just get on and do that."

"That sounds like a great idea."

I turn to him. "So, Ruairidh MacRae, I'd really like to spend time with you and get to know you better, really well, in fact."

"Well, since we both seem to want the same thing, would it be okay if I consider you my companion for the next four weeks?"

"Absolutely! Though I have to say as well as being your companion, I'd love for you to be my teacher and me to be your pupil."

He laughs. "Well, perhaps as far as local history goes, that would work, but I wouldn't want you to see me only as a teacher, because I'd be terribly uncomfortable in that role all the time."

"Okay, maybe for today, and when we visit the museum and Helmsdale, and things like that?"

"Hmm! I think I can just about cope with that. But only if you prove to be a happy pupil. You must let me know as soon as I become a bore and you've had enough of my lectures. I can be a bit of a geek or a nerd, or whatever it is over-studious people are called these days."

My turn to laugh. "Oh, I doubt that will happen. I could listen to your voice all day. You do know, don't you, that you have a delightful east coast, highland lilt? And, besides that, there is so much I shall enjoy learning from you."

So, as we continue our walk along the now familiar beach, that is what we become, good friends, happy companions, as well as pupil and teacher, teacher and pupil, and I'm loving it.

Going back in time

"So, yesterday, you said you were hungry to learn about this area."

"And beyond," I say, smiling up at him, as he helps me clear our continental style breakfast dishes again.

"Well, we talked a lot about the fishermen and the life they led here in Embo, so today, I thought we could take a walk back through time to much earlier settlers here."

"Okay."

As we walk in the opposite direction from which we usually walk, Ruairidh shares the aim of our walk today. "I want you to cast your imagination back, way, way back to when people first came to populate Scotland."

"Like the Vikings or ..."

"Even before that, but after the global flood of Noah's day, when his three sons spread out to populate this glorious planet."

"Oh, you believe in the Biblical flood?"

"Well, I am a Christian and I believe Jesus was who he said he was, the Son of God, and he believed in Noah and the Bible account of the flood, so who am I to disagree?"

"Oh, I'd never thought of it like that. I like to think of myself as a Christian but I've never studied the Bible much at all. I suppose I followed the religion I was brought up in. Our Sunday School teacher read us what she called, 'the story of Noah and the flood' and had us draw pictures of all the animals going into a pretty wee ark, like the one she showed us in the picture in the book she read from. It made it seem like a fairy tale. A myth."

"Another time, I'll show you the passage in the book of Matthew, where Jesus talks about Noah and the flood."

"I'd like that."

"It was Noah's son, Japheth and his descendants who are believed to have wandered towards Europe, over many centuries, eventually reaching islands like Britain."

"How on earth would they have managed it without all the modern modes of travel we have?"

"People mistakenly think the early settlers were uneducated and without proper communication, but that simply isn't so. Again in the Bible, it's clear from the earliest of times they could plan together, design and build houses, cities, even. There were tool makers, workers in metal, wood and stone, and they had units of measurement. The ark itself, far from being a pretty wee boat, was a massive three storied floating wonder. It was a tremendous feat of engineering. True, Noah and his sons worked in accord with clear instructions and measurements from God, but they would have had to learn many new skills to do it. They would have had all that knowledge and more to pass on from generation to generation."

I nod. "Of course."

"And when they came out of the ark and were told to spread across the world, they would not have been without transport. The animals saved from the flood would in time proliferate and there would be plenty of donkeys, horses, camels and all sorts of beasts of burden to load with their possessions and to pull their carts. When they came to water, they would have chopped down trees and built boats, just as the Vikings, the Saxons and so many who came after them did."

"Of course."

"The first settlers in north-east Scotland may well have travelled by sea, but not necessarily from across the North Sea. The archaeological evidence convincingly shows the earliest settlers on this island arrived from

Continental Europe, some of them possibly crossing the Channel. The earliest artefacts are found in the South of England. As those who chose to wander further spread northwards, they would sometimes follow rivers further inland, but often it was easier going by sea, taking shorter hops up the coasts, where they could attack the almost impenetrable forests they encountered from the coast, living on beaches like this at first, chopping the trees down to use for firewood, building dwellings, gradually pushing inland. We are talking about many hundreds of years, thousands of years of migration."

"Wonderful to imagine." I shake my head. "I'd never given it much thought."

"When people first settled along this coast, they would have fed off shellfish of all sorts, clams, oysters, whelks and mussels, as well as the fish they caught, any game they could catch and nuts and berries that were plentiful on the trees and bushes up there." He inclines his head to the rough grasses and scrubby bushes on the skyline above the dunes. "There is not much sign here of the rudimentary shelters they built to house their families, but the shell middens found in places up this coastline are evidence of their presence and activities in the distant past."

"Shell middens?"

"Like ancient landfill sites in the dunes, places to dump the detritus of their way of life."

I peer at the dunes. "Could I stumble on any around here?"

He inclines his head. "Mmm. It's possible, but I'm not sure here would be best to look. I've often walked this stretch, but haven't found any, though I'm assured there are some to be found further than I usually walk. And there are some more to be found walking south from Dornoch. Perhaps a walk for another day?"

A smile spreads through my chest and across my face. "Yes, please," I say.

"The proliferation of things like these would seem to indicate they gradually, over time, became permanent dwellers in this region, judging from ancient structures and ruins found in various places around Scotland. At first they used tools of stone, eventually of bronze as they entered what archaeologists call the Bronze Age."

I nod, taking in what he says, allowing it to stir in my mind, seeking out bits and pieces of learning lurking there from my school days. "If I remember rightly, archaeologists traditionally divide prehistory into three main periods, don't they?" I close my eyes the better to think. "It's the Stone Age, the Bronze Age and the Iron Age, yes? Each named after the main technologies used in their time."

"Absolutely. History – what they call *pre*history has been shown by archaeologists to have followed a logical progression."

"Oh, it's so exciting to find signs of life from so very long ago, right here around Embo and Dornoch." I am filled with the joy many pupils must feel when taught by a teacher who not only loves his subject and is passionate about it, but who also helps you see it, both literally and figuratively.

He teaches so well, he makes me feel good, as though I'm a bit clever too, instead of the dumb housewife I have classified myself as. He helps me dredge up, from somewhere deep inside me, things I must have learned at school or over the years since. Snippets of knowledge I had no idea were hidden there. Not every teacher has that gift.

While finding out so much about the area, I am also finding out much about the man. A man of faith as well as a man of passion, of learning and of joy. A man to be much admired.

The more I look at what he has drawn to my attention, the more I can picture the early settlers. Of course they would have designated places outside their settlement where they could pile up the debris of their foraging, probably digging in any vegetable waste elsewhere, to enrich the soil for whatever they could plant. I wonder if they brought with them bags of seeds from Continental Europe, in case they found land hospitable to the crops they were familiar with. And of course they would have made use of whatever they found in and around the places they landed. I picture the men out fishing in that water I see in front of me, pulling their boats up this beach, up above the water line, possibly even using them for shelter until they could chop down trees and build their homes, probably up there on more solid land well back from the shifting sand of the dunes.

I picture children playing, or helping their parents plant crops and forage for meat. I see it all in my imagination, which is truly coming alive under Ruairidh's tutelage.

I look out at the same sky they lived under, the same sea they saw, the same beach where they would have worked on their boats, the same sun shining down on them, the same moon at night, the same rain that watered their new crops.

Sure, I know the air and the water move round the earth, round and round in perfectly designed systems, but throughout history and prehistory the same air, the same water have always been in and around this planet. It's an awe-inspiring, beautifully efficient recycling system, designed by its creator.

Where I am walking and standing right now will have changed a little from time to time, season to season, with the shifting of the sands and the changing of the tides, but basically, it would have been almost the same hundreds and thousands of years ago. The timeless beauty of all that I see and sense seeps into my soul, into my being and gives me a true sense of belonging.

Closing my eyes, I take a long, deep breath of the same air those settlers might have breathed in, and let it out in a long contented sigh.

What do you see?

Eventually, when I am ready, Ruairidh accompanies me back along the beach towards the caravan site, but before we reach it, he leads me up a path between some of the dunes, pointing out things I'd have overlooked before: wildflowers, variegated horsetail, purple milk-vetch, rue-leaved saxifrage, moonwort and frog orchid, whose names I type into my phone along with their photographs; birds such as sandpipers, shag and cormorant, where I might only have noticed seagulls. He is opening my eyes, helping me look outside of myself, as I asked him to, and I am so filled with gratitude I could hug him.

We pass the local football field, skirting around it because there is a ladies' training session in progress, then all the way to the side of the reception building of the caravan site.

We've been so busy talking, I followed happily without question, trusting he knows where we are going and why.

"What do you see?" he asks.

"Well." I look around myself. "I see the reception building and steps down to the level below from the side of it, the car park …"

"And what else?"

"And, hmm …" I look around myself, somewhat puzzled. "And a pile of stones," I say with a shrug.

"Right. I wonder how many times you will have walked or driven past that 'pile of stones', without giving it a second glance."

"Oh, times without number, I suppose. Why? Is it significant?"

"This 'pile of stones' was first officially recognised as an ancient site in 1956, when a gentleman holidaying here with his family, before there was ever a caravan park, realised that 'pile of stones' was actually the remains of a Neolithic chambered cairn."

"Goodness!"

"The word cairn in Scottish Gaelic, was *carn* and is a group of stones piled up to form a mound. A chambered cairn has at least one chamber inside the mound. This one had two chambers. This cairn was used as a burial place for the local community of settlers here in Embo, many, many years ago. The dead were buried in the chamber, starting even before the Bronze Age. We know that, because one chamber was found to contain two Bronze Age cists, spelled with a 'c' but pronounced kists, which had clearly been added at a later time than when the cairn was first in use."

"A cist being?"

"For individual burials, rather than communal ones, where the remains of the dead were stored, after cremation or lying somewhere until the flesh had been eaten by carrion. Each cist would usually contain the remains of one person, together with some personal items, known as grave goods. One of the cists, found in this cairn, contained a food vessel and some jet beads."

"Wow! I can hardly believe I have gone past it so many times, without really seeing it, never mind investigating it. But you said there were two cists found here?"

"Yes, the other contained the remains of two babies with a food vessel and fragments of pottery."

I automatically raise my hand to my face and step back a little, hurting inside. "Oh, how sad."

"It is sad, but the babies were buried by someone who loved them enough to provide for some sort of afterlife where they might need food. It is also a sign these were organised, civilised people who buried their dead. Not the barbarians many think the early settlers were. They were not apelike creatures with no interest in one another, but, from earliest times, they gathered together, had designated places for their rubbish, pooled resources and buried their dead with some sort of ceremony. This site is now listed as a Scheduled Ancient Monument."

"Wow! That's really rather awesome, to be standing here in touching distance of something that belonged to the ancient residents of Embo. And I always walked right past it, intent on checking in and finding my caravan." Once more, I hang my head, ashamed of my own ignorance as well as my lack of past interest and curiosity. And also the lack of the respect due such a memorial.

We spend a little time here, with Ruairidh walking me around the perimeter of the site to where there is an information board, explaining what I see in front of me. He helps me make out the structure of the ancient cairn. This is so far removed from a 'pile of stones' standing or lying about nonchalantly, unaware that someone would notice them thousands of years later and 'read' their story by examining them.

Again, I try to imagine the people who had built this edifice. They surely must have lived nearby because I can imagine they would have wanted to conduct their burial ceremonies and mourn their dead somewhere they could visit again. So I wonder if some of them were settled over near the dunes we visited earlier. Would they have enjoyed a reasonably quiet life in this peaceful place? Before the caravan park and the fishing village were here, there would only have been a small settlement with all that stretch of beach and open sea. I hope it was a pleasant life. Hard work, maybe, but no one minds working hard in order to care for family and live in peace, do they?

After a while, Ruairidh turns to me. "Enough history for this morning, I think, eh? Let's walk back and gather our bits and bobs, drive to Dornoch and I'll treat you to lunch before we hit the museum to look at some of the artefacts that pertain to our morning's adventures."

Almost reluctantly, I turn away from this simple but amazing 'pile of stones', knowing I shall never walk or drive past again without thinking of the people who buried their beloved babies and others here, in times so far removed from my own.

The morning has proved to be a fascinating one and I stand in awe of the teacher as well as his teachings.

I can't seem to stay away

After the first visit to the Historylinks Museum in Dornoch that day, I mused on what I saw, and what I learned, and enjoyed reading the booklets and pamphlets I bought, becoming completely immersed in it all. I decide I'd like to go back there, to see everything now I'm better informed, feeling I'll have a better understanding of it all and wanting to try to get the timelines sorted out in my head.

To be honest, I can't seem to stay away from the place. It has really captured my imagination.

Not liking to commandeer all of his time, I tell Ruairidh I'm happy to go by myself, since he had been kind enough to take me the first time, but he elects to come with me, which makes me smile, because I so enjoy his company. I love talking to him about what we examine because he always seems to help me put everything in context.

"Besides," he says. "There is something I want to show you."

When we are in the museum, he points out something I'd hardly noticed in passing the first time, because my mind was a bit fixed on finding out all I could about Embo as a fishing village, during my earlier visit.

There was a battle fought on the beach at Embo!

"There was a battle in Embo?"

"So it seems." Ruairidh laughs, not unkindly – probably at my childlike amazement and enthusiasm.

"Fought about the year 1245, in which William 1st Earl of Sutherland defeated Viking invaders," I read. "Fought on the beach, according to the account written during the 16th century and quoted here. Apparently, the 1st Earl of Sutherland arrived at Embo with a large force to help oppose the invaders, who then fled, pursued by the Earl, and during the battle the general of the Danes was killed with many others." I look up at Ruairidh, my eyes wide and my mouth open, making him laugh again. Then I turn back to the information on the wall. "The Earl apparently secured the victory when he killed the Danish general with the severed leg of a horse." I turn to Ruairidh as though he won't believe it, despite the fact he is standing beside me and quite capable of reading it for himself. "The severed leg of a horse?"

"So the account has it."

"But, can you imagine how bloody and gruesome that was?"

"Ugh! I try not to." Ruairidh pulls a face, waving away the images brought to mind.

"Wow! I'm really beginning to see Embo in a whole new light. I've always thought of it as a sleepy wee village with a holiday park and a long expanse of beach, looking out over the North Sea."

"Which it is."

"But I am beginning to realise it hasn't always been. With your help to examine it deeper, it's actually a wee village standing on the ground of rich history. Bloody history even."

"It is indeed."

"I'm totally enthralled and besotted with the area now. You do know I probably will want to revisit it all again?"

Once my attention has been drawn to that information, which had been there in the museum last time too, I shake my head in disbelief that I could have given it so little notice. It seems such an important event in Embo's history. And so hard even to imagine, though of course I set the intention to try next time while I'm walking on the beach.

As we exit the museum, Ruairidh walks me in a slightly different direction to see a rather ancient, broken monument.

"What is it?" I ask, leaning forward to see the small information plaque.

"It used to be in the shape of a cross and is called The Thane's or Earl's Cross, and was erected as a memorial of The Battle of Embo," Ruairidh reads, helping me out while I rake around for my reading glasses and my phone.

By the time I photograph it from every angle, and ensure that Ruairidh is doing the same, in case he snaps the best photo, I'm ready to go – this time.

When we get back to Embo and Ruairidh drops me off at the caravan, after that second visit, I decide to christen my newly-bought sketch pad and have a go at resurrecting an old favourite hobby. I used to spend many happy hours drawing and painting, when I was a girl. I thought it might be interesting to see if I've still got enough skill to enjoy it again.

I'm sitting down to have a try when Ruairidh knocks on the door of the caravan, and I realise he didn't have time to do more than park his car before he's back.

"Ah, I see you're busy," he says. "I'll leave you in peace."

"No, please don't go. I was only going to try to do a wee sketch or two. But, to tell you the truth, it's been so long since I did any form of art activity, I have no idea if I can even still draw anything at all in any recognisable way."

"Ah, yes, it's one of the things you said you'd long ago lost sight of."

"Did I? I don't remember …"

"Yes, it was one of the things you were mourning the loss of when I came across you sitting staring out to sea, looking very sad and pensive. That and poetry and dancing, as I remember. In fact you spoke very poetically of their loss."

"Did I? I had forgotten."

"But I hadn't," he says. "It really touched me."

"How kind to have remembered the ravings of a distressed mind."

"I was very moved by what you said, and I think it's a lovely idea to win these things back into your life."

I go to the shelf and reach down some of the new pamphlets and books we gathered from our foray to Dornoch. "There were some photographs in these. I thought I might choose the one of the fishwives hoisting their creels on their backs to go sell their fish in the village. Though I think that might be a bit too ambitious for a first return foray into sketching." I take my phone from where it also lies on the shelf. "Or I might use one of the photos we took in the museum today. There were so many interesting old artefacts there. I haven't decided yet. Perhaps you'd like to help me look through them?"

"I'd be happy to."

So we spend a delightful hour or so, going through the pamphlets, booklets and the photos on my phone, hoping something will jump out at me, saying, 'Me. Me. Sketch me.'

When I ask to see his photos, Ruairidh is very reluctant to show me, though I'm aware he took loads.

"Ach, they're mostly of the things you photographed as well, only they're not as good," he says.

Assuming he's just being modest, "I can't really believe that," I say. "I bet they're far better. I'm not very skilled at using my phone as a camera."

"Really, I think you have a great selection yourself."

"But I'd like to see yours."

"Och, I don't think there's much of interest for you there."

I hold my hand out for the phone. "I'd like to be the judge of that, please."

But he moves his phone to the other side, away from me.

After trying coaxing, teasing and daring him to let me see, we have a silly, childish play-fight on the couch, with me trying to take the phone from him and him resisting vigorously.

Suddenly, the game feels too intense, so I sit back and pretend to huff.

It's only when I teasingly ask him if he won't let me see the photos because there are too many photos of all the lady friends he's been seeing that he weakens, lets me take the phone from his hand, and gives me the password to access it.

He goes very still and quiet, sitting forward on the couch, his head bent, examining the back of his hands.

They are practically all of me, his photographs, they are practically all of me: me photographing things that interested me; me with my reading glasses on; me with them off to look at photographic displays; me with them on again, reading the information about all the fascinating artefacts and photographs.

None of the exhibits themselves.

I had no idea.

I don't know what to do, what to say.

There are no words.

I'm breathless. Overcome. The emotional impact of what this means stuns me. It's too much.

Handing his phone back to him, I sit beside him with our shoulders touching and my hand in his for a long time before I kiss him gently on the cheek and thank him in a whisper.

Another companionable day

After another lovely morning walk, followed by our breakfast, we decide to relax in the caravan because the day has clouded over and we even felt the need to have the heating on for a while.

"Would you like some time to yourself?" Ruairidh asks. "I'm conscious I've been taking up rather a lot of your time these past weeks. Am I cramping your style a bit too much?"

I burst out laughing. "My style? What style is that, d'you think? I don't imagine I have such a thing. Nope, I'd far rather you stayed to keep me company."

Ruairidh smiles, pleasure showing in his smile. "So, what would you like to sketch today?"

"Oh, I'd planned to do that when I thought I would have no company."

"Nothing stopping you doing it anyway." He spreads his hands wide. "If you don't mind me sitting quietly reading one of your books while you do, we can just enjoy being together. It's a chilly, grey day out there. In fact it's even starting to rain, so we can cosy up in here, if that's okay?"

"Oh, that would be lovely."

Tears rise to my throat. Even Bill didn't take the time to find out what I missed in my life. I think he always assumed he and the girls were enough. And, in many ways they were, and I don't regret the life we had one bit, but, suddenly I am overtaken by a feeling of loss. Loss of the opportunity to let Bill see me as more than his wife and the mother of his children. I wish he'd helped me find ‘me’, the me I should have been if my father hadn’t walked out when I was sixteen, taking the remainder of my youth and the fulfilment of my personal dreams, leaving me with the shell of my mother to nurse.

That with so short an acquaintance, Ruairidh had already listened to the distressed uttering of my personal grief, taken it seriously, and is intent on helping me find my dreams again, is yet another of the most meaningful things to have happened to me in many, many years.

I can’t speak, but only nod as I lift my sketch pad and pencils from the shelf. But he seems to know what I can’t say and draws me into his arms and holds me for a while.

“So, what do you want to sketch?” he whispers as he releases me.

Looking through the few sketches I’ve already done, I’m happy to have found the familiarity of holding a pencil in my hand and creating a recognisable likeness of the things I choose. I’m comforted that particular joy is not lost but is returning to me. I decide to sketch one of the photos I took of the remains of the chambered cairn up by the reception area because the story intrigued me. Standing there looking at it, imagining those early settlers living off the land and the sea, burying their dead in a civilised, almost ceremonial way, was a very meaningful experience for me, and I now feel ready to tackle drawing what they built thousands of years ago.

“Good choice,” Ruairidh says. “That should make a great subject for a sketch.” He has chosen a book from the shelf, but I don’t suppose for a moment, he’s genuinely interested in reading about romance in the world of fashion.

The books I had brought were very much intended for light, holiday reading – for me. However, true to his word, he sits there in the corner of the couch, quietly pretending to read, while I attempt to find again whatever talent I’d once shown.

After a while, I realise he has dozed off with the book in his lap and his reading glasses askew, so I smile and feel less self-conscious about getting on with my task.

I've been working up at the table behind him, and it's not until I put the pad down and stretch out my stiffness that Ruairidh wakes up and turns round. "Finished already," he says, with no realisation he has been sleeping for ages.

I laugh. "Already," I say, closing the pad over and gathering my pencils to put it all away.

"Am I going to be allowed to see it, then?"

I pull a face. "I'd rather not. I'm still very rusty and it's not great, though I did enjoy the exercise. I'll let you see one when I get it right. This one is proving more difficult."

"Up to you, but I'm sure you're being harder on yourself than I would be."

"Cuppa time," I say, putting pad, pencils and reading glasses back on the shelf. I notice with a smile, he didn't get past the first page of the book.

While we have a rainy spell, we spend several idyllically happy afternoons in similar fashion, me sketching the things I've seen, the photographs I've taken, filling my heart and mind with the history of Embo and Dornoch, while Ruairidh sits nearby, reading a book he has brought with him from his own bookshelves.

Sometimes he brings his fiddle or his button box and plays for me. Practice for him, pleasure for me, though Ruairidh declares himself happy we have no near neighbours – the caravans to either side of mine both being unoccupied this late on in the season.

Today, while he plays, I find my mind wandering, thinking through all the things I've seen and done with him.

In the past, when the children were young, I used to love visiting the National Museum in Edinburgh. Sadly, their attention span never quite matched mine and I always felt a little short changed by the time I took them home. There always was so much more I had had no time to see, floors I hadn't had a chance to explore, artefacts I'm certain I could have learned history from.

While we were there, my attention was constantly diverted from something interesting to what had caught Emily's eye, or Abigail's attention, or Donna would be needing to go to the toilet – 'Now, Mumsie, right now!'

Why, oh why, I ask myself, did I never take the time, or make the effort to go there by myself? Did I think it was there for the children only? Did I walk out of its grand, domed exit and forget about it until the next time I was looking for something to do, somewhere to take three young children on a rainy day?

How sad was I? How shut in to the routines of life?

It was the same with the art galleries. Yes, I'd visited them, but never on my own, never viewing things at my own pace, taking my time to go from room to room. Instead I'd be rushed around until it was time to go to the gift shop, where the girls were never interested in postcards of the paintings we had hurried past. Their main concern was how much sweet rubbish I'd allow them to buy.

What a wasted opportunity once they grew up. It simply didn't occur to me to take time out of my, mostly unnecessary, housework to spend a blissful afternoon looking at beautiful things.

I feel such a fool. There are so many things I could have been enjoying all these years since the girls grew up, if I'd only looked outside my own little 'box'.

My mood is quickly lifted when Ruairidh reminds me he's playing in a ceilidh tonight, not a wedding ceilidh, but one I am invited to attend with him, and it's time he went home to get ready.

My heart skips as I contemplate yet something else new to experience. How rich my life is becoming.

What on earth does one wear to a ceilidh?

But what on earth does one wear to a ceilidh, I wonder, as I peruse the meagre contents of my holiday wardrobe. I did ask Ruairidh, but he wasn't a lot of use because he just said, 'Something comfortable, casual and suitable to dance in.' So, starting with footwear, what can I dance in that would be comfortable, casual but still look reasonably pretty? I wish I had thought about this problem when I packed to come this time.

I look at my phone. Hmmm! No time to go shopping. Then I laugh. This is not Edinburgh. I have no idea where the nearest clothes shop is and the supermarkets in Tain have a very limited selection of ladies-wear.

I realise I've discovered the first drawback to living so far out of the way.

There is a very classy shop in Dornoch, but it's pricey and possibly more 'country classic' than I'd want to be. No matter, I really don't have time to check it out for anything I can wear tonight, anyway.

Okay. I turn back to the little wardrobe space in the caravan.

This is it.

My ceilidh outfit will have to be composed of what I have in front of me right here, and I'll have to decide reasonably soon because Ruairidh will be picking me up in a wee while to go to Lybster, in time for him to help the band set up.

I decide to wear a pair of jeans. They're not too dressy, but not too scruffy either, not fashionably 'distressed' with rips and holes, but they do have an attractively frayed hem. The choice of top is slightly less limited, but, having tried on three or four combinations of t-shirts, jumpers and shirts, I settle on a periwinkle blue short-sleeved tee with a plaid shirt over it, the shirt echoing the colour of the t-shirt, the colour of the jeans and a couple of shades in between, as well as a bit of red in its pattern.

Donning my denim deck shoes, brushing my teeth, running my fingers through my hair, a touch of lipstick and mascara and voilà, I'm ready to party. I don't really possess any fancy jewellery, not that I'd wear it with this outfit anyway, so just my usual rings it is to finish off what I very much hope is a suitable ceilidh outfit.

I feel casual and comfortable, and I hope I still look reasonably attractive too. I pull a face at myself in the mirror. Vanity, thy name is Eilidh!

However, my efforts are well rewarded when Ruairidh pronounces the look, "Perfect!" And the approving look with which it's said, brings colour to my cheeks.

I step into his arms to give him a thank you hug, and I have to be honest, the thoughts I was having as we clung together were not of dancing.

So, outfit approved and completed with a blush, I put my jacket on and we set off for the ceilidh.

The ceilidh

The drive up to Lybster is quite, quite beautiful, graced with a wealth of basking seals at the nature reserve, and a pod of dolphins showing off in the Sound of Fleet.

As for the ceilidh, well, it's so much more fun than I could have imagined. Right from the start, I feel at home, my outfit fitting in perfectly, and most of the band members and their wives adopting me into their group as soon as Ruairidh introduces me.

I had wondered how he'd achieve that comfortably, which he does beautifully with the words, "This is Eilidh, who I found washed up on the beach in Embo, the prettiest mermaid I've ever seen as she sat there on a rock looking out to sea. She's from Edinburgh, so we'll need to mind our manners, in the hopes she'll stay around these parts for the foreseeable."

The grin with which he says these words, coupled with the twinkle in his eyes and the warm touch of his hand on my shoulder, certainly make me want to.

While the folks at the table introduce themselves, someone gets a round of drinks in, a soft drink for me, as I'm really not much of a drinker and I know Ruairidh never imbibes alcohol either when playing in the band or is going to be driving.

Ruairidh, standing near the stage, takes a fair bit of ribbing for having brought me along. "Better than your usual driftwood, old man," accompanied by a clap on the shoulder.

"Edinburgh, did ye say. My, my!" says another.

"Bit classy for you, is she no!"

I hear Gloria, one of the wives mutter about me 'hardly being Ruairidh's type'. "I mean, look at her. I'm not surprised she's from Edinburgh." She pulls a rather snooty face. "Nothing doon tae earth about that madam."

Someone else, Jen, I think, says, "Ach well, she may be just someone to take his mind off Catriona being gone."

"We can but hope," Gloria says, casting me a very sullen look as she picks up her glass and takes a long swallow from it. "Anyway, looks like she's married, from the rings on her fingers."

"Widowed, actually," I say, knowing she intended me to hear her remarks and feel awkward.

She sniffs and turns away, pretending interest in the buttons on her blouse.

Ruairidh and Fiona, who sing with the band, gather on the stage with the others to get the party started.

And wow! Do they get the party started.

Without preamble they break into a loud, lively Gaelic fisherman's chorus, which everyone in the hall seems to know, bar me, of course. Those who don't join in the singing are tapping their feet, slapping their thighs or grabbing a partner to get the dancing started.

Another of the ladies at the table, Ina, I think she was introduced as, changes her seat from across the table to come sit beside me. "Pay no attention to Gloria. She can be a bit of a soorpuss at the best of times. You're fine, lass." She leans into me and shouts in my ear, "And pay no heed to the ribbing Ruairidh's getting either, he's a good guy, and it's great he's got a girlfriend after all this time."

"Oh, I'm not ..." But my weak protestation goes unheard, drowned out by the noise.

Ina is used to this atmosphere, and she leans in again and shouts even louder. "There's a few of us here had a try for him in the past." She gives a tiny nod in the direction of Gloria. "But he's never shown interest." And she's gone, pulled onto the dance floor by another of the ladies.

They're good, the band. They're clearly popular and professional.

Without knowing the words of any of the songs, whether Gaelic, Scots or English, I'm immediately totally and completely under their spell.

From time to time, when he can be spared, Ruairidh leaves the stage to invite me to dance, explaining the moves and leading me expertly to make them. I never hesitate to take the hand he offers, happy to be taught all these glorious, happy dances I'd been longingly watching from my seat.

It's been a long time since I've been out socially with a group of people, certainly not since Bill died, and I have forgotten how much alcohol people drink when they're out for an evening. It shocks me a bit to watch perfectly nice people gradually become slovenly, aggressive or incoherent as the evening progresses.

It's something I've always hated to observe and something I vowed many years ago would never happen to me.

Many people seem to think they can't enjoy themselves without alcohol, but I certainly can, so I stick to my soft drinks.

One of the band members, Billy, seems insulted by my refusal to be pressed to accept a rum and Coke, his wife's drink of choice, so each time it's his round, he buys one for me. Gloria, his wife, does the same when he's onstage playing. It sits untouched on the table each time.

When there are four full glasses sitting there, going to waste, Gloria finally leans across the table and asks me what my problem is.

I resist the temptation to tell her it isn't me who has the problem, and also resist pointing out that she is becoming increasingly unpleasant as she drinks, and just say, "I really don't enjoy the taste."

She pushes one of the drinks towards me and encourages me to, "Swallow it over quickly and you'll hardly taste it."

I smile and ask, "Then, what would be the point of that?"

She looks at me, frowning, clearly unable to come up with an answer. Instead, she pushes the drink further towards me. But she has become clumsy as she's become drunker, and the glass topples and the drink spills into my lap.

There is an instant hush at the table while everyone wonders what I will do.

"Oops!" I say, righting the glass on the table and pushing my chair back. "I think I'd best go and clean up a bit."

While I'm in the ladies' room, soaking up the rum and Coke as best I can with paper towels, Jen, another of the ladies who's been sitting at our table comes to see if I'm alright.

"Sorry about that," she says. "I'm afraid Gloria doesn't hold her drink well. On the other hand, you handled her *very* well. How do you do it?"

"Do what?"

"Sit there and let all those drinks pile up in front of you without ending up reaching for one of them."

I shrug. "They don't tempt me because I don't want them. I don't even think of them as mine. Billy and Gloria bought them, so as far as I'm concerned, they are theirs. I told them, 'no thank you, not for me' each time they were getting a round in, so they can't be for me, now can they?" I smile at her reflection in the mirror.

She laughs. "You're absolutely right."

"If they choose to buy drinks for an invisible friend, well, that's up to them, isn't it? But it seems a bit of a waste of money to me." I shrug my shoulders and spread my hands out, palms up.

Jen laughs so much she starts to cough and crosses her legs. I'm afraid she might choke or fall down, but she dashes into a cubicle to relieve herself.

"Oh, that's hilarious," she says, once she emerges. "I love it!"

She keeps chuckling as she washes her hands and we go back through to join the others.

I notice the unwanted drinks have been removed, the sticky mess cleaned up and a clean chair in place where I was sitting, so I sit down as though nothing else happened other than a trip to the ladies' room.

"Sorry," Gloria mumbles.

I smile back at her. "No harm done. I'm just glad I decided not to wear my Gucci blouse tonight."

Everyone at the table laughs, and Jen orders me a lime and soda drink. "Here's to good manners and the sobriety that's needed to remember them." She raises her own *Old Fashioned* in salute to me.

The next time Ruairidh asks me to dance, he whispers close to my ear, "Well done! I saw what happened and stopped playing ready to rescue you, then I watched how well you handled the situation and realised you didn't need rescuing. According to Jen, via Liam, you are 'amazing', 'the best', and 'so funny she nearly wet her pants'." He holds me a little away from himself to look at me quizzically. "What on earth did you do or say that was so funny?"

When I recount the gist of the conversation, he laughs so much, we have to step out of the dance for a moment. "You are amazing," he says as he dances me back into the crowd. "I love it!" He twirls me round in the dance, then whispers, "Jen's right, you are the best. Even though you smell like a rum and Coke."

"Yeah, as I said to Gloria when she apologised, I'm glad I didn't wear my Gucci blouse tonight."

His head goes back in laughter again. “Love it! Just love it, I wondered how you’d got the whole table laughing once you rejoined them.” He holds me close. “I’m so proud of you, so proud you are my date. My girl.”

Time for tea

After a selection of energetic dances, Fiona and Ruairidh take the lead in singing a slow, gentle Gaelic ballad allowing the dancers to catch their breath, followed by another, sung a capella by Fiona. It's hauntingly beautiful, and I truly don't need to understand the Gaelic words to know it's a sad, sensual love song. It's remarkable how silent the audience is after all their hooching and chooching of so little a while ago.

Fiona and Ruairidh finish the set with a bright but not riotous Gaelic song, the audience cheer and clap, and it's time for tea.

No wonder Ruairidh said not to eat too heavily before we came. The buffet spread is generous and diverse, the table heavily laden with all sorts of meats, fish and salad dishes, with one end of it weighed down with the most sumptuous selection of desserts I think I've ever seen.

I'm handed a plate and invited to fill it, so I enjoy choosing some of the things less familiar to me. Ruairidh helps by suggesting some of his favourites he hopes I might enjoy too. "And you can always come back to the table to try some others when you've scoffed that," he says with a cheeky grin.

It takes all of my self-control not to plant a kiss on the side of his face as he leans forward to dig into a bowl of salad to put some on his plate. His nearness, as we're pressed close together against the long table, is making me feel weak at the knees, as the very descriptive saying goes. It's a relief when he offers to carry my plate to our table – gentleman that he is – and I can concentrate on making my legs follow him.

I watch him interact with the others at the table, with much talking and laughing, as we enjoy our meal. It's clear he is a much loved member of the band, and I'm not surprised. He is such amusing and attentive company. He doesn't talk too much, when others are talking he listens carefully, responds appropriately, turning to me frequently to ensure I don't feel excluded from any conversation. He's just a lovely, lovely man and, minute by minute I'm finding myself more and more attracted to him.

So much for me not letting my heart get involved too soon. Ha! Too late, much too late to try to hold back the feelings that sparked in me the first day we met.

Gradually, as people finish eating and tea and coffee cups have been filled, refilled and emptied, the band meanders back to the stage. This time they start with the ballads and some evocative tunes from land and sea, giving time for food to settle before the dancing begins again, more sedately at first, drifting into a few of a more energetic nature, before becoming dreamy and slow again at the end.

When Ruairidh takes me in his arms for the last dance, I am almost weepy with melancholy tears, sad for the past, happy for the present and hopeful for the future.

On the way home, Ruairidh and I both become very quiet after the first pronouncements about what a great evening it's been, and I tell him, truthfully, how much I love his singing and playing. "I'm a big fan," I say.

He hadn't sung the song, 'Eilidh', he'd sung a little of on the beach, and something inside me tells me not to ask why not. It feels personal, something between us and no longer for the general public.

We chat a little about the band and their families and I tell him a little of the table talk, but we are both tired and have a lot to absorb, this having been my first ceilidh and it being the first time we've gone anywhere as any sort of couple, so gradually we fall into that delightful state of companionable silence when two people are comfortable in one another's presence without the need for constant sound.

When Ruairidh drops me off at my caravan door, he draws me to him and looks questioningly into my eyes for permission to kiss me goodnight, while I look back hoping he will. Not a peck on the cheek, not a polite goodnight kiss – I long to feel his lips on mine. I see the same longing there in his eyes, but we each seek reassurance from the other that it will be a welcome next step, so our lips move tantalisingly close, our breathing slows into sync, and at last, we are lost in the most perfect first proper kiss.

It's hard to let him go after that, with no words needed, nothing to break the spell of that magical moment when time stood still.

Good morning

We had agreed we'd have a long lie, falling into the ancient tradition, without intent, designating Sunday a day of rest, Ruairidh having recognised my silence in the car denoted tiredness as well as contentment.

So, when I eventually wake after a deliciously long, deep sleep, I don't even check the time, but lie cosily in the double bed, reliving my happy evening and analysing and absorbing the feelings it provoked.

On one level, I know I am falling for Ruairidh, on another, I am trying to hold back from allowing it, but last night, whether I allowed it or not, I know it totally happened.

People talk about a whirlwind romance and I balk at thinking of it that way. It's such a cliché, but truly, it is the absolute best way to describe it when it happens. I feel as though I've lost my footing and there's a strong wind lifting me in the air and birling and twirling me around, making me dizzy and giggly and silly, like the kind of teenager I never was.

This is a new feeling for me, this floating outside myself.

I loved Bill dearly, but it had been a slow burner. We had been on several dates before I even decided whether I liked him, but he sort of grew on me till I couldn't imagine us not being together and I grew to love him with what should have been a forever kind of love.

With Ruairidh, cliché or not, it was love at first sight, if there really is such a thing. It's actually a misnomer for what happens in such cases because I don't believe you can possibly love someone you know nothing about. But you can know for certain they are someone you want to know everything about. You can know, straight away, that you have found someone who could well complete you if you test the fit.

I suppose that's what we're doing – testing the fit. Are we truly compatible in every way? The attraction is enormously strong, but is it a healthy one? Infatuation can be a hugely strong attraction, but it doesn't stand the test of clicking together in a meaningful, lasting bond.

So, at this point in time, how can I know?

There's a voice screaming inside me, saying, 'Does it matter? Does it really matter? Why not go along with it for however long and however far it takes you? What would be the harm?'

But what I, sensible, level-headed Eilidh Crawford know, is that the harm could be a broken heart.

So I'm back to the same question: how can I know?

If I let myself fall truly and irrevocably in love, how can I know beforehand that the same wind is whirling him in the same direction? How can I know the depth of feeling will be returned?

As I throw back the warm duvet to go to the bathroom, I realise I already know the answer. Quite simply, I can't know. I'll have to learn to trust.

Love is known to be true, not by its declaration, but by its demonstration.

So I shall have to be patient a little longer to know for sure, but all the signs so far are good. Ruairidh has proved himself to be an attentive, kind friend, all you could want in someone you are contemplating building a relationship with.

I was married long enough to know that love is not all about how it makes you feel, but how you make the other person feel too. It's a two-way thing. Any relationship needs both parties to put the work in because a good one cannot be bought, but it can be earned.

I look at myself in the mirror as I finish dressing. 'Goodness, girl,' I say to my reflection. 'These are deep thoughts for a Sunday morning.' I chuckle. 'Getting a bit ahead of yourself, are you not? I mean, it was only a kiss. One kiss.'

But oh, it felt so good.

It has been too long since I melted in a man's arms, so I'm probably reading far more into it than I ought.

That one melting moment might have been mine, and mine alone. Ruairidh may have felt nothing. Why, right now, he could be anywhere, doing anything, without giving a thought to what it meant to me.

There's a tap on the door.

'Or perhaps not,' I say to the woman in the mirror, with a smile and a wink.

"I know we agreed today was to be a day of rest and recuperation," he says, giving me a very sheepish look as he holds out a bag of pastries and a flask of coffee. "But I missed you."

Laughing, I push the door wider and step aside for him to come in. "I was missing you too – and your real coffee."

"I know, I know, it's really the coffee, isn't it?" He puts the flask and the bag on the table. "I can leave you to enjoy these while they're warm and give you peace, if you like?" He would sound a lot more convincing if he could keep his face straight.

By way of answering him, I step into his arms and cuddle close. "Good morning," I mumble into his chest.

"Good morning." He lifts my head and bends to claim my lips.

It's fortunate he's firmly holding onto me, because, once more, I have jelly legs.

When we eventually draw apart, he pulls a face, half reluctant, half hopeful. "So, I wasn't totally joking when I said I could leave you to get on with your day. If you need a quiet day to yourself, you must just say."

I smile. "To be honest, when I'm back in Edinburgh, I have more days to myself than is probably good for me. It's nice to have pleasant company. Please stay."

"Oh good, I hoped you'd say that. The day seemed to loom large and empty without you." He starts unwrapping and plating the pastries. "So, any thoughts about what you would like us to do today?"

"Perhaps a walk?"

"Easily arranged," Ruairidh says through a mouthful of Belgian pastry.

As we stroll along the beach after we've finished eating, I ask him to tell me about the Highland Clearances.

"Are you sure that's what you want to talk about on this delightfully fresh morning?" he asks.

"Yep! I was thinking about it as I got dressed this morning. You'd mentioned your ancestors were caught up in the clearances, and I'd really like to learn more."

"Okay." He pulls a doubtful face and takes a breath. "Where to start." Another breath after a moment or two's thought. "Right. This is by no means going to be a very detailed account of the clearances. More an outline, if that's okay."

"Of course." I nod.

"A large part of the north and east of Scotland, is and was, Sutherland land," Ruairidh explains. "Early in the 19th century, in common with many other highland landowners the Duke and Duchess of Sutherland were advised they should 'improve' their estate to make it more productive and profitable, by farming sheep, large-scale, rather than rely on the small income paid by the tenant farmers crofting the arable land."

"You sound as though you don't believe it was ever going to be an improvement."

"I don't and I doubt the landowners and their advisors honestly did. They tried to pass it off that they were wanting to improve the tenants' lot in life. As far as they were concerned, such lowly people were a disposable source of income that was not yielding the high results they craved. I doubt they ever even considered what the crofters and cotters wanted. True, their life was a hard one, but they knew no other."

"I suppose they just got on with it, if it was all they'd known."

"Exactly. They were settlers, reluctant to leave the land they thought of as theirs, despite the fact they owned none of it. They had no lease, not even a spoken agreement that gave them any sort of secure tenure."

"So, they were totally at the mercy of those who owned the land."

"And, in effect, owned them. So, in order to lease their glens and braes to sheep-farmers from the Lowlands and England, the landowners chose to clear the tenants from the crofts in the inland straths and glens through a series of forced evictions of men, women and children – using police and soldiers where necessary. The claim was they would move the people to planned settlements on the coasts, which the Sutherlands did here in the east, chasing their tenants to what became Helmsdale, Lybster and other small villages all the way up to Caithness."

"Oh, I didn't realise there were settlements made ready for them."

Ruairidh laughs. "Not really. When I say, 'planned settlements', I mean just that. There were vague plans, but nothing much had been done about putting them into practice. Settlements like Helmsdale grew gradually once the tenants were already 'in situ'. It was a traumatic time for these poor crofters and their families. With little warning, they were brutally turned out of their homes."

"That's awful."

"At risk of traumatising you, I'd recommend reading John Prebble's account in his book, *The Highland Clearances.* There, he explains the 'politics' behind it all and he chronicles some of the many acts of brutality and shame."

"Did no one speak out against such treatment of the poor folks?"

"Oh, yes, there were voices advising otherwise, but those voices went unheeded. Throughout the whole operation in the first half of the 19th century, the landowners and their agents made it abundantly clear sheep were preferred to people. And the landowners became impatient for the promised increase of profits."

I am stunned into silence, weighed down by 'man's inhumanity to man'.

"The tenants were at the mercy of the landlords. Highland society had been a pyramid, long before the time of the clearances. Below the chief, who was at its apex, were the tacksmen, an intermediary between the chief and the rest of the clan. He leased the land from the chief and sub-leased parcels of that to the crofters as sub-tenants. A myth grew up over time, until it was assumed everyone in the clan was related to the chief, but that isn't true, even though they often took the clan surname."

"So where did the myth come from?"

"Possibly from the Gaelic word *clann* which originally had the sense of *children* or *offspring.* But, many men bought their way into a clan and many of the landowners married into it and they too adopted the clan name. The Duke of Sutherland being a case in point, he being an Englishman, with property there already."

While I ponder on all this, we reach the pier area, but there are no dolphins today for us to watch admiringly while they leap and arc above the water. We open the beach chairs Ruairidh carries and set them near what remains of the pier, to just enjoy the view anyway. We sit for a while in a familiar companionable silence.

I love that we can do that. After all the seriousness of the discussion, Ruairidh gives me time to digest the information.

I'm trying to picture a settlement of people who lived off of land that was not theirs, but that they felt a deep attachment to, an attachment that went alongside their loyalty to the clan chief, in this case, the Duke of Sutherland. "It's a statue of the Duke of Sutherland that tops the hill over behind Golspie and Brora, isn't it?" I nod to where it can be seen in the distance.

"That's right."

"Yes, Bill used to give it some right dirty looks sometimes, it seemed to be a personal affront to him it being there." I laugh. "Abigail used to say it was because it was a statue of someone other than him. Anyway, he absolutely refused to visit Dunrobin Castle, refusing 'to line the pockets of such a scoundrel', despite the fact many, many years had passed since the clearances. And that particular 'scoundrel' had long passed."

Bill knew about the Highland Clearances. He'd read up about it and clearly, it was something still offensive to him despite the fact his ancestors were from much further south.

As for me, all I knew was the little he shared with me, which consisted of his enduring ill-feeling and judgement. I didn't visit Dunrobin Castle, not out of any principles that I held, but out of loyalty to Bill. In what I now see had become a pattern with me, I didn't ever bother to find out for myself if his judgement of matters was a fair one, though, according to Ruairidh's account, it sounds like it probably was.

"So, tell me, were your ancestors crofters or cotters?"

"They were crofters. They lived in a tiny township, in the Strath of Kildonan. It was really just a small settlement, but it was called a township and it held a portion of the glen and a tract of mountain pasture for thirty or forty black cattle and a small herd of thin and fleshless sheep owned by the crofters. Each of the small settlements in the strath would have had a small corn kiln. These kilns, used for drying crops and sometimes for drying and baking pottery, were the warmest places in the township and were often used as gathering places. Sometimes they were used as schools, which was where my ancestors learned to read and write. I learned their stories from the few writings that were preserved through generations. My father was very proud of these worn, torn, battered old pages containing a mere fraction of our family history."

"Do you still have them?"

"Not me personally, but my oldest brother does, since my father died some years ago."

"Would I be able to see them?"

"Of course, though you'd not be able to read them, since they are written in Gaelic."

"Are your family all Gaelic speakers?"

"Very much so, though it is a language very much in decline, sadly."

"It's lovely that folks like you and your family, keep it alive."

"Aye, lass, we do our best to remember many of the old traditions." He chuckles. "My many-times-great-grandfather was apparently known for the excellent whisky he produced in one of the kilns."

I laugh. "What a rascal he must have been."

"One of many, it seems, since the kilns often housed illicit whisky stills in those days." He smiles. "For that and many other reasons, our ancestors' attachment to the land was deep and strong, and they clung to their history in story, verse and song."

"I noticed that many of the songs you sang at the ceilidh were greeted with what could only be called deep respect."

"Aye, in places like Helmsdale and Lybster, there is still a great pride in our shared heritage. Sadly, Prebble's book says, 'The subtenants of the land held to the spirit of the clan when the chief was bartering it for a house in Belgravia. They retained their respect for him long after he had lost his for them.'"

"I think that's a book I must read. You've mentioned it a couple of times, and seem to have committed passages to memory. Would they have it in that lovely wee bookshop in Dornoch, d'you think?"

"I'm sure they will have it, or they'd certainly order it if they haven't."

"And so, back to the clearances," I prompt, when Ruairidh falls silent for a while.

"Aye, sadly, the Strath of Kildonan was savagely cleared in the years between 1813 and 1819 – so savagely that these clearances provoked the first recorded dissent against the evictions anywhere in the Highlands, Prebble reports. There were riots and mobs when they started, but that only gave the Duke of Sutherland's factors the excuse they were looking for to go in heavy handed. Within three months, large areas of the upper strath had been entirely cleared, and the people offered tiny allotments of poor land on the clifftops near Helmsdale, or sent into exile in Canada. By the time the last inhabitants were cleared from their land, the people had learned by bitter experience that resistance was useless and there was no one willing to help them."

"I didn't know that many emigrated to Canada at that time."

"They did indeed, in their hundreds, some 700 Kildonan clansfolk alone. Many of them didn't make it through the voyage, many of them died soon after landing, but those who survived, went on to the settlements along the Red River, and many settled in the city of Winnipeg, in Manitoba."

"Do you have relatives in Canada?"

"A few. We've lost touch with most of their descendants, but my father spoke of there being long, longing letters 'home' from the original settlers there. In fact, I believe there are one or two secreted in the pages of our family history book."

I raise my eyebrows and grin at him.

"Which I'll show you when we go up to Helmsdale, if they are still there, and Fingal and his missus don't mind the imposition."

Frozen

The bookshop in Dornoch does have both *The Highland Clearances* by John Prebble and *The Silver Darlings* by Neil Gunn and I buy both the next day. It thrills me to have them in my possession and I can hardly wait to start reading them properly to get a fuller picture of that time in Scotland's history. Knowing that Ruairidh's ancestors lived through those times gives both books added interest. I want to understand where he comes from and what his heritage is. I can't explain it, even to myself, but there is a yearning in me to know all there is to know about him. Despite my usual natural caution, I already feel unbreakably bound to this lovely man.

I'm walking along the pavement with a real spring in my step, thinking about what I'm going to wear tonight when we meet for an evening walk on the beach. I love having someone in my life again, someone I want to feel attractive for, someone I want to look my best for. Someone I want to stay in my life from here on in. A startling admission to myself and a hitherto unspoken one, but none the less life changing.

I love wearing scarves, not just for warmth, but chosen well, they can really set off an outfit, and, last time I was in Dornoch, I'd noticed they had some pretty ones in the chemist shop along from the bookshop so I decide I'll treat myself to one today. It's that kind of day. Buoyed up by my blossoming relationship with Ruairidh, I feel like buying something new to wear.

Smiling to myself, almost skipping along the pavement, I'm about to enter the chemist shop when the door is opened from the inside. Preparing to stand back to let people come out, I freeze.

They can't pass.

I'm in the way.

There's nothing I can do about that.

I can't move.

Years ago, I remember Bill and I driving home from Pitlochry one night after seeing a play in the Pitlochry theatre. Suddenly, a young deer crossed our path.

But it didn't cross.

It stood bang in front of the car.

Frozen.

It was only when Bill dimmed the lights, the deer seemed to come to its senses and bound away.

But the couple standing in the doorway of the shop have no headlights to dim.

No way to release me.

I am caught.

Frozen.

This has happened to me before, though right now, I don't know when. I only know the feeling is familiar.

Ruairidh steps forward a little and holds me against him. "It's okay," he whispers in my ear. "It's okay. I'll explain."

Stepping back, he draws the lady beside him forward. "Nan," he says to her. "This is the lady I was telling you about. This is Eilidh." Turning back to me, "Eilidh, this is my neighbour, Nan. I'm taking her to visit her husband in the care home."

"So lovely to bump into you like this," she says in a voice that betrays the fact she's ready to settle in for a chat. "I've been dying to meet you. Ruairidh has told me so much about you." She looks up at him and smiles. "He's a good one. A keeper," she whispers close to my ear.

I look at her, shock and confusion still preventing me from speech.

With gentle care, Ruairidh takes my arms and moves me to the side so they can come out of the doorway to allow others to pass behind them.

He turns to Nan and hands her the keys to his car. "I'll be right with you, Nan," he says.

"Of course," she says with a grin. "I'll give you two a moment. Nice to have met you," she says to me.

Smiling – or I think I'm smiling. Who knows? My face doesn't feel like it belongs to me. I watch her cross the road to Ruairidh's parked car.

"Are you okay?"

I nod, feeling slowly returning to me.

"I have to go," I say as I get into my car. "I need time …" I manoeuvre out of the parking space and drive off.

When I get to the caravan I put the kettle on and make myself a hot, sweet drink. Wrapping myself in the rug from the couch, I sit there and sip the resuscitating beverage willing myself to stop shaking.

I'm in shock, a feeling I remember from three years ago. I felt it happen as I saw Ruairidh come out of the chemist shop with another woman on his arm. There was no mistaking they were together. She was looking up into his face, laughing. He drew her to him when he thought I wanted to pass.

I thought at that moment I'd been made a fool of. I was overcome by a familiar feeling of betrayal.

Closing my eyes, I try to steady my breathing, resisting the urge to cry.

Without a knock, Ruairidh bursts into the caravan, startling me for a moment.

"Oh, Eilidh, what must you be thinking? You got a shock and I'm so sorry. It's my fault. I should have explained what the 'things I have to do today' meant."

I close my eyes, try to stop shaking, determined to be strong.

"I can only think you thought perhaps I had been leading you on and I was married or something?"

"You owe me no explanations. You made no declarations, no promises. I've been a fool."

He takes the empty cup from my hand and puts it aside, then lowers himself onto the couch beside me. "No, my dear Eilidh, you've not been a fool. Neither have you been fooled. Like I said, Nan is my neighbour and I was taking her to visit her husband in the care home."

I look at him, wanting so much for that to be the simple explanation. I see the earnest look in his face, hear it in his voice. Hope steals over me, warmer than the blanket.

"Oh, Eilidh." He takes both my hands in his. "I know it seems too soon to make such a declaration, but I have fallen in love with you and there is not, nor will there be, anyone else for me. I love you, Eilidh Crawford, and I'd dearly love to spend the rest of my life getting to know you better."

When he leans forward to kiss me, as the warmth of his kiss flows through me, all the fear, all the pain leave my body. He loves me. It has been real. This bond that's grown so quickly, and become so strong between us is real. It's not one-sided. It exists, not just in my imagination.

"I'm sorry for what happened in Dornoch. I made a spectacle of myself, didn't I?"

"It was, quite simply, shock. At risk of sounding presumptuous, I think perhaps you thought you were losing someone else important in your life while you were still getting over the shock of losing Bill?"

"Yes." The familiar feelings, being unable to move. Not once, but twice. The first time, when my father walked out on us. I remember freezing as I watched him lift his bags into the boot of the car.

I couldn't move, though every fibre of my being wanted to take the bags from him, throw them to the ground, make him stay, if not for her, then for me. I couldn't do anything. I was helpless. Frozen.

I couldn't speak, though my whole being wanted to cry out to him not to go. To tell him I still loved him. I still needed him. But I said nothing. I was struck dumb.

I remember standing there, with my mouth wide open in a silent scream.

It was only the sound of my mother's terrible wailing and keening that shook me out of my shock and into hers. She was crumpled into a shivering, jelly-like heap on the hall floor behind me. I must have stood looking at her for quite some time before helping her to her feet and upstairs into her bed. I remember she slumped limply against me, heavier than she should be as I half carried her up the mountain of stairs.

What I don't remember is how many days it was before I helped her out of her clothes to have a shower and change into others, which turned out to be wasted effort because she immediately went back to bed.

Someone had to keep us alive, so my shock and distress was pushed aside to be forgotten.

Until that day when Bill died in the bed beside me.

I have a vague memory of sitting on my dressing table chair staring at my dead husband. Unable to close his eyes. Unable to cover his face. Frozen.

I have no memory of phoning for help, though I was told I did. I have no memory of being put to bed, though I was.

Shock. Shock upon shock upon shock.

I close my eyes.

And now the tears come. A torrent. Gulping and gurgling from me like a broken dam.

Ruairidh sits beside me and holds me while I shudder and wail.

"There, let it all out, lass. Let it out."

I could not have stopped if I'd wanted to.

Not for a while.

When the deluge slows to a dribble, I look at him, but find I can't explain. These were tears for my father and for Bill. Both times I had to stem the flood, firstly for my mother, then for the girls. There had been rather a lot dammed up behind that protective wall I'd built, beaver-like, over such a long time.

"I suspect that, normally, it would not have been such a big deal," Ruairidh was saying, "but the way Bill died has traumatised you and your whole system is raw and ready to fall into that shocked state again when provoked."

"Yes." How does he know? How come he understands what others could not?

He smiles. "In a way, it's very flattering and reassuring for me to know I mean that much to you. I've been afraid I might be deluding myself that our relationship was genuine on both sides."

I shake my head and smile. "No. It's real. I've been struggling too, afraid to admit to myself that I've fallen in love again."

He kisses me. I close my eyes. I don't want him ever to stop. I want us to be together forever.

Oh, but he has to go! Poor Nan. Deserted in Dornoch.

"I've thought of a great title for a book or a film." I laugh through the last of my tears. "Poor Nan. *Deserted in Dornoch.* What do you think?"

Ruairidh laughs too. "Great title, but I suppose I should get back to her before she calls out the rescue services."

"Tell her I'm sorry to have commandeered you."

"I'll do no such thing. She saw you'd taken unwell and was happy for me to help you. She'll be fine."

"What about her husband?"

"He'll have no idea who we are, let alone that we're later than usual."

"Poor Nan."

"Which is precisely why I go with her every week. She finds it too hard to go on her own. Sitting there with him staring at nothing, saying nothing the whole time we're there. Well, it's hard for her. But she loves him, and loyally visits every week. She holds his hand and talks to him, telling him all about her week, remembering things from their shared past, just in case there's a corner of his mind still able to register she is there and she still loves him."

"That's so sad."

"Yes, it is." He sighs. "So, if you are going to be okay now, I suppose I better get to it and take her to visit Gerry. He was a good neighbour for many years and I feel a bit like Nan, in that I want him to know he's not forgotten."

'A keeper,' Nan called Ruairidh. I look at this kind, beautiful man, standing in front of me, and know she's right. He truly is 'a keeper'.

Before he goes, he fetches the pillows from my bed and arranges them behind my head, insisting I lie down. "You have a rest and I'll bring you some food when I get back. Doctor's orders!"

I smile and snuggle down, cosy and safe – feeling loved.

To my great surprise I fall into a deep, healing sleep from which I am awakened by my handsome prince – bearing steaming soup and warm, buttered rolls.

Telling secrets

The next evening, after a gentle stroll along the beach, I decide I really must telephone the girls to give them a little more than the two or three sentences I've been texting each day in reply to their concerns.

They deserve more, I know, but once I hear their voices, I'll find it hard to strike the balance between telling them nothing and telling them all, so it's been easier to write a few words to reassure them I'm well and enjoying my break up here.

However, now Ruairidh and I have assured one another that this relationship has a future, I think it's time I gave up some of my secret.

Donna is going to be the easiest of the three phone calls to make, so I decide I'll leave hers until the other two have been accomplished, as a pick-me-up after what I fear will be a series of reprimands, warnings and anxieties from each of the other two.

Leaving me to my task with a goodnight hug and an assurance that I should and could do this, Ruairidh went home a little early and I'm missing him already.

I make myself comfortable on the couch, with a warm drink, the rug over my knees, and a box of tissues to hand.

With a deep breath, I dial Abigail's number.

I've thought a lot since I've been here about what I should say and how I should say it, but while the phone is ringing out, I realise there is not a word of what I'd rehearsed anywhere to be found in my head.

Although I have only been in Embo a few weeks, it feels as though a lifetime has passed, and I suppose in a way, it has. My old lifetime. So when I hear Abigail's voice, the familiarity of it seems quite shocking. Time feels as though it's playing tricks on me.

I remember once seeing an old black and white film where the passage of time was portrayed by the pages of a calendar falling off one by one, getting faster and faster until years had passed in just the few moments it took the pages to fall.

That's how it feels when Abigail says, "Hi, Mum!"

As though I've been catapulted back through a lifetime in moments.

It's been only a few weeks since last we spoke. The reality shocks me as it strikes home. How can I tell her I've met a man and am contemplating spending the rest of my life with him when I only met him a few short weeks ago?

I wonder if she's had time to hoover the sand out of her car since she was here with me in Embo, yet the hours I've spent with Ruairidh feel like years.

I never liked the film, *The Wizard of Oz,* yet I think of it now, how Dorothy thought and felt she'd lived a very long time in Oz, she had so many adventures, yet, when she was catapulted back home to Kansas it turns out she'd only been unconscious for a short time.

Instead of clicking my heels together, I only had to tap Abigail's photo on a screen and I'm connected to home.

When I tell her what I intend to tell her, she's going to think I've lost my reason.

I had known Bill for years before I realised I loved him enough to commit the rest of my life to him.

Abigail knew Trevor even longer before they made that commitment.

How could she possibly understand how I feel about Ruairidh? She's such a practical, down-to-earth person, she'll laugh at the very idea I could make that commitment after knowing Ruairidh for what? Weeks, merely weeks. Having spent days I can still count in his company?

“Mum! Mum!”

I stare at the mobile phone in my hand, betrayed by it, not ready to go back to Kansas.

“Mum! Can you hear me?”

I end the call.

The phone rings.

I sit and stare at my daughter’s name on the screen, until the light goes off and the ringing stops.

Faced with the choice, Kansas or Oz, dreams or reality, I am immobilised, knowing that as soon as I speak to my daughter, the delightful bubble in which I’ve been living for the past weeks will be burst and I’ll be transported back to my old life. I’ll be Eilidh Crawford, widow, again, instead of Eilidh Crawford, girlfriend.

The phone rings again.

I quickly text her to say I’m fine but can’t speak at present, which is true. Leaving the phone there in the caravan, I put my coat on and go out.

Embo

I have no idea where Ruairidh lives in the village, but Embo is a small place so I'm sure if I look for his car I'll be able to find him. So I wander through between the caravans as I've often seen him do after he leaves me.

With no trouble at all, I find a well-trodden grassy path leading me into the village, but I quickly realise I have set myself a difficult task.

This is an old fishing village.

Most of the rows of cottages have no front gardens, many, their front doors open onto a very narrow pavement, some, there is no pavement at all, so the streets are too narrow to have rows of cars parked along them.

Short of hollering out his name, or walking these rows of cottages, peering in their windows or examining each nameplate on each door, I can see I am unlikely to find Ruairidh – the downside of having left my phone in the caravan.

However, it's a charming village, the old part of it with well-kept stone or white-washed cottages in neat rows either side of narrow recently-tarmacked roads, so I decide to explore anyway.

I love the ambiance of this part of the village, where it's easy to imagine fishwives sitting outside their front doors mending nets, talking all the while to their neighbours. Or gutting fish to fill the creels stacked by their doors.

Here, the cottages are small and terraced, so it would probably be a communal, amiable life the fisherfolk led, sharing readily the joys and disappointments, the vagaries of the catch each day, the ups and downs of life.

In the early days of this village I could probably have found Ruairidh with no trouble at all because everyone would know one another and I could ask any of those sitting outside their house, enjoying the last of this balmy evening.

Tonight, the few pavements are as empty of people as the roads are empty of cars.

The sense of peace that washes over me when I'm on the beach extends to this orderly village and I enjoy my walk. I'm guessing any cars there are in the old part of the village must be housed at the backs of the relevant homes, so I start to explore the rows behind the rows, hoping to find Ruairidh that way, but to no avail because here there are small yards or gardens and, as I suspected, rows of garages, hiding many of the vehicles.

There are various newer houses in the outer areas of the village but exploring there yields no easier way to find which is Ruairidh's home.

Foiled in my goal, but happy in the adventure, I walk back to the caravan, having had time and space to explore my heart as well as the village.

Reaching down my sketch pad and pencils, I commit to paper a sketch of what I remember of a row of the cottages, feeling again that peaceful ambiance. I am better settled in myself now and I know what I must do.

Worst case, best case scenario

When Bill and I had big decisions to make, one of the things he had us do was to draw up, not just a pros and cons list, but a worst case, best case scenario list.

Since my thinking can be scattered and veer off at all sorts of tangents, I decide such lists are the best chance of focusing it now.

Turning to a fresh page at the back of my artists' pad, I rule out an appropriate table, under the heading:

<u>'Continuing this relationship'</u>

<u>'Pros'</u> and <u>'Cons'</u>

I start to fill it in.

There is a long list of 'pros'. Every time I go to move across to the next column, I think of another 'pro' to be added as to why I should continue this relationship with Ruairidh. At the top of the list:

He 'gets' me, understands me.

Sympathetic. Empathetic.

He seems to know what I need before I do and he always supplies it.

He is kind and attentive.

Interesting. Knowledgeable. A good teacher without condescension.

Has a love of nature

Fun

Talented

Cool under pressure

Generous with time and material things

Cares about others

Cares about me

Understanding

Upstanding, modest, humble

Well spoken of by others

Respected

Experienced

Can take a teasing

Handsome and fit

Added onto the 'pros' list are things that occur to me as being pretty important in the scheme of things:

If I discontinued the relationship, I would forever wonder if I had walked away from something very special.

Knowing me, I'd go back into my shell, afraid to look outside of myself and my immediate family.

I'd lose out on getting to know Ruairidh better

I'd miss him horribly

My life would be empty without him

It would break my heart

No, these things are not 'pretty' important, I decide, they are *very* important. I'm not sure my heart could ever be mended if it was broken again.

In the 'cons' list against continuing this relationship, there is one thing listed. To me, it feels a small thing, to others, I know it will loom large and dangerous:

We have known one another for so short a time.

Turning to the 'Worst case, best case scenario' page, under 'The Worst Case Scenario' heading, I write:

On getting better acquainted, we find we're not compatible, whereupon we'd say our goodbyes and I'd go back to my life in Edinburgh, having lost nothing but a little time in beautiful surroundings, doing interesting things.

Under 'The Best Case Scenario' heading:

I will gain a soulmate for the rest of my life and live happily ever after.

The family would have somewhere beautiful to visit.

To sum up, I don't feel I have much to lose by continuing the relationship, but a lot to lose by discontinuing it.

Making myself a mug of hot chocolate as a reward for my logical, organised assessment of things, I sit back and think about what it shows. While I'm in thinking mode, using my head instead of blindly following my heart, I search for anything I might have missed in my deliberations. I turn to another page to jot down my findings and what I can do about them.

Firstly, Ruairidh is without doubt a delightful, charming man, with a lot going for him as a prospective life companion, but is he too perfect? That's what I need to make sure of. To have found someone like him at this time in my life seems almost too good to be true, and it's often said that if something seems to be too good to be true perhaps that's because it is too good to be true.

During the three years of my widowhood, I have watched far too much daytime television, particularly once I had managed out from under the duvet. Many films and many afternoon cosy detective series. There was one theme that arose from time to time, where a charming older man made a career out of defrauding older widows out of their life savings, their husband's life insurance policy payout, and their homes.

Without allowing my heart to take over again, I need to work out how I can be certain that's not what's happening here.

True, Ruairidh could not have known I was a widow, or that I had any life savings or anything else, when he first was concerned for me when he came across me in a distressed state on the beach. But, isn't that how some of these unscrupulous anti-heroes in the movies work? They keep the 'romance' going until they find out what there is to gain, then press on full-steam once they find there is.

But Ruairidh has never pressed me to know whether I'm financially well placed or not. It's not been something that's come up for discussion.

Another question: Is he who he says he is? What evidence do I have that he has a house in the village? What evidence do I have that he was once a fisherman, belonging to a fisherman's family in Helmsdale?

I know he's a talented and able musician and singer, he is in a ceilidh band, and he is respected and liked by its other members. I can't see how he could falsify that. I saw it with my own eyes.

In my heart, I feel convinced he is the real, genuine man he portrays himself as being. My head tends to agree, but to prove it beyond all reasonable doubt, and to satisfy myself and my daughters I have been duly diligent, there are a few things I can do.

I want to check out his home in Embo and his family in Helmsdale.

I'm aware I'm at a vulnerable time in my life, but I refuse to be anybody's fool.

Happy with the work I have done, I get ready for bed with renewed determination to be the strong, independent woman I was destined to be before life blew me off course.

Home

"So how did the phone calls go, last night?" Ruairidh asks when we meet for our morning walk.

"Ah, I'm afraid they didn't. After I got through to Abigail, I suddenly realised I wasn't ready to tell them about us yet. When I heard her voice, I knew I couldn't go through with it, so I was very selfish and hung up without saying anything. I did text to say I was okay, but couldn't talk at that time – which was true. Then I went for a walk, without my phone so I couldn't hear if she tried to ring back. I needed to think some more."

"Ah, yes."

"I texted her again this morning to reassure her I was okay."

He nods. "Well, I can understand that. Funnily enough, I'd spent last night, after I left you, thinking too. Perhaps it's as well you hadn't made the phone calls. I think your girls will need far more reassurance when you do drop the bombshell. Do you think you can avoid telling them for a few days more?"

"I think so. I'll drop them a text or two. I've already explained to Abigail why the phone call didn't happen last night, and she texted back to say she remembered how frustrating it was to lose signal in the middle of a conversation. It had happened to Trevor a few times when his work colleague called. Why?"

He turns to look me straight in the eyes. "I think you should check out that I am who I say I am. For yourself as well as for the girls. If this was an afternoon television drama, you'd probably hire a private investigator to check me out, but since you and I probably don't live in that kind of world, I think I'd like you to be your own investigator. I want you to be one hundred per cent sure of what you're getting into getting involved with me, and I want your girls to be certain too."

I stare at him, my heart pumping furiously. I can hardly believe what I'm hearing. It's as though he's read my thoughts, or my pages of notes, which he couldn't have, since we met here, outside my caravan, this morning before breakfast.

"If it's okay with you, I'd like you to start by coming to my place for breakfast this morning, then meet some of my neighbours afterwards. Does that sound reasonable to you?"

I can hardly speak, but I nod enthusiastically until the words find their way to my tongue. "Of course. I'd love that." And I tell him about my walk last night after the aborted telephone call to my daughter, and my deliberations. I finish by shaking my head and saying, "As the cliché goes, 'Great minds think alike.'"

He laughs. "'And fools seldom differ,' the saying goes on to say. But I don't want either of us to be fools or to be made fools of, so let's overrule the passions of the heart and go about this methodically before we declare our attachment to the world, or, in this case, your family."

"Oh, Ruairidh, You can't begin to know how happy this makes me." And, allowing my heart to take back some of the control, I throw my arms around him and hug him, then he takes my hand and we walk towards the village.

"So what did you think of Embo village when you explored it last night?" he asks.

"I love it. But I was a little puzzled by some of the street names. For instance, there is a Station Road." The question as to why is in my voice.

"Yes, the Dornoch Light Railway that was opened in 1902 ran through Embo to where it joined the main line further on at a station called The Mound. Back then, at the beginning of the 20th century, Embo was a thriving settlement. It had five streets, all running parallel towards the sea in traditional fishing-village fashion. There was a railway station, a school, and even a police house."

"Goodness, were there enough people here getting up to mischief, to merit having a police presence?"

"According to the official records of the time, there were between 500 and 800 people living here at the beginning of the 20th century, and the population were just as partial to a bit of poaching and smuggling, fighting and stealing, as any other."

"I suppose." I negotiate a steeper bit of the walk up to the start of the village. "I didn't see any signs of the railway line on my evening wanderings, yesterday. I must have missed that bit."

"Sadly, it closed in 1960. The lines were lifted, and the station building and level crossing demolished. The only thing that remains is the station master's house, though you can see, here and there, where the track once was, when you walk along the coast and past the golf course, heading for Dornoch."

"And the school, is it still here?"

"The building is, but the school closed in the mid-1980s. School kids are bussed to Dornoch now from here. It's a grand old building from the late 1800s, and since its renovation it's being used as a community hall. There's a great story about how the funds for that renovation were raised, but I'll tell you that story another time … because …" He takes his keys from his pocket and opens the door. "Here we are. My humble abode."

I love his house. It's painted pale cream outside, with a red door opening straight into the living room.

Inside, it's a rather different story. The bare walls have been patchily re-plastered and I can see an extension has been added opening the living room up with a window to the front of the house and a bay window with French doors in the extension at the back, the French windows bringing a load of light to what must have been rather a dark room in the past. The room will be great but it's still very much a work in progress.

The furniture is old and mostly covered with dust cloths.

Ruairidh hangs his head. "Probably not quite what you expected."

"To be honest, I wasn't sure what I expected, but I can see it's a not yet what it will become."

"A while after Catriona died, I decided I wanted to stay on here in Embo and I thought I'd like to make the house my own. Up till then, if asked where I lived, I always said, 'In my sister's house, in Embo.' Bless her, Catriona had done nothing to the place over the years and, apart from being like something you could open as a museum piece, everything was well-worn and grubby looking, and very hard to keep clean and tidy. Once I'd decided to make it my house, which it actually is anyway, since she willed it to me, I spent a while deciding what style I wanted. I even bought *House and Home* type magazines. I stripped everything out. But, as you can see, having made a start, I have no idea how to continue. The structural alterations were not so difficult after I had the necessary planning permission for them, but there I stalled."

"I can see this is going to be a wonderfully light, bright room when you get it finished."

"You mean, *if* I get it finished," he says, looking at his feet.

"Oh, don't look so glum. Of course you will. Why shouldn't you get it finished?"

"Because I totally lost heart for it after the alterations were done. It seemed too much work, the more so because I had, and have, no idea at all about home decor or anything like that. I still have all the magazines I bought, but, to be honest, I was quite overwhelmed by choice. So many styles, so many 'ambiances' for each room. I'm happy to do the work, once I know what to do, but don't know where to start finding out what I'd like or want in a room. All I knew was, the room was looking old and shabby and something needed done, so I made a start."

"And a good start. The extension has given you a super space with which to work."

He shrugs. "But, until now, no motivation to get on with it. Bringing you here today, I suddenly want it to be beautiful to show off to you, instead of looking like a building site."

He looks so crestfallen, my heart goes out to him. "Yet you still invited me. I appreciate that."

"Well, in the spirit of full disclosure, it seemed important for you to know the useless part of me as well as the nerdy part of me."

I take him in my arms. "You are far from useless," I say, looking up at him. "Just a little lost." We stand there, in the middle of the room, enfolded in one another's arms for a while longer before I pull back a little, still enclosed in his arms. "Do you want to talk about it?" I say, grinning up at him.

He chuckles. "Not really. But thank you. There's nothing much more to say."

"In which case. Let's have that breakfast you promised me and maybe we can look at some of your home decor magazines afterwards."

While Ruairidh prepares the breakfast, I look around the room and take it all in, then close my eyes and try to imagine how I would furnish and decorate this room. When I open my eyes again, I realise I have found 'my taste'. If it had been me looking through magazines for what I wanted, I honestly believe I'd have chosen something very simple. Light, creamy walls perhaps, keeping the light, bright and airy look of the room. Not too many ornaments or pictures, a bookcase or two, maybe a shelf or two for Ruairidh's musical instruments, enough to show real people lived here, rather than it being a show-home people only tramp through.

Instead of the old-fashioned dark-patterned cushions I had recently donated to the charity shop, I would want to choose lovely cheerful ones, to scatter on a dark brown leather sofa or two.

It occurs to me that Bill's taste, like his mum's, and actually like the home I grew up in, was not only old-fashioned, it was fuddy-duddy and dull. Stifling.

I shudder to realise that is what I'd unwittingly, but not unwillingly, submitted myself to all these years.

In contrast, even unfinished, I love this room. I love the proportions and the shape of it, with ceilings not too high but in good proportion to the room. In fact, so far, I love this house, from the outside in.

There's a table at the back of the room in the beautiful large bay window. The table is delightfully laid for breakfast for two.

I follow Ruairidh into the light, bright kitchen, also extended out to the back, the window overlooking a small yard and the lane behind.

"I see you're admiring my low maintenance garden," he says, with that mischievous grin.

There are pots of flowers and herbs dotted about the yard, turning it into a jolly wee patio, where, if it was warmer, we could easily sit out to have our late breakfast.

"I love it. Is that basil?" I move my position to see better what else there is. "And parsley?"

Opening the back door at the side of the kitchen, he leads me outside. "There you go. You can get the full delight of smelling the herbs as well as identifying them now."

There is indeed basil and parsley, as well as thyme and mint. "So, are you a cook?"

He pulls a face. "Mmmm! Not a very good one, but I had to learn in order to feed myself and Catriona. Over the years, she taught me how to make her favourites, sitting there in the kitchen in her wheelchair, giving me instructions. At that time she had a wee patch of earth under the window, in which she grew her herbs and a few peas and beans. Turns out I wasn't much of a gardener and, when I planted the peas and beans, they failed to do well, but the herbs seemed to thrive with little attention, so in order to build the extension when I had to lose her wee plot of earth, I decided the way to go was pots, so you could say, 'I went to pot.'" He laughs at his own joke, then goes back inside to get on with making our breakfast.

While he makes the coffee, fries the eggs and bacon, and warms the rolls they're going to go in, I watch the masculine grace and familiarity with which he moves around the room, gathering what he needs, using appliances flawlessly. He suits this kitchen, and it suits him.

I feel comfortable and at home in his house and it seems natural to help butter the warm rolls for him to fill, and carry things from the kitchen through to the table.

After we've eaten and are sitting talking, there's a light knock on the door, which is then pushed open by someone calling out, "Hi, Nuncs. It's just me ... oh, sorry. I didn't realise you had company."

"Come in, come in, Jenna." He gets up and goes forward to receive the hug and kiss she offers. "This is Eilidh, my friend who's visiting from Edinburgh."

I step forward and shake hands with her.

"And I'm Jenna, Uncle Ruairidh is actually my great-uncle, but that's too cumbersome, so Nuncs or Uncle Ruairidh he is," she says with a grin. His grin. There's no denying the kinship.

"Nuncs. I like that. Suits you," I say to Ruairidh.

"Coffee?" he asks Jenna. "There's still some hot in the pot."

"Tempting, but no, thanks all the same. I've left the wee one out in the car. I'm going down to Tesco and wondered if you needed anything."

"No, thanks, love. I'm fine. But I'll come out to see Angus and introduce him to Eilidh."

We all troop out and there in the car is a mini Ruairidh, A toddler of three or four with a head of dark curly hair, exactly as I can imagine Ruairidh's would have looked before it was streaked with silver. And there is that cheeky wee grin again, clearly a family trait, and the big, dark eyes.

Ruairidh leans into the car and there's a scuffle of tickling and pretend fighting. "Ha-ha!" Ruairidh says. "I've got you now. Trapped. Just as I like it."

Jenna rolls her eyes. "Thanks, Nuncs, for getting him nicely wound up when I need him to sit quietly in the trolley."

"Ach, he'll be great, won't you, wee man? By the time you drive to Tain, he'll have dozed off, all nice and calm for the shopping."

"Yeah? You think?" She turns to me. "That man should really have had kids, so he knew how hard it is to calm down over-excited kids once their over-sized playmate leaves them to Mum and Dad." But she says it with a broad smile, and whispers to me. "Love him to bits."

I resist the temptation to say, 'Me too!'

"You'll have to bring Eilidh round for a cup one afternoon so I can get to know her, Uncle Ruairidh."

"I will, love. I will."

"Soon," she says as she gets into the car. "Please."

I look at Ruairidh as we wave them off. He is smiling with genuine affection for his great-niece and what I suppose is his great-great-nephew.

"Where do they live?" I ask as we go back indoors.

"Aye, she lives in Golspie, but she likes to swing by this way when she's going shopping. Likes to know I've not popped my clogs, I think." He shakes his head. "Hit her hard when her gran, Catriona, died."

"So where does Catriona's daughter live?"

"She's in Golspie too. Catriona had a son as well, but as soon as he married, he and the wife flew off to Canada. They seem well settled there. But the old girl missed them, even more as the years went by, I do believe." He sighs and shakes his head. There is genuine affection in his expression when he talks of, as well as to, any of his family.

After we've cleared away the breakfast things Ruairidh asks me what I'd like to do this afternoon.

"To be honest, I think I'd like to sit here in this lovely room with you for a bit and perhaps look through some of your magazines and we could exchange ideas till you find how you'd like to decorate."

"Of course, lass. Why don't you sit quietly while I get on with one or two things I've been meaning to get to before I can take you upstairs to see the rest of the house."

Surprisingly, I doze off in the comfortable old armchair he's snuggled me into with my feet up, a rug and cushions. I feel safe here in Ruairidh's home.

Embo to Dornoch

When we set off on our walk to Dornoch a few days later, it was sunny but with a chill wind and I pulled my coat round me and wondered how good an idea this was, but now, we're almost half-way and I'm undoing buttons and contemplating removing my coat altogether. It's not that the day has warmed up a great deal, though the wind has dropped a little, but we decided to set off at a good pace because I want to test how fit I am or am not. I've decided I am not.

I'm delighted when it's time to pause for a drink of water and an apple, and I ask Ruairidh if we could please adopt a slightly slower pace. He laughs and tells me I'm doing great.

"Well it doesn't feel like it," I say.

"That's probably because you're approaching it with the idea that it's a long way to Dornoch, but, in fact, you've walked much further than we've walked so far on other occasions."

"Have I?"

"Often. The trick is to tell yourself you're over half-way and it's really not so far."

"And do you really think that'll fool me into not being so tired from here on?"

"Worth a try," he says with a grin. "Let's go!"

If the pace is any slower now, it's hardly noticeable, but the strange thing is, his ruse works and I'm stepping out with renewed vigour.

Or perhaps it's because I'm in such good company, happily distracted by tales of Embo's day of independence in 1988, when they actually asked and received permission from the Queen and Margaret Thatcher to declare Embo an independent state for a day – on the proviso, according to the Queen, that it was only for the one day.

"There was a 'Custom Point' set up on the road into the village, where motorists could stop and buy a visa for the cost of a donation to the renovation fund for turning the old primary school into a community centre. They could have these visas stamped at the 'Government Building' in Grannie's Heilan' Hame, in exchange for a free dram of Clynlish Malt Whisky."

"Is that when Embo was twinned with – where was it? Somewhere in Hawaii or somewhere like that? I've always loved seeing that on the sign telling you you're entering Embo. It sounds ridiculously exotic."

"That came about because a Hawaiian couple, who spent part of each year in Embo, were involved in the shenanigans and they suggested that Embo become twinned with the village of Kuanakakai, Moloka'i in Hawai'i, where they came from. It wasn't till 1990, the official twinning took place and the sign went up at the entrance to the village."

"It all sounds to have been so much fun."

"Oh, it was, and the day attracted a lot of interest and was widely reported on."

"Did you play any part in it?"

"Although I wasn't living here at the time, I came down to spend the day with Catriona, and I did a couple of stints at the 'Custom Post' alongside, Erchie, her husband."

"How did motorists respond to being stopped by you?"

"Everyone took it in good part, and were more than happy to stop. The best thing about the whole day, was the funds raised were more than what was needed to add to the grant received for the renovations of the old school."

"I love it." I chuckle for ages, thinking about it and listening to Ruairidh's tales of the day, and it seems no time at all till we're walking up the street in Dornoch to the cafe where we enjoy a light lunch and a wander round the town before returning the way we came.

On the walk back, the journey is sweetened by the tale of how Grannie's Heilan' Hame became such a loved and popular holiday destination, as well as the birth of the Royal Dornoch Golf Club, whose golf course we skirt on the route.

After a short half-way pause, I ask about why and when the fishing from Embo came to its end, since there is no sign of it continuing on now.

"Ah, as you can perhaps imagine, the fishing industry was badly hit by the two world wars. Even before that, the boom in the herring fishing was beginning to decline, due to overfishing along the whole east coast. There were hordes of fishing boats taking to the North Sea, from Caithness all the way down the coast. Stocks were running low. Plus the popularity of herring was declining – smoked potted or fresh – so markets for it were becoming fewer."

"I don't even see an occasional fishing boat out there."

"No, you won't. Sometime after World War Two, the Embo fishermen sailed along to Loch Fleet, beached their boats and burned them."

"Wow! That must have made an incredible bonfire."

"Next time we're driving up the coast, I could take you round to where we can walk along the beach at low tide and you'll be able to see the remains of some of the boats, skeletons of a whole way of life that lasted for many centuries."

"A poignant sight, I'd imagine."

"Yes, I saw them some years ago, though time, waves, wind and water may well have made them harder to find now."

We walk in silence for a while after that, while I try to imagine the sadness that must surely have lain over the fisherfolk of Embo at that time. The loss of their livelihood and their whole way of life must have hit hard. They would have had to find other employment, possibly having to move from their homes to find it. Despite all that, I find it hard to imagine the real reason for such a dramatic finishing flourish.

Sensing my sadness, probably in the droop of my shoulders and the fact I keep lagging behind a little as we walk, Ruairidh starts chatting about how there is a football team, Embo FC, who even won the Inchlampie Cup in 2013.

Not being a football fan, it's not something I'm particularly interested in, but Ruairidh chatting on about it eventually sees me home to the caravan. I smile to myself as I realise I am beginning to think of it as 'home'.

When Ruairidh takes his leave and I flop onto the couch, I can hardly believe what it tells me on my phone, that I have walked more than eight miles today, including our wander around in Dornoch. Wow! I'm impressed with myself and text the girls on our family WhatsApp to tell them.

It's with a great feeling of accomplishment that I shower and make myself some dinner, revelling in my daughters' admiration in their responses to my text:

Donna: "Go, Mums! Embo to Dornoch and back, Wow! You'll need to do it again with Owen and me sometime." (Followed by loads of hugging and kissing emojis interspersed with hearts and celebration emojis.)

Emily: "I'm very impressed, Madre Mia! I can't imagine walking eight miles in one day, even broken up with stopping for lunch. Well done!" (Followed by clapping emojis and a couple of celebration emojis.)

Abigail: "Goodness, Mum. I hope you haven't overdone it. Have you had a good warm shower and stretched it out of your muscles. I hope you won't be too sore in the morning. Take care. P.S. Well done, though! I am impressed."

I laugh. If ever I want to explain how different my three daughters are to Ruairidh, I'll show him these messages.

After I've cleared up my dinner things, I spend a lovely time sketching some of the things I took the time to photograph while on the walk – turns out, stopping to take a photograph is a great and acceptable excuse for a micro-breather.

I'm aware that to many people such a walk would be a short stroll, but to me – who had turned, more-or-less, into a couch potato for three years – today marks another step forward in my new life.

I feel so, so alive and I'm looking forward to building on the achievement.

I make a mental note to share this information with Ruairidh later, when I see how he has progressed with his plan to paint the living-room ceiling and make a start on glossing the doors. Unlike me, our walk energised him and he claimed he could hardly wait to open the tins of paint he'd bought yesterday.

Meantime, after sketching for an hour or two, I take a nap before dressing for a light supper at Ruairidh's house, which I know will be the perfect end to a perfect day.

The whirlwind returns

A few mornings later, while luxuriating in my warm bed, not feeling the need to rise until my bladder demands I do, I become aware of voices outside my window and footsteps walking round the caravan and up the stairs to my locked door. Rising hurriedly, I pull my warm robe around me and go to answer the insistent knocking on the door, fearing the worst, I must add.

"Hiya, Mumsie. We've come to see how you're enjoying your holiday." Donna sweeps me into her exuberant hug, kissing me as though it had been forever since I'd seen her last.

The whirlwind has returned.

Before I can dress, they invite me to join them both on the beach. "In the sea, in fact," Donna says, stepping out of her clothes, revealing a full wetsuit underneath.

I shake my head in horror at the idea. "Oh, thank you but, no, I really don't think so."

"Oh, come on, Mumsie," she cajoles, producing a matching wetsuit from a large bag Owen retrieves from outside the caravan door and holds open for her. "It's the most invigorating thing ever. You'll love it once you're in."

Stepping back, pulling my warm robe tighter around me, I shake my head. "No, quite definitely, no."

So how does it come about that, ten minutes later, I am totally kitted out with wetsuit, rubber wet-boots, gloves and hat (all thoughtfully designed for cold water swimming), running down the beach hand-in-hand with my daughter?

She doesn't pause at the water's edge as I hoped she would, but keeps running me straight into the water, slowing at last as the water rises up my legs, allowing me time to acclimatise a little to the cold.

But she's right. Once I am totally in, it's the most amazing, invigorating experience. I look at her and laugh.

She swims close to me and hugs me tight. "I knew you'd love it."

"Oh, I do," I say. "I would not have believed it, but I do."

We frolic about a bit, splashing one another and pushing one another back into the water. Then Donna dares me to dive, something I used to be really good at, as she probably remembers from when we used to go to the swimming pool every now and then when the girls were children. But that was in an indoor pool, in warm water. This is the North Sea, for goodness' sake. However, she has dared me and something inside me pushes me to give it a go. So I do.

I resurface to smiles and cheers from Donna, followed by another hug before she tells me, "Okay, Mums. Enough now. Can't have you getting hypothermia. Abigail and Emily would never forgive me." And she pulls on my arm and leads me onto dry land, where Owen is holding out a large, long, thick, towelling robe for me to put on over my wetsuit, which I do, happily. He then picks up another for Donna and we run up the beach chittering and laughing.

"Right, I'll help you get out of the wetsuit, then you must get right into the shower and warm up," she instructs, unzipping the suit behind and helping me escape from it – no easy task, I discover. These things are skin tight, hard enough to get into, but when wet, murder to get out of.

As soon as I emerge from the shower and go into the bedroom to get dressed, Donna goes in to have her shower.

When I come through to the living room, still rubbing my hair dry, it is to discover that Owen has put the heating on and brewed a pot of coffee, having found the coffee pot and bag of fresh, newly ground coffee Ruairidh bought for me down in Dornoch, as it was too hard to go back to instant coffee after tasting Ruairidh's 'proper' coffee.

Thinking of Ruairidh seems to conjure him up, and here he is, at the door just as Donna emerges from the extra bedroom, showered and dressed again.

Without hesitation or embarrassment, Donna sweeps him into a hug and fairly bounces with happiness to see him, reminding me, for all the world, of a very exuberant Labrador puppy we once owned. He calmed down after a few years and I can't help wondering when Donna might – while simultaneously hoping she never does.

"I hope you haven't made too many plans for the day," she says.

Ruairidh and I look at one another and shrug. "Nothing that can't be done another day," he says, putting down the bag of rolls he was bringing for breakfast.

"Why? Do you have a plan?" I ask Donna.

"Well, we're only stopping by before heading across to Ullapool tomorrow," she says. "But we were hoping you might show us the old cairn you told me about on the phone."

Ruairidh looks at me and smiles.

I shrug and give him a look back that I hope conveys the message that, while my other two daughters have to make do with occasional texts, I have no qualms about chatting on the phone with Donna, even telling her about the progression of our romance, without fear of judgement or censure. It's not that she's my favourite of the three, but she is the one who gets where I'm coming from, and where I'm trying to go.

He seems to get the message and smiles again. "It would be a pleasure," he says to Donna. "And I'll let your mum tell its story. Since she seemed to really enjoy hearing it, I'm sure she'll have remembered it."

"As long as I can get a gold star if I do," I say with a grin, confident I can share my recently acquired knowledge, especially with the help of the information board beside the site. In fact, I'm excited to repeat it to help imbed it in my memory.

So, after breakfast, that's what we do. Wrapping warmly, because the wind is getting up a bit, we walk to the car park.

It gives me a special kind of thrill to explain as much as I remember to Owen and Donna. They both seem genuinely interested and when they ask questions of Ruairidh, he always defers to me, giving me my place as the teacher this time round.

It's difficult to explain how good this makes me feel.

My daughter looks at me in a different way. I suppose she sees me in an unaccustomed role. She starts to ask the questions of *me*, looking to *me* for the answers. It has been a long time since my girls were young enough to believe their mother had the answers to anything – let alone everything.

I'd like to think Ruairidh would step in if I got things wrong, but he stands back and the confidence that gives me is immeasurable. Time and again, I look at him with such gratitude and love. I hope he reads that in my face and body language, as I snuggle against him while Donna and Owen re-examine everything in the light of what I've explained to them.

We have such a delightful morning, the four of us, topped off by a pleasant and tasty lunch up at the wee restaurant at the reception area, chatting over what we've enjoyed about our journey back to days gone by, and about what Owen and Donna have been up to since last we saw them. It feels so right to be sitting, having a meal out as a wee family foursome.

When we get back to the caravan, I see the wetsuits we hung out on the veranda seem to be dry enough to pack back in Donna's bag and suggest we do that now, to get them out of the way.

"Sure, I'll take mine, Mums, but the one you wore this morning belongs to you." She looks over to Owen.

"Yes, we bought it as a gift for you to say thank you for how wonderfully you joined in the spirit of things when we performed in Dornoch," he says.

"Oh, but …"

"No buts, Mums. I already have a wetsuit and have no need of another, so the wetsuit and all that goes with it is yours."

"Including the cosy, after-swim, towelling robe," says Owen. "Which I chose especially for you." He smiles, proud of his choice. "I hope you like it."

"Oh, Owen," I say, giving him a hug. "I love it. It is perfect for purpose and I could not have chosen better. Thank you." I swallow hard, but can't hold back tears. "This is all too much. You're both so kind."

Donna gets up and comes over to gather me into her arms. Kneeling back on the floor in front of me when I sit, she says, "I'm so very, very proud of you, Mum, how hard you've battled through an incredibly difficult three years and are now making a new life for yourself. I want so much to help you do that, and I thought it would be good to introduce you to cold-water swimming as part of your therapy as you heal after all the trauma."

Overcome, I am totally without words. I can only cry the more and hold her close. My beautiful baby girl.

Owen then turns to Ruairidh. "We want to thank you too, Ruairidh, but we weren't sure if you had a wetsuit?"

Ruairidh laughs. "I used to manage to swim here in the North Sea without the comfort of such luxury, but I'm afraid I've become soft in my old age. Perhaps I should invest in such an item now, so I can join your mum for the odd morning swim."

"No need," says Owen, turning back to the seemingly bottomless bag. "We bought one for you, hoping you didn't have one, and hoping we guessed your size right." He pulls it from the bag and gives it to Ruairidh, along with all the other bits and pieces that go with it, including a dark charcoal towelling robe like the pink one they've given me.

I've never seen Ruairidh struck dumb before. He sits holding the bundle in his arms, staring at it, feeling the soft, thick robe, swallowing hard. It's plain he too is overwhelmed by their kindness and generosity.

"But, how can you possibly afford all this?" I say at last. "It's far too much."

"We can afford it for two main reasons," says Owen. "The performance at Dornoch was unusually well attended and so much enjoyed that the attendees were exceedingly generous in their donations, plus those who hung around to be sketched afterwards were so delighted, we received no less than three commissions for proper painted portraits of their families. Having delivered said portraits, we are considerably better off than we've ever been."

"And a lot of that is down to you two," adds Donna. "We have so much to thank you for."

Owen reaches into the bag one last time and brings out a bottle of Champagne. "And we thought, if you don't mind having a meal with us tonight, we could celebrate our recent successes with you."

"Oh that would be lovely," I say.

"On one condition," Ruairidh says. "That you all come to my home and let me cook dinner. Please." He holds up his hand. "As long as you don't expect fancy cooking, and don't mind the house being a bit of a building site."

Donna bounces up and down on the couch. "Oh, I'd love that. I've always wanted to see inside one of the cottages in the village. That would be so great."

I look at her, frowning. "I didn't know that. I wasn't really aware you'd even noticed the village before. Our holidays seemed to centre round the beach when you were a kid."

"Oh, Dad and I used to explore the village whenever we popped up to the wee on-site shop for anything. We used to like imagining what the houses were like inside."

It takes my breath away. So much I missed out on all those years, mainly because I'd be so intent on making sure there was a warm meal ready for them all after a day on the beach, in and out of the water, and running about playing games. It never occurred to me she and her father had this wee secret together.

"I used to think it was just 'our thing', but I think Dad had similar special things with each of us girls. It helped to make Embo such a wonderful place in our memories."

"Yes, I see that now," I say, trying hard not to be jealous, but to be happy they had that.

"It's settled then," Ruairidh says. "Dinner at seven, dress code casual." He grins. "Any dietary restrictions or requirements?"

Owen laughs. "When we're on the road, our meals are simple and sometimes simply whatever we can afford, so we have learned not to be fussy. Whatever you enjoy to make will be wonderful – as long as it goes well with Champagne."

Donna laughs. "Which, as far as I'm aware, absolutely everything does."

"Right. Well, if no one minds, I'll take my leave for now. I have some shopping to do, followed by some meal prep." He gets up. "Enjoy your afternoon, guys, and I'll see you at seven."

I get up too, to see him out, looking for a hug and I want to say my personal thank yous to him for today and the promise of this evening.

Expecting to do that outside the door, I am surprised when he takes me in his arms and hugs me right there in front of Owen and Donna. It surprises and delights me.

When we step outside, he kisses me properly. "Thank you," he says, softly. "Thank you so much for letting me be part of your family. You can have no idea what that means to me. And thank you for the joy you bring me every day. You have gladdened my life beyond what you can possibly imagine. I love being with you. I love watching the joy on your face as we share stories and new things together. I love how you laugh, how you cry, how you move, how you feel things, how you enjoy things and how you share it all with me. From the bottom of my heart, thank you."

He kisses me one last time, then he is gone, striding out purposefully through the caravans towards the path to the village, leaving me weak at the knees once again.

How on earth can I get through the rest of the day till seven o'clock when I can be in his company again?

Dancing

As it happens, we have a delightful afternoon. After Ruairidh goes, we sit chatting for a while, then Donna suggests a walk on the beach, which I agree is a good idea. The wind has dropped a bit and the sun has come out, making it perfect for a walk. Owen explains he has things to do over at their caravan and Land Rover. He likes to check them regularly since they're on the road so much, so he goes off to do that and Donna and I go down to the beach.

As we walk, she cuddles in against me. "Oh, this is lovely, Mumsie. We don't often get much time just you and me, do we?"

I give her a squeeze. "No we don't, and it is lovely. I'm really enjoying having you here. And I'm so glad you're getting another chance to get to know Ruairidh better."

"Oh, me too. He's a lovely man. I like him enormously."

"Oh, I am pleased. He and I are becoming very close."

"I see that."

I turn a bit to see her face better. "Are you okay about that?"

"Absolutely, Mum. I don't think Dad would want you to be unhappy and on your own for ever, any more than I would."

"What about the others? How do you think they'll take it when I tell them?"

"I think they'll take a while to get used to the idea – especially Abigail – but I think she'll be okay with it once she gets to know Ruairidh."

"Yes. I hope you're right."

"Tell you what, Mumsie, why don't you book the caravan for another week or two and invite them up, one at a time, to spend some time with you and Ruairidh? I think they'd love that – to get away from the kids and the routine for a while, some time with you, like this, and get to know Ruairidh – it could only be a good thing."

"That's a great idea! I'll go up to reception later and make the booking to keep the caravan after my four weeks are ended, which they will be next week, then phone Abigail and Emily to invite them up. I wonder if they'll be able to get away?"

"Oh, I think they'll find a way."

"What a brilliant idea." I give her another squeeze. "Clever girl."

"Oh, look! Dolphins!"

And there they are, quite close to shore, leaping and diving, a whole pod of them. It's so exciting to watch and we stand there for ages until they move away, Donna deciding we should run along the beach in the same direction until we can't see them any more. Only we don't run along the beach, she has us dancing along, leaping about not unlike the dolphins.

"Oh, Mum," she says. "Don't you just want to join in their joyful dance?"

And, suddenly, I do. Very much so.

It's quiet on the beach, but I really don't care if anyone sees us or not. I don't care how crazy we seem. It's wonderfully freeing to let go of all inhibitions and dance with abandon, something I've wanted to do all my life but have never actually done.

Long after the dolphins have swum away, we go on skipping along the beach, clambering over rocks, laughing and singing with the complete unselfconsciousness of children.

Later, when we have tired ourselves out and slowed to a gentle walk, we start talking about the music we like to dance to, at least Donna does. Music being another thing I haven't kept up to date with for a long time.

"Owen and I watched a film the other week and I really loved the soundtrack, so I downloaded it onto my phone. I think you'd like it. It's great to dance to."

She finds it on her phone and starts playing it. "It's from the film, *Love at First Sight* and I think you'll like it because track after track actually tells the story of what's happening with you and Ruairidh."

And it's true. It almost takes my breath away, it is so close to what is happening to us. I can hardly believe it, and yes, some of the tracks make me want to dance again, some with freedom and abandon, some with gentle, flowing grace.

"Oh, please, is there any way I could have that on my phone?"

So we stop walking and Donna sends me the link.

I just know that dancing and cold-water swimming are going to become happy additions to my regular activities, along with walking with Ruairidh.

I feel so happy, and again, so alive.

Champagne

When we get to back to the caravan, Donna leaves me to go and get ready for our meal at Ruairidh's, and I put the music on again and dance while I change into one of my pretty dresses, Donna and I having agreed that, even though Ruairidh said the dress code was 'casual', we wanted to dress up a bit. I look through the small selection of dresses I brought with me, and choose a long flowing sundress in aquamarine and blue. With a short, slightly deeper blue top over it, silver sandals and minimal make-up – merely a touch of lipgloss and mascara –my hair brushed till it shines when it falls into place, and I am ready. The only jewellery I add is a silver chain, which picks out the increasing strands of silver through my dark curls.

I add a warm shawl to ward off the evening chill and when Donna knocks, I am ready to go.

Donna looks stunningly beautiful in a dress of warm autumn colours, with several layers, each lying at an angle to the others, dipping in asymmetrical points here and there. When I ask, she tells me it's a handkerchief dress, and somehow, that makes sense. It flows around her as she walks and skips beside Owen and myself. She too has topped the dress off with a shawl, but hers is a gorgeous, vintage silk shawl with long silken fringes falling from its edges.

Owen looks casually smart in dark blue jeans and an open-necked white shirt.

I hope Ruairidh isn't too put out that we ignored his instruction.

When Ruairidh opens the door to us, I'm delighted to see that he didn't pay attention to himself either, because he is more smart than casually dressed, wearing dark navy dress trousers and a pale blue, open-necked shirt.

The house is warm and welcoming and Donna looks at me in wonder. "Wow!" she says. "It seems so much bigger inside than I expected." She spins around. "I love it," she says to Ruairidh. Looking at the beautiful set table at the far end of the room, she says, "How inviting is that?"

"I'm happy you like it," Ruairidh says, with an amused smile.

We look at one another and share another smile, the unspoken acknowledgement between us that Donna is like a delightful, excited child. It's a very endearing quality in a twenty-seven-year-old woman.

I also nod in approval at the work he has done since last I was here. He had already painted the ceiling the palest of cream and the doors and skirtings the same when I was last here for supper, and now he's papered the walls with a softly textured, warm creamy wallpaper. "Ted at the decorating shop in Tain assures me that wallpaper will be a delight to paint over if we choose to change the colour anytime," he whispers in my ear as we briefly embrace.

I blush at the phrase, 'if we choose', inferring we're in this venture very much together. A delicious tingle travels through me.

I notice too that the dust sheets are gone and the worn old furniture buffed up to look its best against the plain, warm background.

I kiss him again and whisper, "Thank you," in his ear, knowing he'll know what for. I love that he has made all this effort to impress my daughter, probably guessing how much it would delight me.

Looking around the room, which as yet has bare walls, Donna offers to paint a glorious Embo sun-rising over the water to grace one of them. Perhaps just here," she says indicating the space above the fireplace. "What d'you think, Mumsie?"

"Oh, that's up to Ruairidh," I say, looking over to him.

"Well, knowing the quality of your art work, I think that would be beautiful in this room," he says with a smile, drawing me close to him. "Don't you think?" he asks me.

Unbidden, I blush under his meaningful smile, understanding the message it conveys. "I think that would be perfect."

"So," Ruairidh asks us all. "What's it to be, dinner first or the tour?"

"Oooh! Definitely, the tour, please – if that's okay with everyone," Donna says.

After she's exclaimed over the lovely big kitchen, which despite being new, has managed still to look delightfully rustic, and she's declared that their whole caravan could fit inside it, which is a gross exaggeration, but no one pulls her up on it and we all just laugh, Ruairidh leads us upstairs.

"Ooh, do the rooms upstairs have sloped ceilings? Oh, I hope they have sloped ceilings," she says as she follows him up.

"Will this do?" he asks going into the main bedroom and standing aside for her to walk in.

"Wow! Oh yes!" she exclaims. "Look, Owen. Look at this! The ceiling is sloped!" She turns to Ruairidh. "Oh, I so hoped it would be. Whenever Dad and I explored in the village, I guessed they'd have sloped ceilings upstairs."

The second bedroom, built over the extension, is declared 'cosy' and 'cute', which could make it sound small when it's not much smaller than the other. The bathroom, also enlarged as part of the extension, is declared 'divine' and, all in all, the whole house is given 'the Donna seal of approval', despite none of it being quite finished. "I can use my imagination to add the colours and textures," she says when Ruairidh apologises for the lack of decoration. "The important thing is these rooms are terrific canvasses on which to create heavenly scenes."

And she's right. Ruairidh has done marvellously with all the structural alterations he's made and the rooms will be fun to decorate once he feels motivated.

Owen is frequently called upon to agree, which, of course, he does, though I suspect his interest in having the tour is less than his wife's. I've tagged along, though I've seen it all before, because I guess Donna will love everything and I want to enjoy her delighted reactions. Besides, it gives me a strange semi-proprietorial feeling to tag along on the tour, almost as though I belong here in this house with Ruairidh. I smile at the thought, delighted to realise that, far from scaring me, it feels good.

Ruairidh takes it all in very good part, and at last, the tour is completed and we can go back downstairs to settle round the table to eat.

While he is in the kitchen, putting the last touches to the meal, Owen following him through to offer help, Ruairidh leaves us listening to some soft music. Donna has to investigate the source of the music, of course, and is ecstatic when she realises he had left a vinyl record ready on the turntable. All he had to do was switch it on as he passed on the way to the kitchen.

I wonder if Donna will think his choice 'cheesy' but, far from it, she declares Beethoven's *Moonlight Sonata* a favourite of hers. Ruairidh already knows it is a favourite of mine.

Just as I had done before, Donna sits on the floor in front of his record cabinet, examining its contents, and again like me, she is enchanted and delighted he still has such a thing as a vinyl record collection and a turntable to play them on. We both thoroughly approve of his choice of music in general.

And we more than approve of the meal he has prepared for us: a gorgeously creamy, gooey cheese and chicken pasta bake, served with salad and garlic bread.

"I'm sorry I'm not a more adventurous cook," he says, as he places the hot casserole dish on the table. "But this easy oven-bake became a firm favourite of Catriona's when I used to make it for her. 'Comfort food Italiana,' she used to call it." He laughs.

"It looks perfect," I reassure him, understanding now how he had time to remove the dust sheets and buff up the furniture while the dinner was slowly cooking in the oven.

"Totally perfect," Owen agrees, his eyes lighting up as Ruairidh dishes it out.

And it is, 'totally perfect'. Cooked to perfection and delicious.

Owen opens the Champagne amid a great deal of hilarity because he looks almost afraid of the whole exercise, his shoulders and face all scrunched up as though expecting an explosion. Instead, the cork exits with a very satisfying 'Pop!' and Donna is ready with a glass to catch the first of the foamy, sparkling wine.

It is a meal I hope I never forget: the four of us sitting cosily round the table eating delicious food, laughing and joking, enjoying conversation every bit as sparkling as the wine, listening to beautiful music.

The whirlwind blew in with a wealth of joy before settling into a mellow, sleepy sunset evening.

Another perfect end to a perfect day.

Heading for Helmsdale

At last, the trip I've been looking forward to this week. I will meet Ruairidh's family and see where he was born, brought up, and worked for many years.

We take a brief detour, timing things perfectly to be just right for low tide, though Ruairidh has explained we have little chance of discerning the remains of the Embo fishing boats since it's quite a few years since he found them before.

Littleferry is a quaint little village that got its name from the fact it is no more than a few houses from which there used to be a little ferry across the narrow channel of Loch Fleet.

Ruairidh points out the last standing supports of an old wooden pier across the water from the stone one on which we're standing. The ferry itself is long gone.

Driving back up the narrow road a little, we turn off and drive into a carpark from which we can walk along the beach after donning our walking boots.

It's a fair walk, at first on a well-worn path through the rough grass running along the top of the dunes, then down onto the beach.

I found it very poignant when Ruairidh told me about the burning of the Embo fishing boats, and find it no less poignant to see their remains now.

When we catch sight of the first of them in the distance, I feel my heart lurch. It's great that we have found them, but it feels as though I am walking through a cemetery where the coffins have long worn away. There are spines of boats lying embedded in wet sand, ribs sticking up here and there just as Ruairidh said before, 'skeletons of a whole way of life that lasted for many centuries'.

We linger there for some time in silence.

Did the fishermen hold any sort of ceremony here? Did they take the time to grieve as the flames devoured their livelihood? Did their wives and children join them on the beach having parked where we did and walked towards the bonfire? I can imagine the families' silent walk back to their transport, a funeral procession.

When Ruairidh leads me back to the car to change our boots and continue our journey, I feel heavy with memories that were never mine, sad for a life I never lived and people I never knew.

It's a while before I can even enjoy the scenery we pass through as we continue up the east coast of Sutherland.

Thankfully, I've passed this way before.

Eventually, "I've been reading John Prebble's book," I say. "I was wondering, why 'Sutherland', do you know? I keep reading about the 'Duke of Sutherland' and I know this area is called Sutherland, but I was wondering how it came to be called that."

"The place name and clan name of 'Sutherland' came from it being the 'land to the south' of the Norse Earldom of Orkney and Caithness. So, it's been known as Sutherland for a very long time."

I look at him and smile. I honestly am falling in love with this man. I love his passion, his wealth of knowledge, not just on Scottish history, but Bible history, prehistoric history, and a load of other things we've touched on in passing. I feel as though I could listen to his lovely, lilting voice forever.

But he's not only interesting to listen to, he's incredibly easy to talk to. He really listens. He listens with understanding, without judgement, and without trying to 'fix' everything. He helps where he can, but he helps me work through the things he can't do anything about, for instance, my widowhood. He's helped me see that I'm not required to bury my life with my dead husband.

When he starts talking again, I listen happily as we drive along this beautiful part of the country I've always loved but am only now learning much about.

"I've been reading about some of the forced evictions in the book," I tell him. "Some of them were not only brutal, but barbaric too. Not always great bedtime reading, I'm afraid, so I've decided to read a little each afternoon, when I can."

"Aye. The first thing, once they were driven all the way to the coast, was to build a house. A fore-sighted few had taken their roof beams with them, if they had a cart available and time to dismantle their house before it was set ablaze by the manager of the land and his gang."

"Taking the roof beams must have helped with the building."

"Right, but until they could get some kind of basic shelter built, they had to spend the early days as best they could, living rough, more or less exposed to the elements, the old and infirm huddled under blankets."

"Oh, my goodness."

"Yeah! But I'm afraid 'goodness' had little if anything to do with it. They cooked whatever they could forage from the land or the sea on fires built of whatever material could be found, like fallen wood, peat or heather. Organising that would have been women's work, gathering and burning kelp among the other things."

I pull a face, imagining the smell of their fires would sometimes be rather pungent and unpleasant when they had kelp on them.

"The women were having to cook food they'd never cooked before, all sorts of shellfish and seaweed, working in cold, wet conditions, their stomachs full of foods they were not used to eating. Unsurprisingly, many of them became very ill. Some died from the cold, wet conditions and lack of shelter, some from dysentery and other diseases. Not just the women and children, but the men died too. They had no experience of the sea and how inadequate their wee home-made boats were, and no idea of how dangerous it could be fishing off slippery rocks."

"It doesn't sound as though they had much choice in the matter."

"Oh, there were choices, but not necessarily better choices. They could explore the woods around them for prey to hunt, they could fish in the rivers, or another alternative occupation was to use any tools they'd managed to salvage when torn from their homes to clear narrow strips out of the patches of grass among the heather. But that was, at best, a long-term solution. Anything they planted may or may not do well, but it certainly would take time."

I frown, trying to imagine the horror of it without 'seeing' it too clearly. "The phrase that comes to my mind is 'out of the frying pan into the fire'. Their lives before sounded pretty hard, but their new life, even worse."

"You're right enough there, lass."

"So your family became fishermen."

"That's right. They would have also tilled the land for a few generations until they became more skilled at the fishing and began to build what has become a family business."

"You said after Catriona died you had no desire to rejoin them in the business."

"I never was enamoured of the life. I followed my father and my brothers into it and it was all I'd known, and perhaps that's part of my trouble now. Apart from that and then looking after Catriona, I've never been on my own before. I lived and worked with my father and brothers when I was in Helmsdale and then with Catriona, when I looked after her. You said I seemed a bit lost when you first came to my house, and that's how I feel sometimes. I don't know what to do with myself when I'm not out walking or playing at the ceilidhs." He turns a moment to look at me, before looking back to the road. "But that's all changed since I met you. Where I felt I had no point or purpose to my life, you've given me both. Finding you on the beach that day turns out to be the best thing that's ever happened to me. As you saw, it has even got me caring again about the great wee house Catriona left to me. I can see it now for what it is, rather than just being somewhere my sister used to live."

I snuggle against his arm. "Aw, Ruairidh, that's such a kind thing to credit me for, though I do believe time alone could have brought you to the same conclusions."

"I doubt it." He points to the Helmsdale sign we're approaching. "But we're nearly there, so perhaps I should prepare you for meeting the family. I did phone ahead to make sure Fingal and Bonnie would be home, but I'm guessing word will have gone round and they'll *all* be there."

I gulp. "So, who is 'all'?"

"Well, there's Fingal and Bonnie, who live in the house we were all born in, he being the oldest surviving son. They have five grown-up children, three sons, two daughters, and seven grandchildren, who mostly live in and around Helmsdale and are always up for a party. Mhairi, the oldest of my surviving sisters, lives with Fingal and Bonnie as her carers. Some of her family are still in Helmsdale, most are not. I should think that will be about it."

"Wow!"

"I did ask Fingal not to tell everyone we were coming, but I doubt he could resist telling most of what he considers to be his immediate family – immediate in the sense they live closest." He laughs. "Fingal's little brother bringing a lady-friend to tea – now, that's news they will all want to be in on, I'm afraid."

"Phew!" I mop my brow. "Then I suppose I'll just have to be on my best behaviour and tolerate being given the 'once over'."

He looks at me, his face screwed up in sympathy. "I hope they're going to be on their best behaviour and won't totally overwhelm you."

"So do I." I grimace. "I've become rather a solitary person, day to day. Still, I have been to a ceilidh with you and that was a fairly rowdy affair."

"True, and you coped well with that."

"I doubt Fingal's house is quite as roomy as the hall was, though."

"Er, no, not by a million miles," he says as we draw up in front of a small terraced house down by the harbour. "As you can see."

What I see is a well-kept, upstairs-downstairs mid-terrace house, painted a bluish grey, with white window frames and front door painted green, looking every inch the fisherman's house it is. And, strangely, because I'd never lived by the sea, I feel at home here already.

As I get out of the car, I look around myself. The house overlooks a truly picturesque, working harbour, part-filled with fishing boats, some still being unloaded of their catch, one making its way into the harbour heading for a space along the wall. Ropes, creels, fishing nets, bouys, it's all there. All the paraphernalia of the fishing industry, stacked up on the harbour wall or still in the boats. My heart is dancing. I want to explore it all.

"Don't worry, love," Ruairidh says. "If it gets too much for you in there ..." nodding towards the house, "I'll make our excuses and we'll escape to the harbour. I promise you'll get time to look around it."

I turn to him and smile. "Thank you, Ruairidh. Oh, thank you for this; the opportunity to meet your family, Helmsdale, the harbour ... everything." I'm giddy with a mixture of delight, joy, pleasure and apprehension.

"Last thing, we need to decide fairly quickly before we're spotted – how do you want me to introduce you?"

"Whatever you feel most comfortable with. Or you could just call me your 'lady-friend', since that's a more mature version of 'girlfriend' and it seems I'm at least that, yes?"

"Oh, at least," he says, leaning in to kiss me as we stand there at his brother's front door.

I can't seem to stop smiling.

Helmsdale

When Fingal opens the door, I'm still smiling, and he is too. "Welcome, welcome, Eilidh. Come away ben." He ushers me straight into the living room. Like Ruairidh's, there is no hall at the front door, but a tiny square of space where boots and coats are neatly stored, so as soon as he steps aside and I step in, I am 'ben', as in 'through to the room'.

Thankfully, the living room is devoid of the people Ruairidh thought might fill it, apart from Mhairi, who is sitting quietly by the fire. She holds tightly to his arm when Ruairidh bends to kiss her cheek then gently raises her hand to stroke his. He draws me forward to meet her, making it clear that I am his 'lady-friend' with signs and the way he holds me close. She gives me a shy smile and holds my hand to her face, nodding at us both.

"She lost her hearing a long time ago and stopped speaking after her children were all grown and husband dead," Fingal explains.

"She seems such a gentle soul."

"Always has been."

"It's good that she's here with you and Bonnie, Fingal."

"It's not the way of our family to allow strangers to care for those of us less able," he says. "It's not a duty, it's a blessing that we can care for Mhairi."

"Just as Ruairidh cared for Catriona," I acknowledge.

"Exactly." Fingal steps away and calls to Bonnie to come greet me, and she comes through from the kitchen, taking off her apron.

"Here, let me get rid of my pinny, and have a look at you, lass." She puts the apron down, smiles, and holds out her arms.

As I step into her embrace, I'm aware she is considerably shorter than I am, but much rounder and cuddlier. I feel very warmed by the strength of her cuddle. Nothing perfunctory about it. It's a proper, genuine hug of welcome.

"So, Eilidh it is they call you?"

"That's right."

"Well, I'm Bonnie, and you know that yer man here ..." She indicates Ruairidh. "He sings a grand song about an Eilidh. Has he tickled your ears with it yet?"

"Aye, that I have, Bon," he says, giving her a hug. "But only in the Gaelic, as yet."

"Ah, well, you've that to look forward to, lass. But sit yourself down and I'll bring ye a welcome. Tell me, is it tea or a tot ye'll be havin'?"

"Oh, Eilidh and I will be happy with tea just now, if that's okay, Bon." He looks to me for agreement.

I nod.

"We're neither of us much for the hard liquor."

"Aye, well, you'd maybes not try this last batch. It's mighty strong." She bustles off to make the tea, leaving Ruairidh giving me a very meaningful look, which I take to mean, 'Don't ask.'

During this exchange, I notice Fingal has taken the opportunity to scrutinise me as he stands back, allowing his wife the floor. He smiles at me, which makes me blush, with pleasure rather than embarrassment, because in his smile there is approval for his youngest brother's choice.

Instead of the thick mugs of tarry brew I was half-expecting, given the fact this is a fisherman's home, Bonnie wheels in a trolley, prettily laid out with dainty cups and saucers, a matching teapot and milk and sugar set. There are plates of home-baked scones and pastries too. All set on a beautiful embroidered cloth.

"Oh, that's gorgeous," I say. "What a pretty tea service."

"Aye, I plagued hissel long enough to part with some of his earnings to send for it from the catalogue. It fair took my eye when I was new married."

"You've had it a while then?"

"Aye, near forty-five year now, I've been learning to be a lady." She roars with laughter at her own joke. "But ye can tak the woman fra the travellers, but none sae easy for to tak the traveller out o' the woman." And she laughs the more. "Ye'll maybes have guessed I wisnae born and bred here abouts. It's no kent whar ah hail frae."

As we sip our tea from the dainty, delicate china, I quickly realise that Bonnie MacRae may sound rough and ready, but she is an honest, straightforward woman I feel very comfortable with. As we chat about the life of a fisherman's wife, both now, in modern times, and how it was when she married Fingal nearly forty-five years ago, I realise she has been a hard-working woman who is now enjoying a gentler life, and I'm happy for her.

She's as proud of her children as I am of my three girls, who she declares she must meet and issues a sincere invitation for us to bring them with us next time we come.

"Well, lass, I'm right sorry to break up the tea party, but I have to store some nets and creels I left lying after unloading today's catch. I wanted to be here to greet you, but I'm wondering if you and yer man here would care to join me to see 'The Bonnie Lass' to bed." Fingal is pulling on his oilskin trousers in the kitchen doorway. He nods towards Ruairidh. "He tells me ye're keen to check out the harbour and now might be the best time, while there's yet some light, and afore the family arrive to meet Ruairidh's bonnie lass." He chuckles as he shrugs into the oilskin jacket.

"Oh, I'd really love that." I look to Bonnie.

"On ye go, lass. Hisself's been right eager to show off his pride and joy."

As we walk across the narrow road to the harbour, excitement grows in me. I remember little from when I was here before, when the girls were young. However, I do have a memory of a very picturesque place, and so it proves to be. It's getting late in the afternoon, so most of the boats seem to be home for the day, leaving one or two spaces for latecomers.

I laugh, remembering how hard it was to hold onto Donna. She was so curious to look into the boats that she'd go dangerously close to the edge of the harbour wall, and Bill was so busy doing the same himself that he couldn't be trusted to hold her back. Emily was no trouble at all because she found it all rather 'disgusting and smelly' she exclaimed, and stayed well clear of the boats and the creels and lobster nets stacked beside them. Abigail accepted responsibility for looking after her, holding her hand while still enjoying the scene.

Today, I feel free to take it all in.

When Fingal arrives at his boat, a pretty standard one compared to the others, I see that it is beautifully maintained, with the name, 'The Bonnie Lass', displayed proudly on its side.

"Well, well, well," he mutters. He turns to us. "I left the lads finishing off their chores and told them I'd be back to see to mine, by and by, but it seems they've done them for me. All is neat and tidy."

"I see that," Ruairidh says. "Aye, my brothers were always good workers."

"The best," Fingal agrees. He climbs aboard and goes into the wheelhouse, reappearing wearing a life vest and holding two extra ones aloft. "If yer none too fussy about your clothes getting grubby, and dinnae mind wearing these, I could take you out for a bit. Let you see how she performs."

Ruairidh looks at me, his face radiant with pleasure to be asked. "What d'you think, Eilidh. Are you fussy?"

"Not at all." There's no way I'm going to miss out on such a fun adventure. After all, there are such things as dry cleaners, these days.

"And are you a good sailor?"

I shrug, stepping forward and taking Fingal's outstretched hand as he helps me climb aboard. "We'll soon find out."

They both laugh and Ruairidh follows me aboard, to help me put the life vest on. "I know you are a good swimmer, but rules are rules," he says as he clips me into it.

Fingal throws us some oilskin suits, saying, "In case you want the full fisherman's experience, and are still no fussy, here you go, lass."

I laugh and choose what looks like the slightly smaller of the two suits.

I have to turn the trousers over at the waistband and roll up the sleeves and trouser legs, but I couldn't be happier with my outfit, and ask Ruairidh to please take a photograph of me to show the girls, whereupon Fingal also takes one of us both together, Ruairidh with his arm round me and me snuggling against him contentedly with a smile fit to burst the camera.

When we're all suitably dressed and photos taken, Fingal starts the engine and begins to manoeuvre out of the busy harbour, hailing the captain of another ship they pass at the entrance, the crewmen ready on deck to berth the ship and unload the catch.

Once clear of the harbour, Fingal gives the boat 'a bit o' welly' as he calls it and we gradually pick up speed.

It seems I am a good sailor.

I relish the way we cut through the water, the ups and downs of it as we chug through the waves not bothering me at all.

"Aye, she's no speedboat, but she can fair cut the mustard when given her head," Fingal says proudly. He throttles back a bit once we're a fair way out, and he and Ruairidh point out various landmarks to me.

Once again, I look far out to sea and wonder aloud how long it would take a boat like this to sail across to Norway.

"Ah, lass, ah reckon she'd need to take a few days to make that journey, maybe sixty or more hours sailing time. Ah canna say as I've ever thought to try, since there's never been a need."

I look out across the North Sea, imagining such a voyage being undertaken thousands of years ago by the Vikings crossing the endless expanse of water for the first time, probably with little idea of where or when they'd find land, long before the time of engines. The power coming from a mixture of wind and many arms plying many oars.

While I'm contemplating such an amazing feat of human endeavour, Ruairidh comes to stand beside me. When I share my thoughts with him, he chuckles, "You do realise you're not looking straight across to Norway?"

I laugh. "So where am I looking out to?"

"Well, if we turned our helm around to take that line." He points straight ahead of where we stand. "And steered a straight course, we'd probably end up in Brora."

"Hehe! That could save us a bit of a drive come home time," I say, laughing.

Taking my shoulders, he walks me across the boat and adjusts my direction. "There you go. You're now looking out to Norway, some sixty hours sailing distance away."

"I wonder how many days you'd have to be out here, without an engine, till you sighted land on the horizon."

"I suppose that would depend if you took the time to sleep most nights," Fingal says as he joins us at the rail. "Right you two, okay to head back to harbour?"

I gloried in the beautiful wide sweep Fingal made to turn us around and head back into the sunset and a safe harbour.

"Aye," says Fingal. "Nearly home, and you'll rare eat a fresher supper when we get there, for Bonnie is cooking us some of the cod from today's catch."

Fresh fish and family

Fingal was right, Bonnie cooked us an amazing dinner. When I said how tasty it was she took delight in explaining how she'd skinned and boned the fish straight from the catch, then cooked it slowly in butter and cream made from the milk of their own cows, with a little garlic and herbs. She served the fish, which fairly melted in your mouth, with potatoes, carrots and mixed cabbage and onion, all from the garden. Delicious, amazing comfort food of the highest order.

"We'll cut into the dumpling when the family are here," she says.

"Aye, they shouldn'a be long now. Best choose a comfy seat while there's some tae be had," Fingal advises, so we take him at his word and Ruairidh and I get ourselves comfortably ensconced on one of the two sofas in the living room.

Gradually, the family start arriving, Ruairidh's brothers, their wives and children, and Fingal's children and their spouses. It seems word had spread to the wider family after all.

The house gets busier and busier, the noise gets louder and louder, until Bonnie brings through the trolley, laden with an enormous clootie dumpling and a huge pot of custard. She sets them on the table with plates and spoons and starts dishing them out. Miraculously, it seems, the house quietens and the family start queuing up for the dessert.

As guests of honour, Ruairidh and I don't have to queue but are served ours by Tilly, one of Bonnie and

Fingal's granddaughters, while another granddaughter serves Mhairi. Having had and enjoyed clootie dumpling several times before, and having even made it myself in the past, I was not expecting the taste sensation awaiting me. This is in a different league to anything I've had before. Moist, fruit-filled, spicy, light as a sponge cake, it melts in your mouth, yet it is as filling as a steamed dessert should be, it is 'Clootie Dumpling', deserving of capital letters. There has to be a secret ingredient, but, when I ask, Bonnie laughs and winks. "Ach, it's all in the mixing, lass. All in the mixing. That and my great-grannie's steaming cloth."

"And?" I prompt.

She laughs heartily. "That a willnae tell," she says. "No till I'm taking my last breath, and even then, it'll be hard wrung from me."

All who are in hearing distance laugh with me, and the women nearest confess, "Aye, we've all tried." "Aye, I've booked to sit nearest her bed, come that day."

As for the custard, it also deserves a capital letter. Custard. This is no dessert made from a packet or a powder, but is a smooth, thick, creamy plate of deliciousness. "Made with milk from my own cows and eggs from my own hens," that much Bonnie will own to. "And a wee pinch o' this and that spices," she adds.

I smile at her. "I'm almost afraid to ask about the brown sugar so liberally sprinkled on the dumpling."

She laughs and leans in to tell me her secret. "It's from the Co-op up the street."

I laugh with her and she draws me towards her to hug me where we sit.

The doors, back and front, lie open. The windows are open. The fire has burned low and the sun has long set, yet the warmth in the room is almost tangible, and it's not just the warmth generated by many bodies, it is also the warmth of human, familial, affection.

I've been watching Ruairidh as he interacts with his family. He's clearly much loved, and much teased as the youngest of his siblings. The children all love him, and the adults seem delighted he's brought a lady friend to meet them.

As gradually as they all arrived, so they start to take their leave, those with young children going first. Never in my life have I received so many hugs and kisses.

When there's only a handful of us left, Fingal brings out a large bundle wrapped in soft leather, the tanned hide of a once strong and majestic stag, I'm told. Inside are the pages of the family history. I'm shown them, but asked not to touch them until I've donned the white cotton gloves Bonnie takes from a drawer in the old oak sideboard. To be honest, even then, I'm almost afraid to touch.

As Ruairidh had told me, the writing was indecipherable to me.

"No fear, lass, Ruairidh shall read some to you." Bonnie hands him a sheaf of papers enclosed in an old, but more modern folder.

"When but a lad at school," Fingal says, "he set himself the task of translating the Gaelic written here into the tongue of the Sassenach to which we've all had to become accustomed. And a fine careful job he did of it too. He'll not like to tell you hisself, lass, but a copy was made of it and put on display in the museum for some time after, so proud of it was his teacher."

"Ach, away wi' ye man," Ruairidh says, his blush rising to belie his words. "Sure she knew nothing. Was she no a Sassenach herself?"

"Aye, but she had a good grasp o' the Gaelic too." Fingal tapped the folder. "And now, I'm sure your bonnie lass would enjoy to hear a wee bittie o' the fruits o' yer labour."

Bonnie led Ruairidh to stand by the newly-lit fire, facing those left in the room.

He cleared his throat, took a breath, and began reading a story written generations ago:

"A History of the MacRae family as gathered by me, one Dougal MacRae, in the year of our lord eighteen hundred and ninety-five.

When first they were driven from the land where they and those before them had lived for generations, leaving behind the charred ruins of their homes, to live if and how they could, it seemed they were sent here to die.

Lachlan MacRae, my great-grandfather, having loaded his home onto the cart and the backs of his sons and daughters, set them to walking toward the coast, while hisself carried his old mother out of the cottage she'd lived her whole life in, and loaded her onto the back of his tired old donkey, then tied it to the back of the cart when he caught up with it.

He told his weans, that they might remember the barbarism of the happenings, the roof was ablaze already and sparks flew around as he ran with Grannie MacRae, showing the scarring on his face and neck as proof. There was no time to bring her belongings bar the blankets he'd wrapped around her wasted old body as he lifted her from her bed.

No matter he was afeared for her great age, he could find her no better shelter than under the cart with the children each night, and one fearful cold night, they found her dead and frozen into the huddle she must have curled to warm herself. They lost a day of travel to dig in the frozen earth deep enough to bury her, and to grieve her.

When they could walk no further without walking into the sea, they tried as best they could to make rough shelter for their young ones. The able bodied built dwellings of stone and turf. In the middle, a ring of stone in which to light a fire to warm their feet and cook their food, what little they could find of it – a rabbit or a hare, a pigeon or two, wild boar if they were successful in the hunt. They sowed seeds and prayed the stony earth would sustain their growth, knowing they planted, not for today, but for a distant tomorrow.

They learned which shellfish made good eating and which were good for baiting a hook to catch fish in the river running through their land to drain into the North Sea. They learned how to live off seaweed when there was little else. They learned all this by trial and error, the errors causing much sickness and discomfort.

They sold all they could spare to buy the building materials to fashion small boats to try their luck at the sea fishing, knowing fine there were fish aplenty a distance out, praying the rudimentary vessels would hold together under the battering of the waves.

By a year into their forced exile, many had lost their lives to the raging sea, many more had died of the cold winter and malnutrition.

The memory of life in a far more pleasant land of rivers and glens, deer and mountain goat was hard to think on, easy to wish for when times were so bitter, though their memory told them it had been hard work and the rewards of their labours were enjoyed by those they must bow to, rather than by them and their hungry families. But they had become used to that. This new life was hard to feel affection for.

Into this was born my grandfather, Murdo MacRae, a lusty child, by all accounts, who grew up to be a bright and happy child despite his circumstances and surroundings and despite the fact his mother had not survived his birthing.

Murdo hisself tells how he became an adult in more hopeful times, when those evicted had become more settled in their coastal land.

His sisters cared for him as a child and his father taught him as he grew, and told him all that was written in his pages that he might not forget and might teach his children from whence they came and how their forefathers tamed both land and sea where they were driven.

He took interest in the building of the harbour at the mouth of that same river his own grandfather had fished in far upstream.

He took interest too, in the building of sheds in which the women could gut and clean the fish when their husbands and fathers brought home a good catch. These women would load their creels, hoist them onto their back and carry the fish from door to door of the homes in the town that was growing behind them.

Believing no one could lay claim to own the sea as they had the land, the men thought that what they blistered their hands and broke their backs to catch would be their own to eat or sell, but the landlords even levied the produce of the wild, wide North Sea, once they realised the wealth these poor besieged people had found in it.

Herring.

There was a herring boom and it was a busy, fabulous time for those such as Murdo, and he planned that he, his father and his older brothers would profit from it as much as any.

As a lad, he learned to make the best nets, as a teenager, he grew strong enough to shoulder their weight down to hoist into the boat his father had helped to build. As a man, after many mistakes costly to his pride, he became a most canny and experienced fisherman. His shoulders grew wide and strong from rowing the boat through the roughest, toughest of seas, and he could draw in a net full of fish no bother at all.

Murdo MacRae was a man much admired and popular with the ladies. Once he chose a wife he treated her well and Maggie MacRae bore him five strong sons and a daughter.

I myself was born of one of those sons and I listened rapt to his and Murdo's recounting of the history of our forebears.

What I've recounted on these pages is the fraction of past sufferings, as true as I remember fall from their lips, added to what was already written.

Aye, there was much painful groaning for what our kinfolk suffered at the hands of one who was duty sworn to protect them.

The hills behind the village bear many markers of the cruel life to which they were exiled, while the harbour boats declare their victory over the sea. Those who survived were the pride of Sutherland, of the Clan and its bonnie land, but sadly not of its greedy owners.

These words are penned by me, Dougal Macrae, with pride for our kinsfolk who suffered much and are exploited still, and shame for those charged with caring for them."

Ruairidh stops reading and downs the glass of cool water his sister-in-law hands him. "Enough?" he asks, his voice roughened by emotion. "Enough for tonight?"

Fingal rises and embraces his youngest brother.

Bonnie leans into me. "Aye, no matter we've heard it many times, it's a hard-hearted man who's not brought near to tears by the truth of it."

"I noticed he didn't read every page of what he translated," I say, somewhat puzzled.

"Aye, he spared you much of the harsh details written there. Perhaps he'll read more another time."

I look at the man before me, the man I want to spend the rest of my life with and I know with unwavering certainty, this man, the man who read the pages he'd carefully translated as a boy and reads now with such true emotion, this man is no fraudster, no fortune hunter, no cheat. This family he hails from are good people who love and respect him.

This is no act.

This is my future.

Along with my daughters and their families, these are my people. I belong with them, I belong with Ruairidh.

I doubt I've ever felt more certain of anything in my life.

Reaction

And now it's time to phone Abigail and Emily to tell them I am extending my stay another two weeks, explain why, and invite them to visit to spend time with me and to get to know Ruairidh. I've even made a note of these three main points and have my notepad open to the page they're on. It's sitting right in front of me to make sure I don't chicken out of any part of my agenda.

All three of them loved their father dearly, but they each showed their grief in different ways. Donna lay in bed and hid with me – she cried oceans, I could not cry at all.

Abigail became stiff and held her grief tightly to her chest as she went about organising the funeral and everything else that had to be done.

Emily's nature falls between their two. She cried a lot, but was also better able to function and be a help to Abigail.

For the first year and a half, Donna managed to let her grief out, with many tearful outbursts every time something reminded her of Bill, or we spoke of him.

Emily continues to get a bit weepy from time to time, but her outbursts were and are more contained and private.

Poor Abigail is the one I worry about most. As far as I'm aware, she has never given the grief freedom from its prison, locked in her heart. I asked Trevor once if Abigail had been able to grieve and he told me he thinks she has, but in her own, very private way. She is the one who most wants to keep me safe, to restrict my freedom so she can keep it in her control. She once confided in me that the thought of losing me as well as her father sends her into a tailspin. I can see that in her, and I sympathise.

I understand. But I can't live that way any longer.

I need to break free.

Having had a delicious taste of how full and interesting my life can be, I can't possibly go back to my old demi-life. I became a bit of a Pandora's box character, up here in Embo. Weeks ago, when I sat looking at the anchor, I acknowledged for the first time that I'd lived without curiosity. When Ruairidh came along and satisfied that small curiosity, I realised how much more there was to explore in my surroundings. Once that process started, there was no going back. It's not possible to cram all the opportunities I've become aware of back into the box.

In order of seniority, I decide to phone Abigail first.

I dial her number on my mobile.

As I wait while the phone rings out, I get up and start pacing. I'm about to give up when Abigail answers. "Sorry, Mum, you caught me just when I was carrying a bundle of newly ironed clothes through for Forrest to put away when he gets in from football practice." She sounds breathless.

"Sorry, love, have I caught you at a bad time? Shall I call back later?"

"No, not at all, it's all done. Let me unplug the iron. There. Done. I'm glad you phoned, actually. I was just thinking of you. I've taken your advice, you see, and started looking at college prospectuses – or is it prospecti in the plural? Anyway, I've printed some out to study more closely, but I could do with someone to brainstorm with me. I'm looking forward to you coming home so I can talk it over with you."

"About that …"

"Every time I pop round to yours to make sure there's nothing needing attention in the mail, etc., I think how much I miss our chats."

"Yes. About that …"

"In fact, I was thinking as I was ironing – it's hardly something you need to give your whole attention to, is it, ironing? Anyway, as I say, I was thinking about what you said about me needing to find out what I'd really like to do. What I'd enjoy doing. I've started a bit of a list, but I can't seem to settle to actually think properly about it all. There's always so much to do, isn't there? I wish I could ignore everything else and simply get time to think."

"About that, I'm not …"

"It's just that, when we're sitting in your kitchen with a cuppa, there's nothing for me to do. You're always up to scratch on the housework, so I can relax when I'm in your place. Give myself time to think as we talk things over. You know?"

"I do know, love, and I'm looking forward to hearing what you're thinking about courses and things."

"Is it Friday or Saturday you'll be home?"

At last, she's asked something and has paused to get my answer. The floor is mine! "About that," I start again. "I've booked the caravan for another two weeks."

Silence.

I hear her sit down.

Up till now, I've been conscious of her moving around, putting away the ironing board, putting other things away, gathering yet other things onto the kitchen table.

She's right. When she comes to my house, she sits down. When I go to hers, she's on the go all the time. Always doing something. As soon as her bottom hits the chair, she spots something else that needs done and she's up again doing it.

"But I don't understand," she says. "What do you mean you've booked another two weeks? And why on earth would you do that?"

Taking a deep breath, I just say it. No preamble. Straight to the point, pressing home my advantage now I've properly got her attention. "I've met someone."

Again, silence.

"I've met someone I want to get to know better."

"Someone. As in, a man, do you mean?"

"Yes, I do. A gentleman I met on the beach when we were all up here. I'd like you to meet him."

"Why?"

"Because he's someone special, someone who's becoming rather special and important to me."

I hear her indrawn breath. "Oh, Mum," she says. "I hope you're not making a fool of yourself."

"Pardon? Making a fool of myself? Why would you even think that? Am I in the habit of making a fool of myself?"

"No, but, well, I hope this man, whoever he is, isn't making a fool of you."

"What makes you think either of us is being a fool or fooling the other? Don't you think it's possible we actually really like one another? That we enjoy being together? Would like to stay together?"

"Ugh!"

"Ah! Is that the trouble? It's only the young who can have fun, can enjoy the company of a member of the other sex, who can fall in love?" It's my turn to be unable to sit at peace. I'm up and pacing about the caravan. I stop in front of the mirror and look at my reflection. "I'm not so old, am I?"

"I didn't say that."

"But it's what you mean, isn't it?"

"It's not just that, but really, Mum, let's face it. You're not sixteen anymore. You're just playing at being sixteen again. I know you had to grow up fast at that time, but you can't turn back the clock and relive your youth."

"I'm not trying to."

"Aren't you? Are you sure? You're talking about falling in love. Can you even hear yourself when you say it? It's ridiculous, Mum. Really, wake up. 'You met someone.' Mum. You met him on the beach!"

"So?"

"Mum! Think about it. How ridiculous to believe you could fall in love with someone you met on the beach at Embo? Embo! I mean, it's just ridiculous!"

"Why? Why is it any more ridiculous than to fall in love with someone you met at a party, in a bar, or on a dance floor, or on an internet dating site?"

"But don't you see, Mum, it's the age-old cliché of a holiday romance."

"No, that's not true ..."

"Of course you don't think it's true. You're in the middle of it. Instead of booking another two weeks in Disneyland, Embo, I dare you to come home for the next two weeks and face reality, real life. See how quickly you forget this guy you've only recently met. This guy you know nothing about!"

"But I do know ..."

"No, Mum, you don't. You only know what he wants you to know."

"I know this feeling is real."

She laughs. Abigail, my daughter is laughing, cruelly laughing at me.

"Honestly, Mum, I credited you with more sense than that. Can't you see, you're just lonely, you're missing Dad. But as soon as you get back home here, you'll forget about this, this silly holiday romance." She says it with such distaste, I find myself recoiling.

"But ..."

"Come home, Mum, please. We need you here. Please, come home. Give it a try before you embark on something you might regret. Something you feel silly about, something you might feel ashamed of. Ashamed to have made a fool of yourself."

I hear her tone change, the wheedling in her voice. But I also hear the caring there too. She's genuinely afraid for me.

She misconstrues my silence, thinking I'm doubting my feelings, which I'm not at all, but I am wondering whether or not going to Edinburgh will banish some doubts for her and for Emily – because I know for certain, as soon as I put this phone down, Abigail will be on to Emily to make sure she's alongside her.

She must think she senses a softening of my resolve. "Do you want me to phone the caravan park and cancel this coming booking," she says. "I can do that for you if you like."

"No, that's okay. I am perfectly able to do that myself if that's my decision."

"Okay, Mum, but please do. You're needed here. I've been trying to keep abreast of your mail, the bills and things, but there are some affairs you need to sort out. There is a stack of letters here I didn't like to open, but have been leaving for you to see to. And you need to be here to do it. And there's a reminder for your annual dental appointment next week." More arguments hard to refute. "And besides all of that, I need you. Emily needs you. Your grandkids need you. Emily probably told you, Francesca has been accepted into music school, starting next week."

"Oh, I didn't know. Nobody said." Guiltily, I put my hand to my mouth, knowing there were several texts sitting on my phone I hadn't got around to reading, let alone responding to.

"The family were waiting for you to be here for the celebration dinner we've planned for her. Even Donna said she'll be here for that."

At the mention of Donna's name, another spasm of guilt hits me, knowing Donna already knows about Ruairidh, which is bound to upset Abigail's sense of fair play. Closing my eyes and taking a breath, I prepare to explain.

"And I'm guessing she's probably been in on your secret affair. She didn't say anything, but I know she's been back up there to see you."

"Yes."

"Did she meet this man?"

I square my shoulders. "Three things, Abigail: I am not having 'an affair'. I am a single woman with every right to become romantically involved with whomever I choose, and secondly I will not have you calling Ruairidh 'that guy' or 'that man'. His name is Ruairidh and I'd like you to dignify him by using it in future, please."

Silence.

"Thirdly, yes, Donna did meet Ruairidh and she likes him very much. Perhaps you feel I owe you an apology about that, but really, I don't."

I hear Abigail draw a breath as though she has something to say, but I press on.

"I didn't tell you because I wanted to be sure of my relationship with him before opening the door to all your well-meant but misplaced doubts, concerns and interference. I am your mother, not your child, and, while I understand your concerns, I will not be chastised by you about my life choices."

Hearing nothing from the other end of the phone line, I take a breath before I continue, steel in my voice now. "I have no need to put my relationship with Ruairidh to the test, so if I do postpone my extra weeks up here for a week or two, it will be for reasons other than that, I can assure you."

There is a long silence after my impassioned speech.

I've surprised myself, and I'm guessing she's even more surprised, having no notion of how much inner strength and certainty I've developed in the past weeks.

"Mum, I'm sorry if you feel I've been chastising you. I hadn't meant to, but none of us were prepared for you staying away as long as you already have. The whole unexpected scenario has thrown me and got my adrenalin flowing into fight mode. Perhaps it's me who should be apologising."

"Not necessary. How about we agree this has been a difficult situation to discuss over the phone and leave it at that?"

"Yet another good reason for you to come home, Mum. It seems to me you have a lot of unfinished family business here before you should stay away longer."

Responsibilities

Ruairidh is great when we meet on the beach. He listens while I paraphrase the conversation I've just had with Abigail. Understanding how important my girls are to me, he doesn't want me to lose or damage my relationships with them. "Abigail is right," he says. "You should see to your affairs back in Edinburgh, family and otherwise before staying up here longer. She's right. I've actually been a bit selfish, keeping you to myself up till now."

"I wish you could come with me."

"I do too."

"I know you have a wedding ceilidh booked for tomorrow, don't you?"

He pulls a face. "Afraid so."

"But after that?"

"Well I ..."

"Sorry. I'm being selfish. This would not be a great week to leave Nan in the lurch, would it?"

"No, not really. But I could maybe ask Jenna to help out this week."

Nan's husband is not doing so well, struggling to come through a bout of pneumonia, and Ruairidh planned to take her to visit him more frequently this coming week.

"No, Jenna has the wee one to see to. She and her mum already go in as often as they can." I draw myself up. "I'll just have to put my big girl pants on and go down the road myself."

“Another time?” he asks, taking me in his arms. “I’d love to come with you, see where you live and meet your family.”

"Meantime, we each have things to keep us busy for a while, I know.”

“It’s for the best all round if you sort things out in Edinburgh without having me there as a distraction, anyway.” He grins at me, knowing full well how much of a delightful distraction he’d be. I’d want to show him around, go sightseeing with him. Do the whole touristy thing as well as the romantic restaurant dates.

“I suppose.” I sniff, dangerously close to tears of frustration and self pity.

So, instead of a few more weeks of blissful holiday, I’m having to pack all my things and return to my responsibilities. Thankfully, it was no problem to rearrange the caravan rental, and I’m delighted I can have the same one when I come back.

The drive ‘home’ is not the joyous journey I enjoyed a few short weeks ago. It is not filled with happy anticipation but is heavy with sadness and I’m having trouble holding back my tears as I drive.

Deciding an accident is the last thing I need right now, I draw into the next lay-by, have a jolly good cry, then seek out tissues, blow my nose, wipe my eyes and take a breath.

With a long sigh, I choose some cheerful music and make my way back into the steady stream of traffic.

By the time I’ve driven to Edinburgh, and up to my front door, weaving through familiar streets, passing familiar shops, familiar landmarks, I feel flat and tired. All I want is to curl up in my bed and sleep for days.

The house smells musty. I know the girls have been popping round occasionally to pick up my mail, water the plants and make sure everything is safe and well, but I don’t suppose they’ve been opening the windows every day, as I usually do, so before I even unload my things from the car, I go from room to room, opening windows.

When I go out to the car, I open the boot, put my hand on my holdall, then stop.

I close the boot again.

This is not where I want to be.

Perhaps, if I leave everything in the car, I could go straight back to Ruairidh in the morning, after resting my weary head on a soft pillow.

Without further ado, I lock the car, go back into the house and up to bed, where I fall, fully-clothed, into an uneasy sleep for several hours, wakening shivering and hungry, deep into the evening.

I check my phone, only to be greeted by a raft of texts from Abigail and Emily: "Where are you?" "When did you set out?" "You'd have had to be out of the caravan by ten this morning, so by my calculations, you should be home by now." "Please let us know you're alright." And so on.

I throw the phone on my bed and go downstairs to get something to eat, closing the windows in each room I pass. I'm not ready to deal with my daughters yet.

Of course, when I open the fridge, there is nothing much in it. The freezer it'll have to be then. Trouble is, I don't know what I want. I pick something up and put it back, pick something else up and put it back. Nothing at all takes my fancy.

I look through the kitchen cupboards, opening door after door, having a cursory glance in the cupboard and closing the door again. By the time I hear Abigail's key in the front door, I have given up looking and am slumped on a kitchen chair, stricken by the realisation, even if there should be all sorts of delicious delicacies available in my kitchen, I would want none of them. The gnawing hunger inside me is not for food, it's for what I drove away from today.

I want to get in my car and go back up the A9 and into Ruairidh's arms. If only I wasn't so darned weary.

'Tomorrow,' I think, hearing the echo of our parting after each wonderful day I'd shared with Ruairidh. 'Tomorrow.'

"Tomorrow," Abigail says as she strides into the kitchen, "you can do a proper shop, but meantime, I've brought you some bread and milk and such, since I don't suppose you thought to stop and get anything on your way down the road."

I look up at her.

I feel washed out. Such a neat expression. Washed out. Someone or something has power-washed all the energy and motivation to move out of me, leaving me, a limp wash rag hanging over the chair.

"Oh, Mum," she says. "You look awful. Here." She helps me off the chair and through to the living room, where she sits me in a more comfortable recliner chair, puts my feet up and a rug over my legs. "Let me make you a cuppa and some toast and you can tell me what on earth has happened to you on the journey home, to leave you like this."

Revived by the cup of tea and toast, I feel a lot more charitable towards my daughter and when she asks me what happened, I am able to reply more noncommittally than I might have before, "Oh, I'm just a bit tired, and it was hard to leave Ruairidh, so I started out a bit later than intended."

"I wish you had thought to drop me a text to let me know you were alright. It's such a long way to drive all on your own, and as time went on, I began to get seriously worried. Emily and I were both getting anxious, particularly as the light started to go. I was ever so relieved to see your car on the drive as I drove up behind it. I've texted Emily to let her know you're safely home. I wish you'd had the same thoughtfulness."

I close my eyes, trying not to listen. One of the hardest things to bear as your children grow up, is how the tables turn and they somehow think it's permissible to chastise their parents.

"And what on earth have you done with all your cushions and ornaments? Emily and I got a bit of a shock each time we walked in to check everything was okay in the house. For a while we actually wondered if there had been a break-in, butthen Emily pointed out the TV and everything were still here, and besides, why would anybody take the horrible, tatty old cushions instead of the valuables?"

Is this what she wants me to give up my chance of happiness for? To allow her to run my life, to tell me what to do, when to do it and how?

If I wasn't so extremely tired, I'd walk out and climb into my car right now. 'Tomorrow,' I say to myself. 'Tomorrow.'

Keeping family happy

After a good night's sleep, I feel well enough to make myself some more tea and toast in the morning. Only having instant coffee in the cupboard, I decide tea is the better option now I've become used to 'proper' coffee as Ruairidh taught me to make it, even buying me a good coffee pot to make it in.

But that will be for another day.

For today, I have to decide what to do.

My car is still packed.

Tempting as it is to lock up the house and drive up the A9 again, I know that will only turn out to be procrastination and prevarication: a postponing of facing my daughters' displeasure and their haranguing of me as well as the inevitable time I have to stand firm and tell them this is my decision and they will have to accept it.

So, with a deep sigh and a grudging attitude, I drag my luggage into the house, put things away and put a wash on.

I was not about to confess to Abigail that I texted Ruairidh last night before I even entered the house, but he was the only one I wanted to communicate with at that sad and weary moment. But now, texting is not enough, I want to talk to him. I want to hear his voice.

I feel more grounded after a long conversation with him. He is so good at helping me see things from the girls' perspective. His innate empathy allows him to put himself in their position – much more successfully than I have been doing lately. So much of my life has been about caring for other people, which is not the same thing as being empathetic.

For the next few days, I make enormous efforts to see things from their standpoint. I parry all of Emily and Abigail's questions, haranguing and entreaties, exhausted by them, but determined I am not going to do as I did before, and take to my bed. After Bill died, I was in shock and incapable of doing anything else. But I realise now it weakened me in the eyes of my daughters and gave them the right to look after me. I handed it to them on a plate: my independence, my self-assurance, my life. And I am determined to show them those days are past, those needs are no more.

I continue to read the Prebble book, even sharing bits with the girls, who are pleased I have a new interest. They humour me and fain interest themselves, which is fine by me if it keeps them off my back for a bit.

Funnily enough, though, it does capture the interest of Forrest and Marco. While I am at Abigail's for dinner one evening, Trevor says, by way of making conversation, "Abigail tells me you've been reading about the Highland Clearances. The Prebble book, isn't it?"

"That's right."

"Yes, I had to read that when I was at school. A tough read, I thought at the time. Not really my cup of tea."

"I wouldn't have thought it would be mine," I admit. "But I'm finding it interesting. I didn't know before just how awful the clearances were, how much that time changed Scottish history, and how much it had to do with the mass emigration of highlanders to America and Canada."

"I have a Canadian penpal," Forrest says. "He reckons his ancestors came from Scotland."

"Oh, that's nice, Forrest. Does he know whereabouts in Scotland they came from?"

He shrugs. "Dunno, but I can ask him, I suppose."

"Some of Ruairidh's family emigrated to Canada as a result of the clearances and they ended up in Winnipeg back then."

"Does he write to them?"

"Oh, I think they lost touch with that part of the family, eventually, though Ruairidh tells me they have some of the early letters they wrote when they first emigrated in the 1800s."

"Wow! Wicked!"

"Oh, don't get her started, Forrest, or we'll be here all night," Abigail says. "It's your gran's new hobby, Scottish history." She tries to make it sound like a joke, but it makes me surer than ever that she and Emily have been humouring me.

"Is that why Grandpa wouldn't go to Dunrobin Castle?"

"Yes, that's right. The Duke of Sutherland back then, in 1812, drove all his tenant crofters off the land to make way for raising sheep. The crofters had to start again over on the east coast – or emigrate to Canada."

"Why?"

I see Abigail roll her eyes and glare at Trevor for raising the subject. "How about I hand the book on to you? I'm almost finished it."

"No need," says Trevor. "I've still got my copy on the bookshelves over there." He points to the shelves over by the hearth.

Forrest starts to get off his chair.

"Not till we've finished dinner," his mother says. "Unless you want to forfeit dessert?"

He sits back down. "I'll get it later." And he winks at me.

"Next time we're all in Embo, I can take you to where the crofters had to learn to become fishermen."

"Cool, Gran." He high-fives me across the table, making me feel so good about myself. At last, I have found something to share with my grandson. Something we can talk about and share thoughts on.

Later, I find he has talked to Marco, and they are both reading the book. Abigail tells me the pair of them, being quite competitive, are keeping reading even when they hit boring bits. Marco has always been an avid reader, but Forrest hasn't, so she even thanks me for getting him interested in the subject in the first place. I have to try not to look too smug. Inside I'm delighted.

I read the other book Ruairidh recommended too, *The Silver Darlings,* about the herring boom up the east coast in the later 1800s. It makes me want to go back to learn more about it from the family history in Fingal's house. I recommend *The Silver Darlings* to the boys too, buying them each a copy when I go out to the shops.

I keep thinking about Embo, what I've learned about it and the other fishing villages up the coast, and I can't help but try to imagine life in a fishing village when shoals of herring were so plentiful that the men and their families thrived. I feel they deserved that period of prosperity. Sadly it didn't last, but it must have been great while it did.

Abigail worries I'm romanticising the villages and the life up there. She hoped I'd settle back to life in Edinburgh, and gradually even the pretence of interest in my reading material falls away and she doesn't want me to talk about it any more. So I don't, but she can't stop me reading and imagining, and longing to be part of life as it is now in Embo.

I try to put myself in her position. She must see this new-found interest as a threat. Something that is pulling me away from her, and I try to be understanding and respect her wishes.

But I am a strong, independent woman, capable of taking care of myself, making my own decisions and taking the consequences of them if they turn out not to be all I hope. Now I need to gently remind my daughters of that truth.

Unfortunately, in these present circumstances, I raised a strong, independent daughter in Abigail, and she doesn't give in easily. And her strength of will strengthens Emily's. They make a formidable pair.

Edinburgh

As the days wear on, I find I am no more enamoured with the thought of picking up the threads of the life I led in this beautiful city, than I was when I walked through my front door two weeks ago. Yes, there are theatres and art galleries, expensive restaurants and shops, plenty to do and plenty to see, but there is no one I want to do or see it with, nowhere here I want to go, only my daughters here I want to see – and they are making that less and less inviting a prospect as the weeks see them coming through my front door every day for another round of arguing or gentle persuasion.

"What kind of man is this Ruairidh anyway? He could easily be the kind of man who sees his chance of catching himself a well-off widow, someone to look after him in old age, for all you know."

"You're just missing Dad. He always said you were a bit dippy. That's all this is! You being a bit dippy."

Sometimes they talk to me as though I'm a child, unable to make up my own mind, unable to know what I want. At first, each time they talk like that, I'm left deflated when they leave, sitting on the couch, feeling lost and doubting myself. Eventually, I realise, it is bullying tactics. They are trying to organise my life, claiming it is for my own good.

"I am a strong, capable woman, and you are making me feel like a helpless old lady, fit only for a retirement home," I tell them.

"No, we don't mean to make you feel like that, Mum," Emily tries to reassure me. "All we want is for you to be happy and safe where we can look after you in the years ahead."

Abigail sees it differently. "Dad didn't see you that way, as a strong, capable woman. He said you needed someone to look after you."

"No, don't you see? He didn't want to see me that way because it made him feel needed if I was dependent on him. But, in actual fact, I was the one who looked after him. I was the one who paid the bills, called the plumber, the electrician, or whoever was needed. I was the one who did the shopping, the cooking, the cleaning. I was the one who balanced the books. I was the one who ran this house. I was the one who looked after him," I repeat.

The girls don't realise that by haranguing me like this, they are helping me come out of my grief and waking me up to past realities. I loved Bill, but he was far from perfect.

I'm quite sure Ruairidh is far from perfect too, but if I am blessed with another forty years of happy marriage to realise it, I think I can go with that.

But the girls change tack when they feel the argument slipping away from them. "What about the winter? What will you do when it's pouring rain or snowing and too cold to go swimming or walking on the beach?"

"I'm sure there is as much to do up there as here in Edinburgh in bad weather. I mean, what do any of us do when it rains for days?"

"Not a lot, I don't suppose," Emily admits.

"You wouldn't have all the shops," Abigail tries.

"You know I'm not a great lover of shopping. I only do it when I need something specific, never for fun."

"Oh, I love shopping," Emily says.

I smile at her. "Something you had in common with your father, rather than with me."

If I'm going to shop anywhere, I have to admit I'd rather it was in Edinburgh than anywhere else, but window shopping has never appealed to me. If I need something, I go to the shop most likely to have it, if they have what I want, I buy it and that's me done. However I recognise it's very much a case of 'to each his own'.

Bill loved shopping, he loved window shopping, he loved hopping in and out of various shops, up and down on escalators and lifts, seeing what there was for him to choose from, whether he needed it or not.

When the girls were young and we all went 'into town' to shop, I would take Donna, who also hated shopping, to the gardens across the road, where we'd feed the squirrels and enjoy the peace of the gardens, while Bill took Abigail and Emily to have fun in the shops. We'd arrange a time to meet up in Jenner's tea room for their scrumptious afternoon tea, Donna and I usually arriving first, making our choices and securing a table. Bill and the other two were always late, always loaded with parcels, and high as kites.

It was always a great day out for us all in our different ways. And Edinburgh is good at that. Good at providing any sort of day out you could choose: art galleries, cinemas, theatres, restaurants with food from practically every country you can imagine. There are parks, gardens, castles and grand houses. There are special streets, like Princes Street, Cockburn Street, The Bridges, and so on. Not forgetting the Royal Mile with its quaint, unusual shops rubbing shoulders with ancient monuments. There are wynds and closes leading to secret places, John Knox's House, the High Court, old taverns, modern pubs, hotels, restaurants, Camera Obscura, whisky shops and The Scottish Whisky Experience, all filling the Scottish mile that runs from Edinburgh Castle to Holyrood Palace. So much to do, so much to see in such a relatively small area called the 'Old Town'.

For most of my life, I lived happily here. I did the open-topped bus tours, walked The Royal Mile, visited theatres, galleries, cinemas, restaurants, all of it. I played at being a tourist in my early teens, laughing and giggling with the girls from school. Truly, I did it all, much of it at Bill's pace. This was where my home was, this is where I felt happy.

But now, I am ready for a quieter life. I believe my happiness resides two hundred miles away in a cottage, in a quiet little village, with the beach on my doorstep and a country to explore.

The girls even suggest asking Ruairidh if he'd be willing to come and live in Edinburgh with me, instead of me going up north to live with him. "If and when you marry," Emily says.

"Have you asked him that?" Abigail says. "If he really loves you, he should be willing to live anywhere you want to live." She folds her arms and nods to Emily, thinking, I suppose, that they've got me there.

"But why should I ask him to live here when I no longer want to live here?"

Emily frowns. "Don't you, Mum? Why ever not?"

"Because I have woken up to the fact there are other places I can be happy and foremost of them at the moment is Embo."

"Because Ruairidh is there?"

"Well, I'll not lie to you, he is the biggest draw, but not the only one. I have come to love that way of life up there. It's slower and gentler. The air is cleaner and the space is wider and bigger and I feel free up there. Free to be me." I get up, the better to demonstrate the freedom even thinking of life up there gives me. "Free to dance on the beach, to sing in the shower, to draw and paint, to swim in the North Sea and run back up to the comfort and warmth of my home – oh – just to be me," I say, hugging myself.

"Why can't you do these things here? Nobody is stopping you singing in the shower."

"True but I've never felt like doing it before."

"You could get in your car and go to Crammond or Musselburgh, or Portobello and find a beach to dance on, from which to swim in the North Sea, to sit and draw, whatever." Abigail's voice becomes less and less convincing as she lists these places.

"You know why that would not be the same. For one thing, the people. Too many people. How could I feel free to dance, and how could I run up the beach to my warm home after my cold swim? Oh, Abigail, in your heart you must know it isn't the same."

She sighs. "I suppose. But tell me, would you still want to uproot and go there to live, even if there was no Ruairidh?"

I barely have to hesitate. Even before my relationship with Ruairidh grew, I already felt so at home there. It was the beach and the sea. It was the anchor and the history, it was the solitude and the freedom. I knew that first day, if I moved to Embo, after remembering all I needed to, I could leave the past sorrows behind me. My hesitation is only to close my eyes and remember how it felt, even before a kind gentleman helped me off the rocks.

"Yes," I say. "Absolutely, yes. And that's what these weeks are helping me know for sure. I am going to sell up and move to Embo, to live there with or without Ruairidh. I very much hope it is with him, though, because another thing this week has helped me know for sure is that I've fallen deeply and truly in love with him."

"What about Dad, then. Don't you still love Dad?" Emily says through gathering tears.

I sit down. "Of course I do. You know I do. I'll always love your dad."

"Exactly! So how can you fall in love with someone else? Why would you even want to?"

"Because your dad is dead, love. He's been dead for three years, and I'm tired of being dead with him."

Sometimes people use the phrase 'bursts out crying' when really they mean someone simply started crying.

Abigail literally bursts out crying. The noise is explosive. Not a river bursting its banks, but a dam bursting, suddenly, without warning: a weakness erupting. I reel from the sudden force of it.

I can't remember the last time I heard my oldest daughter cry, but it's hard to hear her now. Hard to bear her pain when I can't put my arms around her and hold her. When I try, she pushes me away. When, far from trying to make it better, I'm the cause of her pain and I can do nothing to ease it.

Her tears come loudly, in great gulping, gasping sobs. They're the tears of someone who thought she'd forgotten how to cry.

"Oh, Abbie, Abbie, precious, I'm sorry. It's okay, love, it's okay." I move forward on the couch, reaching my arms out to her, trying to soothe her. I want to hold her, rock her in my arms, as I used to all those years ago. She's my wee girl. I never found it easy to see her tears. I can hardly bear to see them now.

"Sorry, Mum, I'm sorry," she says between great gulps, though still not letting me hold her. "I just miss him. I miss him so much."

"I know, love, I know. I miss him too."

"We all miss him," Emily chimes in, tears running down her cheeks too. I suspect her tears are partly for Bill but also for her big sister, who she may hardly remember ever crying, and certainly not like this.

"But you've found someone else." Abigail's crying intensifies.

"Yes, I have, love. But Ruairidh will never take your dad's place. That's the great thing about love, it's not exclusive, it grows as you need it to. When I was expecting Emily, I didn't believe I'd ever love her as much as I loved you. Same again when Donna came along. But I did, and I do. Love grows. It expands. It doesn't restrict itself to only one person. You know that. You love Trevor and Forrest. You love your sisters. You love your dad. And I hope you love me too."

She's beginning to sound a little calmer. The gulps and sobs are more restrained. She reaches for a tissue and blows her nose.

I go on speaking, praying the sound of my voice is doing what she won't allow my arms to do right now. "Love isn't something you turn off when you're done with it, like turning off the kitchen light. Just because your dad isn't here with us any more doesn't mean we won't go on loving him. But that doesn't stop us loving one another too, does it? Nor does it mean we can't love someone new."

"You say you love Ruairidh, but how can you possibly know that already?" Her voice is tired, small and tired.

"I just do. I knew from the second time I met him. I want to be with him all the time, and I truly believe I love him." I smile.

"Is he kind to you?"

"Very kind."

"Does he make you happy?"

"Yes he does, very much so."

"Then I shall try to be glad, Mum. Really, I will."

"I was hoping you could come up for a few days when I go back to Embo so you can meet him. You too Emily."

They both look at me, new light dawning.

"I suppose that might be helpful," Abigail says.

"I'd like to meet him." Emily is first to come to me and give me a hug. "If you honestly feel you want him to be part of your life, then I think I want him to be part of mine too."

Slowly, almost grudgingly, Abigail moves towards me and allows me to put my arms round her. I feel the shuddering of more sobs, but she gradually relaxes in my arms. "Yes, I'd like to meet this man who has stolen you away from us."

"Oh, darling, Abbie, he hasn't stolen me from you. He is a lovely man and he wants so much to be your friend. He wants us all to be able to have good times together. His family are lovely too, and both of you already have several invitations to meet them."

"That's nice." Emily always did like the thought of having an extended family. When she was a wee girl she was somewhat miffed she had no aunties and uncles, grandparents or cousins on my side of the family, and only one grandmother and one aunt on Bill's side.

"So, do you think you might come up soon? Embo is a great place for getting a chance to think, I've found. You'd have time and space to work out your way forward, Abigail, as well as getting to know Ruairidh. And you'd be able to get a bit of much needed rest from the children, Emily."

"Ooh! Tempting."

"Do you think you could swing it?"

"Oh, I'm pretty sure I could." Abigail blows her nose again. "Trevor's mum is always asking if she could have Forrest stay over for a few nights. She enjoys the company. Forrest enjoys hers too, bless him. So, yes. I think I can swing that. I'll have a word with Trevor tonight and get back to you."

"And I'll ask Bryan."

"That's great."

"And, Mum, thank you." Abigail gives me another, more willing hug.

"That's okay, love. I'll truly look forward to your company."

"Not just that. Thank you, I needed that cry. I've needed it for a while." She laughs, ruefully. "Three years, in fact."

"Yes. I think that's true."

So we sit talking until the afternoon light starts to go and it's time for them to go home to feed their families.

Much has been accomplished this afternoon. At last, they have accepted my decision to travel back to Embo in the next day or two, and to stay there in the caravan until the site closes for the winter. All of that being a precursor to me making plans to stay there permanently.

Provisional plans have been made for them to visit me there during the next couple of weeks in an effort to help them become accustomed to this planned future of mine.

After waving them off, I am exhausted, and I have a real longing to be on the beach, walking, thinking through the monumental shift that came over my oldest daughter. Instead, I warm up some left-overs for my dinner, eat them, then fall into bed, for a change hoping not to sleep, but to think it over. I need to process it all before I can even contemplate phoning Ruairidh to update him on things down here in Edinburgh.

Meeting Abigail

There's something exciting and special about meeting someone off a train. It's not something I often do these days but as soon as I walk from where I parked the car, into the station, I get that delicious flutter of excitement I remember from years ago when Bill used to have to go down to London for his work from time to time.

We were newly married and I missed him dreadfully for the five days he'd be away. Standing at the ticket barrier at the end of the appropriate platform where the train was due to come in, the butterfly flutter would start in my chest and stomach. As the train approached, my excitement would grow and I would go on tiptoe to try to catch sight of him stepping off the train when it stopped.

'There he is! Oh, there he is.'

He'd look for me and there I was, jumping up and down, waving as though I was welcoming him home from years at war. He'd laugh and sweep me into his arms after coming through the barrier.

That moment of reunion was the sweetest thing, making the trip worthwhile, the moment special enough for the trip to be looked forward to.

And here I am now, waiting for my precious daughter to alight from the Edinburgh train in Inverness. I've located the platform, I'm at the ticket barrier, up on my toes as the train comes in, feeling that same delicious flutter of excitement.

When Abigail told me she'd be coming by train because Trevor would need their car, I knew, I just knew meeting her off the train would be a special thing, and I've been looking forward to it.

'There she is! Oh, there she is.'

I start waving as she approaches and watch as she catches sight of me, not knowing how she'll react. Will she be embarrassed by my exuberance? Is she too grown up and sophisticated to feel the flutter in her chest too?

To my delight, as soon as she sees me, a wide grin spreads across her face, she waves back enthusiastically and starts hurrying towards me. Once again, there is that feeling of an elongated separation being ended. We cling together like long lost lovers.

At last, I can hold my daughter while she cries. A week ago, it hurt so much to hear those gulping sobs and not be able to comfort her in my arms. Now I can.

She clings to me and sobs.

We both know why.

I am soothing and whispering to her as a mother does when her child is hurting, tears running down my face too, standing in the middle of Inverness train station.

Three years of pain have been released at last. Strange, and what to many will seem inappropriate, that the release should be achieved in such circumstances, but to many mothers and lovers the world over who have ever welcomed their loved ones home from war, it is not strange at all.

There is so much unspoken meaning in that moment of reunion. There never was, and never is need for words. Everything is said in the tears.

Once we eventually compose ourselves, I take her trolley bag and lead her to the car. We are still holding on to one another, her arm linked through mine, her side pressed against mine, smoothly in step with one another.

I put her bag in the boot of the car, climb in beside her, and awkwardly lean across to kiss her cheek. Once again, the welcome needs no words, the ‘Glad you’re here’ is clear.

The first part of the journey is passed in comfortable silence until, eventually, the beauty of the scenery we pass through brings peaceful serenity to turbulent emotion.

Abigail takes a long, deep breath. “It’s so beautiful up here, isn’t it?”

“Mmm, I love it. I always feel as though, once we cross the bridge out of Inverness, we’ve left modern civilisation behind and entered a new world, free from the necessity to count our day in fifteen-minute increments.”

“I’d never thought of it like that before, but yes, it’s true. That’s how it feels today.”

“I didn’t used to feel that quite so strongly before, because in the past, as your dad drove us up here I’d be thinking about the unpacking there was going to be to do, and what I’d make for dinner once it was done.”

“Yes! That’s it. That’s what’s different this time for me. I only have a few changes of clothes in my case to unpack this time, and that’s hardly arduous.”

“And Ruairidh has promised he’ll cook dinner for us.”

“Oh, that’s lovely! I can hardly wait to meet this man who has won my mother’s heart.” She laughs. “It’s so funny to think of how that could happen to you after all these years.”

I smile back at her. “But it has. It well and truly has.”

“Yeah, well that’s as may be, but I want to see for myself that he’s all you think he is. Just because he’s won you over doesn’t mean I’ll happily allow him to run off with you without a fight.”

I look over to see if she’s joking, but I can’t tell from her neutral expression whether she is or not, and the lurch I feel in the pit of my stomach informs me her opinion matters more to me than I’d like it to.

Over the years, I always felt the thrill of excitement grow as we crossed the bridges the further north we went, it's always been most intense when we're on the bridge across Dornoch Firth, after passing Tain. Today is no exception.

As we drive through Dornoch, "I love that it never changes here, does it?" Abigail says. "There's a tremendous feeling of permanence and dependability about Dornoch that I just love."

"Me too." I am delighted to hear her say that. To know she feels the same as I do. All these years, I had no idea she did. She'd never expressed it before. I smile to myself. This is shaping up to be a very special few days.

What's in a name?

"So you must be Abbie," Ruairidh says, welcoming her without ceremony by drawing her in for a kiss on the cheek.

"Abigail," I say, the correction automatic after all these years.

"No, it's okay, Mum. Abbie is fine," she says. "In fact, I prefer it."

I look at her in surprise.

She blushes. "I like the way you say it," she says to Ruairidh. "It's much softer." She smiles.

There is no wariness, no judgement in her smile.

My heart lurches at the realisation she likes him, she is open and ready to accept him.

So was her stern warning in the car earlier to tease me?

I know Ruairidh has a winning smile. Didn't it win me over the first time I saw it? But Abigail? Really? Or had she already decided to be a softer, more open version of herself? An Abbie instead of an Abigail?

She continues to chat in a friendly manner as he shows her into the house.

I smile at her, hoping my smile conveys the love and gratitude I feel right now.

While Ruairidh busies himself in the kitchen, once again leaving us with music playing softly in the background, Abbie explains why she has changed what she wishes to be called.

"I don't know if you are aware, Mum, but over the years, whenever I've been going through a hard time or when I've hurt myself and you are comforting me – which you have always accomplished beautifully, by the way – you always call me Abbie. You did it again when we spoke when you were home and I broke down."

"Oh, did I? I'm sorry, I was hardly aware."

"No, don't be sorry. It never upset me. It was always soothing, and I always felt safe and comforted by it."

"I'm glad."

"When I started school, I felt very vulnerable. It was hard to be wrenched from the warm, gentle environment of home, where I felt loved and protected, and thrown into a world where no one knew me or cared tuppence about me and there was no one in my corner. I hated it."

"Oh! I had no idea." I feel suddenly terribly ashamed of my own lack of insight at the time. When my darling little girl came home from school that first day and told me excitedly about the things she had done and the friends she was making, I thought she was settling in easily, no qualms at all.

"When the teacher read out our names from the register, she called me Abigail June Crawford. I didn't answer, as I was supposed to, with a 'here, miss' because I didn't know she was calling my name. I'd always been Abbie up till then. She called me again, much louder, much harsher, and she stared right at me, looking for the correct response, which I gave her the second time, suddenly realising that the name Abigail was a much stronger, more imposing name. I felt empowered by it, less vulnerable. I decided that's what I needed to be called from then on, if I was to survive in that strange world."

"Goodness! What a perceptive little girl you were!"

"Ever since, the use of my full name made me feel stronger, almost invincible. But I now realise it was distancing too. Helped keep people from coming too close. Fine when you want that distance, but not when you need to feel loved. After our chat, you, me and Emily when you were down – I shouldn't say 'home' anymore, should I, because I'm fast becoming aware you want up here to be 'home' for you. Anyway, I know I pushed you away and couldn't let you hug me for a while. That was because I was too raw. I needed time to let it all go, not to stifle it with comfort."

"Still perceptive."

"Yet I badly needed to be loved, comforted and held close, and I was comforted in the end when you continued to call me Abbie and we all three of us hugged. But afterwards, these past few days before I came here, I kept getting upset. I think there was so much more pain I'd been holding in. So I turned to Trevor to comfort me. As you know, ours has not been a demonstrative marriage. We've never been overly, or openly affectionate. We're happy enough, but not in a touchy, feely sort of way. I could sense he felt uncomfortable to be put in that position, though he did put his arms around me and try to be what I needed. Later, I told him I'd decided I'd like to be called Abbie again. No explanation, just a request. He shrugged and said, 'Okay!' but I didn't hold out much hope of it making any difference at all. But, surprise of surprises, it is making a difference. His tone when he addresses me is much softer. I like it. I'm becoming softer myself and I feel we will become closer, in a gentle sort of way through time."

Ruairidh had come through from the kitchen during this long speech. Abbie had noticed, but didn't seem to mind and went on with what she was saying without pausing. She simply smiled at him, acknowledging his presence and that it was okay for him to be there, hearing this.

He speaks now. "What a beautiful insight. Thank you for allowing me to share in it." He is visibly moved and holds out his arms to her.

To my surprise, she goes to him and accepts the comfort of the embrace, before turning to me to accept the one I also proffer.

To say I am moved is a gross understatement. I am wrecked. I feel I am receiving the comfort of the embrace rather than giving it.

To understand my daughter so much better after all these years, is beyond words.

My heart breaks for the little girl she was, for how she dealt with the situation she found herself in at only five years old, for the years she hung on to the protection of a name – it's tearing me apart.

Set against that is the joy of her readiness to accept and even bond with the man I love.

I feel I'm on shifting sand right now.

That feeling you get when wave after wave washes over your feet, taking the sand from under them as the tide withdraws, only to regather and surge over your feet again.

"Oh, Abbie," I say. "I had no idea your first day at school was so bad. I wish I'd known and could have helped you."

"But you did help me, Mum. The teacher, a rather stern lady who obviously was never a mother, instructed me to sit beside this boy, David, who wouldn't stop crying – probably couldn't at her sharp instruction for him to do so. 'See if you can make him stop crying,' she told me. I looked at the poor boy, sobbing his wee heart out and put my hand on his shoulder, as you so often did to me. 'It's okay, David. It's okay, I'm here now and I'll look after you.' Again, echoing your words so often said to me. I had noticed him in the playground before we filed into the school. He'd been clinging to his mum and she had a little girl in a pushchair who was also crying. It was a very moving scene and nearly set me off crying too."

"I remember them," I say. "I was worried they would upset you."

"So you knelt beside me and Emily in her pushchair and cuddled us both to you and told me what I then told that little boy in the classroom."

"Which was?" I shake my head. "It's so long ago I don't remember."

"I told him, 'We have to come to school so we can learn things to teach our mum and our little sister. Do you have a little sister?' He nodded. 'Well, if she's your little sister, she'll be stuck at home, too little to be here yet, and she'll be waiting for you to help her, to teach her what you learn.' He looked up at me then and stopped crying. 'Do you think so?' 'I know so,' I said. 'That's what Mummy told me and she never tells me lies.' As far as I know, he never cried about going to school again."

"Oh, my goodness! Is that really what I'd said to you when you started school?"

"Absolutely. I can remember it like it was yesterday. And, true to your word, you always asked me what I'd learned each day when I got home and you and Emily (and later Donna) always sat at the kitchen table with me, eating home-made biscuits and hanging on my every word."

"Oh, my goodness!" I take her in my arms again and remember how hard it was to let her go that first day of school, and how much I didn't want her to be unhappy. I remember it and I feel it again.

When we finally manage to compose ourselves and sit down to eat, it feels so much like a happy, comfortable family mealtime that I struggle to hold back my tears.

Abbie puts her hand over mine and smiles at me. "It's okay, Mum. Everything is going to be okay."

Ruairidh comes to me and gently wipes the few tears that have escaped with a fresh, clean handkerchief. I feel it soft on my face, soft and soothing, and remember the first time he did that, and I am comforted again.

When I can look up at him and smile, he smiles back and returns to the kitchen, leaving Abbie and me to sit close to one another, wordlessly telling one another we are entering a whole new phase in our lives, one filled with a new, deeper understanding and even more love, though I'd have thought that hardly possible.

Morning on the beach

I'd slept well, woken early, as is my habit now, and come through, made a pot of coffee and am enjoying watching the sunrise, as I drink from my favourite mug.

My mind goes back to our eventful evening at Ruairidh's last night. It seemed such a pivotal one for Abbie, but I wonder how she'll feel about it this morning. Sometimes, when you open your heart like that, it can feel embarrassing on reflection, especially when it's something you rarely, if ever, do.

"Morning, Mum," she says as she comes through to the kitchen. "Mmm! That coffee smells good."

"Plenty in the pot, love. Did you sleep well?"

"Like a log," she says, pouring herself a mug of coffee. "It's the sea air, I think."

"That and a long overdue release of tension."

"You look ready for some exercise," I say, noticing what she's wearing as she joins me on the couch. "I love your yoga pants and top."

"Yoga or Tai chi. I do one or other every morning. Care to join me?"

"Mmm! Nice idea, but I'm not really into martial arts, though I have been known to do some of the yoga exercises."

"Me neither. I only do both of them for the exercise. I find both of them great for keeping me fit in a very gentle way. And doing them at the start of my day makes me feel more focused and ready for whatever else I plan to do afterwards."

"I've never tried Tai chi. Is it difficult?"

"Not difficult but the exercises can seem complicated at first and can be a challenge. But when you get the hang of it, I think you'll enjoy it. I could teach you a few moves if you like." She smiles. "That would be fun, eh? What d'you think?"

"Well, okay. As long as you go gentle with me, remembering I'm an older lady."

Abbie laughs. "A pretty fit older lady, I'm guessing, with all the walking you've been doing, according to the texts you've been sending me."

I laugh too. "Walking and dancing! Did I tell you, Donna had me dancing along the beach when she dropped by recently?"

"That sounds like fun!"

"Oh, it is. I've been putting ear buds in and listening to music on my phone while I dance a little. At first, I thought I'd be too embarrassed in case anyone saw me, but the caravan park is pretty quiet now we're heading into autumn, and I decided I wasn't going to let it bother me if anyone saw me anyway."

"Way to go, Mum. I'm proud of you."

"Okay. You can teach me a bit of Tai chi – if we do it down on the beach – and as long as you are very patient with me. I doubt I'll be quick to pick it up."

"Deal," she says. "Though I suspect you'll do fine."

And what a delightful time we have. True, it doesn't take me long to get the hang of it, but we have a lot of laughter and fun until I do, and I'm surprised at what a great, patient teacher Abbie is.

"Oh, Mum," she says. "How wonderful to be able to do my morning routine on the beach. I've never felt so free, so uninhibited in my life. It's a real tonic." She takes the bottle of water I hold out to her and drinks deeply. "I know some folks do Tai chi in the Meadows. I've seen them. But I've always felt I'd be too embarrassed to make a public exhibition of myself like that, and I've no idea if I'll ever be able to exercise outdoors again, but I'm so glad I did today. Like you, I feel I'm coming alive up here."

"Good. I'm really pleased."

She's right, of course, she has achieved in one morning what it took me several weeks to achieve. Freedom to be oneself.

In my case, circumstances trapped me in a life and a persona not of my choosing. In hers, she trapped herself by shaping her life to immature choices.

The results were the same.

She lays back on the sand, star-shaped, with her eyes closed for so long I think she's fallen asleep. But no, she hasn't, and slowly and deliberately, she starts moving her arms and legs in and out across the sand, in and out, in and out, her arms reaching up beside her head and back down to her sides through the sand. She carefully gets up and looks down at the shape she's made. "Look, Mum. A sand angel."

I stand up to look down on it. "Oh, yes, it is," I say, laughing. "It really is."

"Do you remember we used to do that in the snow when we were kids?"

I laugh. "Yes, I do. You used to love it."

"You taught us that."

"Did I? Are you sure it wasn't your dad?"

"No, it was definitely you. I thought you were so clever. I remember being so impressed when you did it to show us how to."

"Did I really? Are you sure?"

"Positive."

And, suddenly, I remember.

I lower myself onto the sand again, the better to review the things whirling in my mind.

I did teach the girls.

Then I remember doing it as a child. My father taught me how.

A strange thing happens when you shut out painful memories. They take the good ones with them, holding tight to them as they walk out the door. My father could actually be fun, he could be kind and loving. I'd forgotten.

But I'd also forgotten I could be fun too. I had become so accustomed to thinking it was Bill who had all the fun with the girls, I'd forgotten I ever had.

I feel so grateful to Abbie for reminding me.

"I'm starving," she says, pulling me to my feet. "Come on, old girl. I'll race you to the caravan. First there gets choosing what's for breakfast."

And she runs off at a sprint, leaving me far behind to bring the empty water bottles.

As it happens, neither of us gets to choose what's for breakfast, because Ruairidh is there waiting for us, kettle on, croissants warming in the oven with slices of brie and avocado ready to go in them.

Fish 'n' chips for old times' sake

"So what's it to be, girls? A walk on the beach or a forest walk in Skelbo?" Ruairidh says after breakfast.

We look at one another and with one voice say, "Ooh! Let's go for the forest walk for a change."

"Skelbo, it is then. And I'll treat you both to lunch in Golspie afterwards."

"You're on," says Abbie.

It turns out that Skelbo Forest is a fun forest, with chainsaw-carved woodland creatures here and there along the trail.

"Forrest would love this. I can't understand why we never came here before," says Abbie.

"Me neither. We often drove this way en route to Golspie, but never visited here. I've no idea why."

We walk on for a while.

Then I remember!

Bill wasn't keen on forests or woods. There was something about trees and their environs that always started off his asthma. 'Nervous asthma,' he told me. 'There's something sinister in the way trees whisper,' he claimed. Personally, I'd always found it friendly and soothing and often longed to whisper back, sharing my secrets, just as they shared theirs.

Ruairidh and Abbie lead the way, happily engrossed in conversation, with me lagging behind to give them the opportunity to get to know one another better, so I take the opportunity to whisper my happiness to the trees.

It's a forest full of interesting twists and turns, with some lovely open views, nice points at which to pause, which we always do, admiring the view and taking delicious wood-scented deep breaths.

We come across the remains of an Iron Age broch, giving Ruairidh opportunity to delve into that part of Scottish history, and me the opportunity to watch how his eyes light up and his face beams with pleasure while talking about a subject he is passionate about.

I look at Abbie while he shows her the different parts of the broch outlined by the rocks with which it had been built. I can see she's loving his enthusiasm as much as the information.

Even some impressive drystone walls we come upon have history, it seems.

The walk itself is fairly easy, with the climb up to the ruins of Skelbo Castle offering the only smallish challenge.

"Well," declares Abbie, when we get back to the car. "Thank you, Ruairidh, that was delightful, and next time I'm in Embo with Trevor and Forrest, I shall happily bring them here. I think they'll love it and they might even be a little impressed that I can point things out to them on the way round."

"Always a plus."

After three or four minutes driving from Skelbo, on the way to Golspie, we pass the Loch Fleet viewpoint.

"Ah, we've timed it well," says Ruairidh, drawing into the viewpoint lay-by.

And he's right, there are loads of seals basking on the sandbanks and some others slithering into the water, while others climb out. We watch for a while, until Abbie confesses, "I've never much liked watching seals. They always remind me of giant slimy slugs, and I have no liking for them when I come across them in the garden."

"Funny you should say that, I'm not that fond of them myself," I agree. "Do you remember your dad always stopped here when we used to go to the Golspie chippie."

"I do, and he always made it seem fascinating. I was just plain bored, but Donna seemed to love them for some reason. Either that or she was sucking up to Dad."

We all laugh and move on.

"What's your opinion on seals, Ruairidh?" Abbie asks.

"To be honest, as a fisherman, I'm rather fond of them. They're a pretty accurate indicator of where the fish are plentiful. However," he adds, looking over at Abbie and grinning. "From now on I'll only ever see them as giant slimy slugs." He pulls a totally disgusted face and wipes his hands, one after the other, on the legs of his trousers, as he drives. "Yuck!"

As we near Golspie, he looks at his watch. "You mentioned the chippie in Golspie. That's one of the places we could choose to lunch in, if you like."

"Ah, now that would be lovely, but to really remind me of my childhood, we'd have to eat them out here, in the car, out of the brown paper." She looks at Ruairidh. "How preciously do you guard the interior of your car?"

He laughs. "For you, as long as you don't actually throw the food about, I reckon I can cope with the all-pervasive smell of fish and chips for the week it'll probably take for it to wear off."

"Aw, Ruairidh, you really don't have to," I say, leaning forward from the back seat and putting my hand on his shoulder.

"That's okay," he says. "You can help me clean the car out later." He winks at me in the interior mirror.

Abbie laughs. "Fish 'n' chips it is then." She turns round in the seat to address me. "I'm helping you out, you see, Mum. Now, among everything else you know about Ruairidh, you know he's a good sport."

Before we open our warm, deliciously smelly brown paper packages, Ruairidh suggests we drive the couple of minutes down near Littleferry, to have a nice view while we eat.

It turns out to be a great idea, because, although the tide is not still sufficiently low for us to go looking for the skeletal remains of the old Embo fishing boats, Ruairidh gives me the joy of explaining what I remember about why the fishermen burned them there.

The fish and chips turn out to be even better than remembered and we thoroughly enjoy them sitting outside at a conveniently placed picnic table in the delightfully natural carpark overlooking the Sound of Fleet, a little before Littleferry itself – respect for Ruairidh's car being paramount, despite his sporting gesture for us to eat in it.

"Why Littleferry?" Abbie asks. "Did there used to be a ferry from the village? Where did it sail to?"

"Yes, there once was a wee, or 'little', ferry which ran from the pier in the village across the narrow channel of Loch Fleet, to a wooden pier on the other side. When we've finished eating, I'll take you down into what is a truly 'little' village to see the pier on this side and you will be able to look across at the remains of the one across the water."

"Was it a long sea crossing?"

"As you'll see, it was a very short one, but it would have saved a considerable distance for people to travel round the whole loch back then. It's nothing for us in the car, but a lot if you're walking or pulling a cart."

"Well, that was scrumptious," I say, licking my fingers before dipping into my handbag for some wipes, which I share with the other two. "I don't know about you guys, but I doubt I'll want much for dinner tonight."

"Me neither," says Abbie. "I'll make us a salad later, if everyone's okay with that."

"Not for me," says Ruairidh. "I have a date with a clootie dumpling tonight." He grins and rubs his tummy. "If I can squeeze a slice in, with custard, of course."

I laugh. "Nan?" I ask.

"Who else."

While we walk back to the car, I explain to Abbie that, once a week, Ruairidh takes Nan, his neighbour, to visit her hubby, Gerry, in the care home in Dornoch.

"And she usually makes a clootie dumpling to take some in for him, and saves some for me when I drop her off afterwards."

"Yummy!" I lick my lips.

"Yeah, hers is always rather good!"

"Lucky you," Abbie says. "Mind you, it sounds like you deserve it."

Littleferry delights Abbie, with its pretty white-washed houses and it's ancient stone pier. Once pointed out to her, she can see the skeletal remains of the old wooden pier across the water. "It's incredibly peaceful," she says, looking out to the water.

"And very sheltered," I agree, enjoying the lack of a cool sea breeze and the warmth of the sun on my face.

After we leave Littleferry, Ruairidh takes us back to Golspie to a delightful wee coffee shop for a cuppa to wash down our chips.

Both while we're having it and all the way home, I delight to see how well the two of them are getting along together, and when Ruairidh drops us back at the caravan, as we wave him off, Abbie leans against me and whispers, "A keeper. He is definitely a keeper."

Future security

As I walk up the caravan steps, Abbie's words ring in my ears. 'He's a keeper.' And that's the third or fourth time that phrase has been applied to my Ruairidh. By his neighbour, Nan, by his friends at the ceilidh and now by my own daughter.

That knowledge has been there in my heart for weeks and I smile to myself as I unlock the caravan, wondering when I started thinking of him as 'my' Ruairidh.

"Can I show you something?" I ask Abbie.

I take down my sketch pad and flick through the many sketches of the anchor and of Ruairidh I've enjoyed making, as well as various others.

"Oh, Mum, how wonderful. I had no idea you were such a great artist."

I laugh. "Neither did I. It's something I used to enjoy when I was in my teens, but thought I'd probably lost. Since being here, I've found many of my old passions still bring me joy. And, as you know, I've found a new passion too. My Ruairidh." I turn the sketch pad over and open the back pages. "And I want to show you that I have not just let myself dance to the tune in my heart, but I've carefully considered my steps." I show her the various tables I made, the pros and cons I considered, the things I weighed carefully before allowing the music in my heart to become the music of my whole being.

"Oh, Mum. I hardly know what to say. This is amazing. When you told me about Ruairidh, I knew in my heart you were a sensible woman. I know I said some terrible things. I know I inferred you were being made a fool of.

But I was taken by surprise. In my heart, I think I knew deep down you could not be made a fool of so easily – you are far too wise to allow that to happen, but the sudden revelation of your life up here shook me to my core and I couldn't accept it right away." She shakes her head. "I never imagined you being with anyone else after Dad."

"I know, love. I know."

"I can see Ruairidh's a lovely man now I've met him." She taps the pad. "And this is proof positive of what I suppose, on some level, I knew to be true."

"Thank you, darling. It means a lot to me to know you have faith in my judgement. Especially because it has all happened so quickly. And I know it *has* happened quickly, but when you know, you just know. It's a bit like looking for a new pair of shoes. When you try on the ones that truly fit and are exactly what you need, you don't walk away just because it was the first pair you tried on. When you know, you know." I laugh. "The funny thing is, I wasn't even looking. In fact I never for a moment thought I could fall in love again."

"To continue with your analogy of the shoes, you went up on your toes, tried a little jump, wiggled your feet this way and that to make sure they remained right for you in various circumstances." She pats the pad again. "This is what this was. You made absolutely sure before you committed to the shoes, and absolutely sure before you committed your heart to Ruairidh. I see that now."

I nod and smile. She understands. My girl understands. How precious is that? "Something else I think you girls should know – before we get married …"

"Yes! I knew it! He's asked you already, hasn't he?"

"Yes, he has." I blush, remembering a few evenings before Abigail was due to arrive.

I was nervous and Ruairidh took me in his arms to reassure me everything would be alright. He lifted my head up and kissed away my tears, then kissed me long and passionately. 'Please,' he said. 'Will you marry me? My life is meaningless now without you. It's becoming harder and harder to leave you each night. I toss and turn in my bed, waiting for the morning light, so I can be with you again. Every thought I have, I wonder what you'd think of it. Every food I put in my mouth I wonder if you like it. When you smile, my heart skips a beat, when you cry, I want to have the right to kiss away your tears. Please, my dearest Eilidh, will you marry me?'

'You had me at the first, "please". Oh, yes please,' I said, clinging to him as I want to for the rest of my life.

"You're blushing, Mum. I take it you said 'yes' then?"

"Absolutely!"

Abbie pulls me to my feet and hugs me. "I'm so happy for you. So, so happy for you." And she dances me round the room, almost making me forget she's Abigail and I'm not cavorting around with Donna.

"You were saying ..." she says once we collapse onto the couch to catch our breath. "You started to tell me something about before you and Ruairidh marry."

"Yes, he was very insistent that before we get married, everything should be worked out as he feels it should be, so we've already been to see the solicitor in Dornoch for me to make a will, making sure your inheritance is well protected. In other words, all my savings, the money I get when I sell the house, everything will be equally divided between you girls. He insists nothing will go to him. On the other hand, if anything happens to him first, everything will come to me and will be added to your inheritance."

"Wow!"

"We are maintaining our own separate bank accounts, and have opened one joint account into which our pensions will be paid each month, giving us a current account from which to work on a day to day basis. As you probably know, I have a generous pension through your dad's work. That will go into that account. And any money

Ruairidh earns from ceilidhs and such will be added to that joint account along with our pensions."

"This is amazing."

"Ruairidh never wants there to be any doubt in anybody's mind that he is marrying me for anything other than his love for me." Ruairidh's love and assurances are overwhelming sometimes, and I feel so blessed. Doubly blessed now, to know that my precious oldest daughter approves of the match.

What the future looks like

"And now, down to business. I know you've been looking and thinking things over, so let's see all these prospectuses you brought with you. We've talked about how my future is shaping up, let's see how yours might shape up."

So we pore over the catalogue prospectuses for various colleges, offering various courses in various subjects. "See what I mean? It's totally overwhelming. I don't know where to start."

"Let's start by making pros and cons and lists of likes and dislikes." I draw her as yet empty note pad towards me. "Likes and dislikes? A decent enough place to start." I mark out the columns. "So, are there any subjects on this page that you know you would not like to do?" We study a list of what one college offers. "And any that you might fancy."

She takes her pen and starts crossing subjects off the list, without bothering with the columns I've made. I smile to myself, realising that the old assertive Abigail is still very much alive and will do things her way, thank you very much.

There are very few subjects with a positive tick beside them.

We move on to another prospectus and she does the same. And the same with the others she brought.

"Okay," I say, having written the ones she ticks in each catalogue in the likes column on her pad.

She studies the list I've made. "Hmmm!" And she starts going through it, crossing some subjects off. "Too much studying required." Scored through. "Too intellectual." Another crossed off. And so it goes on until we are left with a handful of courses.

"Do you notice what these all have in common?"

"That's it, isn't it? You clever woman. Doing it this way has exposed the fact I really don't want to be very studious, do I? I want to be active. Creative, in fact." She looks down the shortened list. "Art, music, gymnastics, dance ..." She thumps the flat of her hand on the pad. "I know what I want to do! I want to learn to teach Yoga and Tai chi." She searches back through the prospectuses to find who offers such courses, but isn't much taken by any of the ones that haven't already started.

"You know, it doesn't have to be a college course. Why don't we look online, for who else does classes?"

"Yes! You're really on fire, here, Mum." She pulls her phone out of her pocket. "This one looks good. Mind you, so does this one."

"It's great there are several in Edinburgh that look right for you. Now you know what you want to do, why not look at their websites, and even phone them up and ask about what they provide and see if you feel you'll fit in to what they're doing, before you decide on any one of them."

"Great idea. As I said, on fire!" She offers me a hand to high-five, which I do, chuckling softly at her liveliness, delighted to see the difference in her from the way she's been since Bill died.

"Right." I get up. "While you're doing that, I think I'll go through to the bedroom and phone Emily. She sounded a bit tearful when I phoned her before. I think she's upset you made it up here to meet Ruairidh before she did."

"Oh, my fault. She couldn't make it soon enough for my impatient soul, so I booked myself on the train and came. I think she thought we might come together." She pulls a repentant face.

"I already explained all that, but she was rather distracted with Chiara, who was crying copiously about some slight she'd suffered at pre-school." I look at the time on my phone. "Hmm! Chiara will be home again now – hopefully not crying this time but playing happily so I can get a proper chat with Emily, to see when she can manage to come."

While I'm waiting for Emily to answer her phone, which keeps ringing out for ages, there's a knock at the caravan door, and when I open it, there she is.

I look to the phone in my hand, then at the one ringing in hers, and burst out laughing. "I don't believe it. I just don't believe it," I say, gathering her into my arms. "But how did you know where I was, which caravan I mean?"

"I knew it was on the front so I looked for your car." She escapes from my hug into Abbie's. "Oh, I hoped you'd still be here. This'll be fun. Okay if I bunk with you?" she asks her sister. "I mean, I know there's a whole other bedroom lying empty, but ..."

"Great! Roommates! Just like old times." Abbie grins.

"Are you on your own? How did you get here?" I ask.

"I drove myself all this way," she says, with a delighted grin. "I'm so chuffed. I left the kids with Bryan."

"Oh, is he at home just now?"

"Well, if you wouldn't mind putting the kettle on and making us a cuppa – I'm absolutely gasping for one – the one I had in Aviemore was pretty disgusting – then I'll tell you what's been going on down our way, if you tell me what's going on up here."

"Deal," I say, putting the kettle on.

"I'll take your bag through to our room, sis."

"Oh, thanks, Abigail."

Abbie stops, with her hand on the handle of Emily's trolley bag. "Actually, I know this is going to seem weird, but I've decided I'd prefer to be called Abbie now."

Emily shrugs. "If that's what you prefer, then so be it. I'll call you Abbie. I actually prefer it. It sounds more friendly, sisterly, even."

Abbie smiles. "Which is why the change. Mother has waved her magic wand and given me a whole new outlook on life, never mind the glass slippers."

When the tea is ready, we sit ourselves down and Emily tells us her news. "Well, I think Mum waved that wand over us too." She laughs. "You asked if Bryan was home this week, which he is, but Bryan has decided he's going to be home every week. After chatting up here, with you, then talking to Bryan about my fears and suspicions, he's decided to hand in his notice. He's leaving the orchestra so he can work from home with me. He was intending to still go to orchestra rehearsals, for a while, but there really is no point, because he'll not be with them for the next performance."

'You say he's planning to work from home. What does he plan to do?"

"He's going to join me, offering music lessons. He used to be great on the flute, but hasn't played it for a while, so he feels he might be a bit rusty. Once he feels his playing is up to scratch, he'll be able to offer clarinet and flute lessons."

"You'll soon have a right wee music school, sis."

"That's certainly the long-term goal."

"Wonderful. I'm really happy for you, love." I get up to hug her.

"After your last phone call," she says when we both sit down again. "When you said you were staying up here, I just wanted to be here and Bryan said to come. We have two cars – something we'll be able to save on now he's home for the kids, and he and Francesca are covering my lessons."

"That sounds like a great arrangement."

"It is. He'll be able to practice the flute and keep up with clarinet practice too, while the kids are at school, in between taking the lessons already booked in for me, which, at the moment, are mostly piano lessons. He's great on the piano, so no problem. Francesca will pick up on the violin lessons after school. So it's all worked out. And here I am waiting to meet this boyfriend of yours. I phoned Abigail, I mean Abbie, sorry, hun."

"No bother. On you go with ratting me out." Abbie puts her hands to her face, covering her eyes.

"So you phoned Abbie? Of course you did," I say. "What are you two like?"

"Sisters?" Abbie suggests.

I laugh. "Okay." I sigh in resignation. "On you go."

"I phoned Abbie last night and she told me Ruairidh's lovely. Bryan reckoned he'd seen you talking to an older gentleman when we first arrived, and then again a few days later, so we did wonder. Was that Ruairidh?"

"Yes. It was."

"He sounds great, your Ruairidh. I'm dying to meet him."

"And you're okay with it?"

"Of course I'm okay with it. If you and Abbie are sure he's okay, I can't imagine I'm going to hate him."

I look over to Abbie.

She shakes her head, and gives me a look of encouragement.

I take a deep breath.

"I was just telling Abbie, Ruairidh and I plan to marry soon."

"Oh, wow. So now you need to fill me in on anything else Abbie hasn't got round to sharing."

So, I show her the pages at the back of my sketch pad and tell her about the bank and the solicitor.

While I'm bringing her up to date, Abbie gets to work making us a delicious salad to go with the bread and cheese, Emily had thoughtfully brought from my favourite Edinburgh deli. There has not been much I've missed since being here in Embo, and though there is a small deli in Dornoch, I miss the larger ones in Edinburgh with their enormous choice of products from all over the world, so it is a treat to have my favourite breads and cheeses tonight.

To round off a full and delicious day, Ruairidh arrives later in the evening with clootie dumpling and custard for us to warm up for supper. Since I had alerted him to the fact Emily had arrived, he even had enough for her too. "But no more for me," he says with a laugh. "I feel like I'm turning into one." He pats his stomach and puffs his cheeks out.

He greets Emily in the same way he had greeted Abbie, drawing her in for a warm hug and a kiss on the cheek, much to Emily's surprise and delight.

"Oh, it's great to meet you Ruairidh, I've heard so much about you."

"And I you," he says. "Now tell me, I've been wondering this ever since your mum told me you teach music, how do you get on teaching violin?" He pulls a face. "Such a wonderful instrument when well played, but can be a dreadful instrument in a beginner's hands."

"Oh, I so agree," she says. "But Mum tells me you play the fiddle. Is that not the same?"

"Like a cat being strangled, my father described it when I was a wee boy learning to play."

"And Mum says you also play the accordion."

"Like ten cats being strangled, my father said when I took it up." He laughs.

"I've never tried to play the accordion, but I've had a try using my violin to play like a fiddle – with some success, but not a lot. Tell me, I know the instruments are basically the same, but have you modified yours at all to make it easier to get the fiddle sound."

"By and large," says Ruairidh. "Fiddling is simply a different form of playing."

"True."

Ruairidh nods. "Fiddlers often use alternative techniques, such as string bending and extended double stops and triple stops."

"Where two or three strings are bowed simultaneously."

"That's right," he says, then looks at me. "This lass knows her music," he says, clicking his tongue in admiration.

"I've noticed sometimes fiddlers hold their instruments differently, too. Is that to accommodate their playing style?"

"Aye, oftentimes, you'll find fiddle players prefer to rest the palm of their left hand against the neck, and maybe hold the bow a bit up on the stick instead of at the frog."

"I get it. I think I've noticed that too."

"Aye, a skilled fiddler and a skilled violinist are simply two different breeds of musician."

Emily's turn to nod in agreement.

"While the primary difference is in playing style, you're right in what you said earlier, sometimes there are tangible physical differences between the violin and fiddle. For instance, what is your violin strung with?"

"Mine? With gut, but some of my pupils use synthetic-core strings."

"Exactly. Fiddle players more often use steel strings, because they make a sharper sound."

"Is that what you use?"

"I do indeed, lass."

"Are there other modifications fiddlers make?"

"Some flatten the curve of the bridge to make double stops easier or cut the bridge lower for easier action since, as you'll know, a flatter bridge decreases the angle between strings, making it easier for fiddlers to play two or more notes at a time, an asset for the fast nature of fiddle music."

"That all makes sense," Emily says, her brow furrowed in thought. "No wonder I find it hard to reproduce the sound. I've learned a couple of reels, but they just don't sound as good as I know they can be."

"I'll show you my fiddle, and let you try out your reels on it when you come for dinner tomorrow evening." He looks up at me. "You will all come to dinner tomorrow, won't you?"

"Of course. We'd love to, wouldn't we, girls?"

"And you'll bring your violin and we can compare the two," he says to Emily.

"What makes you think I've brought my violin?"

He leans in closer to her. "Because you are a serious musician, and would never dream of being somewhere without the wherewithal to play every day."

She laughs. "True."

He stands up. "So, ladies, I shall love you and leave you tonight and I'll pop by for breakfast in the morning, if that's agreeable?"

I nod.

"Then we can enjoy a morning walk on the beach, or at least, everyone who's up for it." He turns again to Emily. "Especially you, lass. You and I have a lot of getting to know one another to do." Then turns to Abbie. "No disrespect to you, my dear, but your sister is behind in the exercise, despite our musical chat tonight, which I trust you will excuse us the indulgence."

"Of course, Ruairidh. I found it fascinating, having always assumed a fiddle and a violin were two completely different instruments." Abbie shakes her head. "There, they do say you learn something new every day, and that's just one of the new things I've learned today. Thank you." She gives him a hug.

"Nice." He nods. "And you, my dearest," he says to me. "Now, you know me too well and we probably have nothing more to talk about, tomorrow or any other day." He pulls a face, his eyebrows raised high, his lips pursed, and throws his hands in the air in a gesture of surrender.

We all laugh, and continue laughing as Emily also gives him a hug, and I see him to the door. In fact, I can hear the girls still laughing and talking when I step outside for my goodnight kiss. Ruairidh is so right. It is getting harder and harder to have to go our separate ways every night.

When I eventually close the door, after waving him off as he weaves through the caravans, the girls are already in their pjs.

As she gives me a goodnight hug, Emily says, "Oh, Mum, he's a delight. Along with everything you and Abbie have told me about him, he's also such fun and such a gentleman. He's definitely a keeper."

Music al fresco

Once again I waken in time to watch the sunrise. I'm enjoying this new routine that appears to be establishing itself; enjoying a deep, refreshing night's sleep, with an early morning rise. I try not to have too many cups of coffee through the day, especially later in the day, which is possibly what helps me get such a good quality sleep at night, but I do enjoy this early morning coffee while I watch the sunrise. It's a great time for reflection.

"Morning, Mum." Emily is the first of the girls to show her sleepy face this morning. "Mmm! Smells good through here." She lifts the pot and smiles. "Okay if I help myself?"

"Go for it, love. Did you sleep well?"

"Best sleep ever." She curls up in the corner of the couch, sipping her coffee.

"Good morning, good morning, we've slept the whole night through. Good morning, good morning, to you," Abbie sings as she comes to join us. "Or words to that effect," she says, pouring herself a coffee.

"And good morning to you, sis. You always that bright in the morning?"

Abbie laughs. "If he could see me now, that old man of mine," she sings. "Dah-dah-dah-da-da-dum-deda-da-dah-dah," she tails off, pulling a face that has us all laughing. "In other words, Trevor would be amazed if he saw me now, up with the lark and ready to go." She indicates her exercise wear. "You up for it, girls?"

I explain to Emily that Donna got me dancing on the beach when she was here, then Abbie taught me some

Tai chi down there too, and we've been getting great benefit from the fresh air exercise.

Emily pulls a face. "I'm no dancer, but I'd happily join you on the beach. I could even play for you while you exercise, if you like." She smiles and mimes playing the violin.

"Hey, live music al fresco! Fantastic! Right, soon as you're ready, you two. Let's go!"

With Abbie's urging, Emily and I go and get suitably dressed, and we all head for the beach.

I lock the caravan and hide the key on top of the front tyre of the car.

"Ah! I did wonder how Ruairidh got in the other morning," Abbie says, tapping the side of her nose. "Clever!"

"Saw it in a film." I smile.

Once down on the beach, Abbie and I do some fun stretches while Emily tunes her violin.

And we're off!

Emily plays a medley of violin pieces, some of which I recognise, some of which are new to me, while Abbie leads me through the Tai chi moves I learned yesterday, then begins to incorporate them into dance-like moves in keeping with the music.

Moving north, towards Loch Fleet, there is a gorgeous long stretch of firm, wet sand, perfect for dancing along. As we travel a little that way, with lovely, long, easy steps, Emily walks along with us so we don't lose the reach of the music. When we turn to dance back along towards where the caravans start overlooking the beach, Emily moves back with us, and I notice with a smile she's not so much walking as swaying.

At last, Emily plays a long, last chord and we all take a bow, surprised to hear a scattering of applause. It seems we have gathered a small but enthusiastic audience, watching from outside the caravans up on the balconies and the grass overlooking the beach.

"That was magic," Emily says as we walk back to the caravan. "Pure magic. Dad would have loved to have seen that."

Abbie puts her arm round her sister as she walks. "Sorry to burst your bubble, sis, but he would have hated it."

"Why on earth would you say that?" I ask, somewhat shocked she would say something so unkind about her father.

"Because he didn't instigate it, nor would he have been the centre of attention. Dad loved fun times, but only when he'd planned it and all eyes were on him. Did you never realise that?"

I had. But I had no idea any of the girls had.

Emily stares at her for a moment, then turns to me. "Sorry, Mum, but Abbie's actually right, now I come to think of it. He would have gone for a walk to hide his huff and missed all the magic."

"Exactly, sis, and thank you for providing the music. That, dear sis, was the real magic."

I am dumbfounded.

All the years I had tried to protect them from the truth when their dad went into one of his huffs, never realising that they knew.

They knew the reality and loved him anyway, just as I did.

I shake my head as I follow behind the girls as they laugh, discussing the merits of the magic, and whether it was in the al fresco music or the 'dancing' Tai chi.

For me, the most magical thing of all is when I look up, and there at the top of the stairs, is my lovely Ruairidh, wearing the biggest, proudest smile you can imagine. Turns out, drawn by the music, he was there to watch almost our whole performance and was one of our appreciative audience.

“Beautiful,” he says, giving me a hug. “Magical and beautiful. And I couldn’t be prouder of you. I can’t believe my luck that you’ve agreed to be my wife.”

He doesn’t seem to have noticed anyone else on the beach. Nor does he mind that he wasn’t part of it and it clearly didn’t bother him he was not at the centre of it. It was probably not something that would even cross his mind.

But I noticed and stored the realisation in my heart.

Foggy day, but clear thinking

The next morning, if there was a sunrise, which logic tells me there must have been, I certainly didn't see it. And not because I wasn't here, sipping my coffee in time.

Thick fog must have rolled in off the sea sometime during the night, obscuring that luminary whose rise I've been enjoying every morning.

However, the coffee is still good and I've had time for reflection before the day starts in earnest.

When we were saying our goodnights, last night, after a delightful long phone call to bring Donna up to speed, Ruairidh asked if I'd like to be thinking about a date for our wedding – keeping in mind that we have to give the registrar at least a month's notice – and also what kind of wedding I want us to have.

So that's what has happily occupied my mind this dark grey morning, and I'm hoping he and I can winkle out a wee bittie time on our own to discuss it, not so easy with the girls here to meet him and spend time with us.

When I go through to my room to get dressed, I can hear the girls talking as they lie in the two single beds and I smile. It's been a very long time since the two of them shared a room and I always did love the sound of their chatter.

I'm especially happy to hear it now, because I want to go down to the beach alone.

I dress quickly and leave them a wee note on the table to let them know where I've gone so they don't worry.

There is something very special about walking through mist or fog. For one thing, it deadens all sound, allowing you to believe you are the only living being awake this morning, something I find oddly comforting.

When I come to the anchor, despite hardly being able to discern it through the mist, I stand for a while, remembering.

Memories crowd in on me, some from a good number of years ago when we used to holiday here when the girls were young, some from only a couple of months ago.

It was a good place for children. Bill had everything planned. He became their playmate. His time off work had become all about the children for those few weeks each year, and he truly gave them all his attention till the evening each day, then he and I had a little time to talk over the day and plan the next.

I smile.

Those were good times.

My smile widens as I think back a few months to meeting Ruairidh here.

"It's nice to find you smiling to yourself," Ruairidh says as he catches me up in his arms and swings me round.

"That's not fair," I say, laughing. "You sneaked up on me. I didn't see or hear you coming because of the fog."

"That was the point. Once I detected you were happier than the first time I saw you staring at the anchor, I decided it would be fun to catch you off guard with a sneaky hug."

"Anytime. Always up for a hug."

As we stroll back along the beach, we take the opportunity of time alone to decide on a provisional date for the wedding, what sort of wedding we both want and also where we want to live when we're married.

When Ruairidh asks me that last question, he prefaces it by saying we have limitless free choices. "I can sell my house and we can move to Edinburgh to be near your family."

"No thanks. I'd rather sell my house and live up here."

"Or I could sell my house and we could look for another that had never been just mine, anywhere you like."

"Oh, Ruairidh." I take his lovely face in my hands. "Thank you for your thoughtfulness, but there really is nowhere else I want to live but here, in Embo, and I love your house. I long to make it my house too. Our home."

He kisses me. "Well, if you're quite sure …"

"I am."

"I mean, you've already started the process of making it our house rather than mine, because, did you notice, the living room is decorated in the colours we'd chosen together when we looked through the catalogues?"

I turn and kiss him. "Of course I noticed, and I look forward to us sharing that process for all the other rooms."

"Then that's easily settled."

Easily settled too is what sort of wedding we want: small, family only at the registry office in Dornoch, followed by a glorious ceilidh up in Helmsdale a few weeks later, for family, friends and all who are drawn in by the music.

The dates we decide to keep provisional until we've consulted the girls, the availability of the band members, and what date is possible at the registrar's.

"Unfortunately, I can only have the caravan till the park closes for the winter, which is the end of October. After that, I'm afraid it will have to be a long-distance relationship, with you popping down to Edinburgh, if and when you can. Abbie has already offered to put you up any time you're there."

"Well, that's kind of her and yes, I can go up and down to Edinburgh quite happily whenever the ceilidh commitments allow. I actually have some in Edinburgh early December."

"Great." I sigh. "I'd far rather stay up here, but there, it won't be forever till I can."

"True. But leave it with me. I have an idea."

"Oh?"

"As I say, leave it with me."

"Breakfast time?" I ask as we near the beach stairs.

"The makings are all there on the kitchen table, waiting for us."

"And I'm sure the girls must be up by now. I left them lying in their bedroom laughing and chatting. It was lovely."

"Yes, I saw the note you'd left them, but no sign of life yet in the living room, so I tiptoed back out, after adding to the note, telling them to touch that bag of breakfast things at their peril."

"Hehe! I bet they'll love that. It's probably well hidden by now."

"Ah! Hadn't thought of that."

No show without Punch

As we near the caravan, it becomes apparent the girls are up and having some sort of carry on. There is certainly plenty of laughter.

The moment we open the door, the source of the hilarity becomes abundantly clear.

"Hello, Mumsie. How d'you like my hat?" Donna bounds towards me wearing a court jester's costume including a long pointy hat with a bell at the end, which she takes delight in making ring by jumping up and down excitedly. "As soon as I knew my sisters were visiting, I decided there is no show without …"

"Punch!" all three of them shout together, whereupon they all collapse in laughter, rolling about on the couch.

I turn to go back out the door. "I think we must be in the wrong caravan." I laugh. "There seems to be a bunch of kids in this one." Which, of course only serves to increase the hilarity.

Donna extricates herself from the other two and launches herself at me, encasing me in an enormous hug. "Oh, Mumsie. I've missed you. And you, Ruairidh MacRae." She drops me and launches herself on Ruairidh instead.

By the time we're able to get properly into the caravan, things are calming down a little – not a lot – a little.

"We've been drinking your delicious coffee," Donna says. "Can you guess?"

"Ah, that's what's got the three of you high."

"It's all Donna's fault. She arrived here when we'd already had a cup, made a fresh pot for you guys, and went to get dressed. When we came back through, we found someone hiding behind the curtain."

"We could, of course, see her stripy legs and funny pointy shoes peeping out from under the curtain." Emily takes up the story. "But, when she jumped out and said, 'Boo!' Dressed like that, well what else could we do but fall about in confusion."

"And have another cup of coffee."

"What they didn't at that point realise is that I had been drinking coffee most of the night with Owen, to keep him awake as we drove all the way up from Cornwall."

I laugh. "So you're well and truly wired."

"And none of us have had anything to eat yet."

"Because we waited for you guys to make it."

Once again, that seems to be enormously funny and the three of them collapse in a heap again.

"Oh, dear," says Ruairidh, with the biggest grin. "I'd better get to it then. Bacon rolls, egg rolls or both?" He takes the makings out of the bag he'd left on the table earlier when he came to find me. He takes the order and sets about making it.

"So when we told her last night we were both here …" Emily starts.

"Owen and I hooked up the caravan, jumped in the Land Rover, and drove all night."

"As you do." Abbie shrugs.

"We'd just finished a very successful week's run of our adaptation of Punch and Judy, down in St Ives, so I had the costume ready …"

"So if you are Punch, please tell me poor Owen isn't Judy?" Ruairidh asks.

"Don't be silly. He's the postman who delivers the baby to Mrs Punch – which happens to also be me." Donna pulls a face. "Funny thing is, you never see Mr and Mrs Punch together, till right at the end."

"And, dare I ask, how that is accomplished?" I enquire.

"While the audience's attention is on the lovely big box, in which the baby is hidden, who, by a clever sleight of hand and curtains, is also Owen, he has already inveigled one of the dads in the audience to don my Punch costume, which is, of course, far too small for him, adding to the children's delight when he appears onstage to help Judy open the box."

"Oh, it sounds like a whole lot of fun."

"It is, and it goes down ever so well with the audience. Some of the kids came back every day. The mums like it because there is no cruel stuff as in the original nasty version."

"Oh that sounds really charming," I say.

"And, as I said right at the outset ..." She holds her arms wide, palms up.

"There is no show without Punch!" we all say together, while Donna sweeps off her tinkling hat and takes a bow.

Three little girls, sitting in the backseat

...

It's fun having my three daughters sitting in the backseat of the car. So much like old times.

I felt a little apprehensive that the girls would find it uncomfortable, even distressing to be in the car with me sitting beside Ruairidh instead of their dad, but I'm relieved when I get no sense of that.

"Are we nearly there yet?" Donna whines from the middle seat, just as we drive out of the caravan park.

"Mum, tell her to move over a bit," Emily says. "She's squashing me."

"It's not fair. Why do I have to sit in the middle?" Donna whines again.

"Will you two stop wriggling," Abbie orders. "I'm trying to read."

Ruairidh laughs. "Is this really what it was like?"

"No," I say, also laughing. "It was so much worse. At least they didn't start the reenactment until we were underway. They left out all the arguments of who sat where before we even got in the car."

"And the argument over whether we can have the windows up or down," Abbie says. "We really scored today because it's raining."

"Ah! Every cloud has a silver lining." Ruairidh laughs. "Who'd have thought the rain could keep the peace."

"What was it like growing up as the youngest of eleven, Ruairidh?" Abbie asks.

"Well for starters, we never had a car. Athair had a truck, but there was only room for him and two others in the front, and it was filthy and stank of fish all the time, so no one was fighting to go with him just for the ride when he was delivering fish. It would usually be him and one of my older brothers who went as his helper."

"Athair? Was that one of your brothers?"

He laughs. "No. Athair is the Gaelic equivalent of 'Dad'. Our family were all Gaelic speakers at home. It was only at school and places like that we used English, or as my athair called it, the Sassenach tongue."

"So you are totally bilingual."

"I suppose so."

"Impressive. Gaelic sounds such a hard language to learn, but I suppose when it's your first language, it would be the English that would be hard to learn."

"Not so bad, though, when you learn it young, as we did. We grew up with the two tongues. So not really that impressive."

"Oh, I still think that's impressive," Emily says. "I tried to teach my three Italian and English as they learned to talk, but it didn't really stick. Possibly because they heard far more English that the smattering of Italian I introduced them to."

"Oh look, there's loads of seals over on the sandbank today," Donna says.

"I really don't know why you get so excited over ugly giant slugs!" Abbie pulls a disgusted face.

"Aw, but they've got such cute wee faces," Emily coos.

Donna leans forward, poking her head in the middle between Ruairidh and me. "Is there time to go to Littleferry to look for the boat skeletons?"

Ruairidh looks at the time on the car's clock. "Sorry, the tide will be too high by now. We'd have had to leave a bit earlier."

"Sorry, my fault." Donna holds her hands up. "But I didn't think it was quite the done thing to meet the future outlaws in fancy dress. I thought we should show up as nice, sensible girls, at least till they get to know us better."

"Fair enough," I say. "Besides, I wouldn't like to keep Bonnie and Fingal waiting. I'm laying odds there'll be fresh scones timed to come out the oven as the car draws up." I laugh.

"Yum!" is the chorus from the back seat.

I think it's actually Ruairidh who starts the singing. All I know is it got started and is accompanying us all the way up to Helmsdale. Every time someone thinks of a suitable song, they sing the first verse, then everyone else joins in, which doesn't work when Ruairidh sings in Gaelic, except when he sings songs the girls and I know in Scots, such as 'Flow'r o' Scotland', 'The Bonnie Banks O' Loch Lomond', 'Will Ye No' Come Back Again?', and 'Wild Mountain Thyme'.

The girls insist he sings more Gaelic songs, even those they have never heard before.

"You have such a great voice," Emily says. "And the songs sound so beautiful."

"Often the better for not being understood," he replies. "Since many of them are laments for someone special who has died or gone off to the Americas, never to be seen again."

The journey passes in no time at all and is thoroughly enjoyable and entertaining.

And I'm right about the scones. The smell curls round our taste buds as we enter Fingal and Bonnie's cottage, cheese scones, fruit scones, blueberry scones and plain scones, all served with lashings of hand-churned butter and home-made jams and chutney. The smell alone makes us hungry.

But before we sit down to eat them, we have all the introductions to make. Thankfully the house is not filled with relatives, just Fingal, Bonnie and Mhairi, who is almost deaf and doesn't add much to the noise level once we all start talking and laughing while we tuck into

Bonnie's delicious scones, which actually manage to taste even better than their amazing smell.

Without being asked, Abbie butters a scone as Bonnie instructs, takes it to Mhairi and sits beside her to help her enjoy it and feel part of the happy company.

When Fingal learns that Emily plays the violin, he fetches his fiddle for her to compare.

"Oh, I see you have made similar modifications to those Ruairidh has made to his."

"Has he gied ye a try on it?"

"He has, but it feels so different in my hands when I'm playing it."

"Aye, I daresay it will that, lass. But we'd fair enjoy to hear you, if ye feel ye could play us a wee bit music ye're familiar with. We promise we'll allow for the different feel in yer hands if ye mak a wee mistake or two."

After a little more coaxing from everyone, Ruairidh in particular, Emily accepts the challenge, stands up and says she'll play 'Flow'r o' Scotland', if we all sing along to it.

Finding herself playing better than she thought she would, she goes on to play a couple of popular songs we can have a go at singing along with her.

"Aye, yon's fine," Fingal says, applauding her. "But now, I'd dear like to hear ye play a wee bittie o' a sonata or two."

Bolstered by everyone's encouragement, she plays part of Beethoven's Violin Sonata no.1, followed by one of Mozart's shorter pieces. She plays them beautifully before declaring herself finished. "Phew!" she says. "I'm amazed I was able to do that, especially without the piano accompaniment, but I'm afraid it's exhausting adjusting my style all the time." She hands the fiddle back to Fingal. "And now, please, will you play this fine instrument the way it should be played."

So the party spirit continues, first with Fingal playing, then Ruairidh. I can't help feeling 'meeting the family' is going swingingly, reels and all. Any apprehension has been well played away and when the playing's finished, the conversation flows just as freely.

By the time we are ready to leave for home, we have eaten our way through most of Bonnie's scones and the delicious fish pies and veg she also produced for dinner, as well as managed to set a provisional date for our wedding that suits the girls as well as Fingal and Bonnie, the most important members of our families we decided to have with us in the registrar's office. Thankfully, everyone present is happy with those arrangements, which was, after all, the main business we hoped to accomplish on this visit.

But we have accomplished so much more.

The girls are delighted to have met that small section of Ruairidh's family and feel totally at home with them.

"Oh, we've had such a great time, Ruairidh," Abbie says. "Thank you. This has been a most memorable day."

"But now, I hope no one minds if I fall asleep on the way home," Emily says, patting her full tummy.

"Me too," Donna echoes. "The thanks and the sleep. I do hope you're good and strong, Ruairidh. We three girls may well need carried in from the car. Night!"

Ruairidh's left hand seeks mine and gives it a squeeze.

Nan

The caravan feels very quiet and empty after the girls go home. It was so amazing to have them all here together. A bonus to have them without kids and spouses. Although, technically, Owen was here, he mostly left us to our own devices while he slept, then serviced and sorted out the Land Rover and caravan for the winter months before joining us for some of the shenanigans.

They were all here for almost two weeks and we had a great time. They even persuaded me to hire bikes and go cycling with them. I suggested they go without me, but they were insistent and swore they'd look after me, which they did.

It turned out I was not a good cyclist and I think their patience was sorely tried. Hills were a no-no for me and at the slightest incline, I was off the bike and pushing it, with them waiting for me to catch up, apart from Owen, who took it upon himself to help me each time, waving Ruairidh to go ahead with the girls.

Downhill was not a lot better. It involved a lot of tense screaming and squealing of brakes all the way down.

Ruairidh called our route, 'pretty flat' and I suppose it was, to them.

To me, I felt I'd cycled in the Alps.

Now the girls and Owen have gone, things are set to return to a more peaceful, probably less fun, state.

For a wee change, since the weather has been a bit colder, windier and wetter, Ruairidh has invited me to breakfast with him, so after my sunrise coffee, I dress warmly and walk up to the village.

When we've eaten, Ruairidh asks if I would mind popping in to see Nan next door, which is fine by me. I haven't seen her for a wee while and she's delightful company.

"Yeah," he says. "She's been a bit down lately. Gerry seems to be getting worse and is not usually even sitting up when we get there. Sometimes the nurses manage to help him do so in the bed, but it's become more like a hospital visit than a care home visit."

"Poor Nan."

"Anyway, she asked if she could have a chat with you."

"No problem." I look at my watch. "Is it too early for her, do you think?"

"No, she tends to be up fairly sharpish and I heard her letting the cat out the back earlier."

She is delighted to see me when she opens the door and ushers me in to sit down, without preamble, starting a long excited monologue all on one breath as she goes ahead of me. "I was just telling Eddy on the phone, that's my son, I was telling him the other day that I was a bit lonesome with his dad in the home, and he suggested I take in a lady companion, a bit like having a lodger except I could do with some help around the house too, so more like a home help, only not quite, because Ruairidh does the hoovering for me and any heavy lifting."

I didn't know that, and am very touched to learn it.

"I wasn't sure about it and asked Ruairidh what he thought, and he was telling me you might be interested. He says you'd need to be looking for somewhere once the caravan park closes for the winter, if you're looking to stay up here."

"That's right, I've started looking already."

"Now, I'd feel better about hiring somebody if it was you. I feel I know you, him next door talks about you that much. What d'you think? Would that suit you? I've got the room. Eddy's old room it was. We decorated it when he got married and went to Australia, thinking it'd be nice for him and his wife when they came back over, but they've only been a couple of times in all those years so it's not been much used. I'd really appreciate the company."

"I'd love to be your companion/lodger/home help, Nan. Whatever you need. Thank you."

"Because it would suit me well to have someone here, especially at night, I wouldn't want to charge you as a lodger because you'd be doing me a favour."

"And I wouldn't want to be paid as a home help, because you'd be doing me a favour too, but I'd want to contribute for things like food and gas and electricity."

Waving the suggestion away, "We can talk about that when we see if it works out okay," she says. "When would you like to move in?"

"Well, I'm booked in the caravan till the end of October, when they close, so how about after that?"

"Perfect. That'll give me time to freshen up the bedding and make sure everything's tickety boo in the room and everything."

"I could help with that. I wouldn't want you to be changing the bed and heavier things like that."

"Oh, him next door helps me change my bed every week. I'm sure he'll be delighted to do it in the spare room, your room, for you." She laughs. "I told you, he does the heavy stuff." She gives me a wink. "He's a good 'un you've found there, lass. Kind."

I smile. "Oh, I know. You told me when I first met you that he's 'a keeper'."

"Aye, and he is too."

"Oh, Nan, it will be so lovely to stay with you. I really do want to stay up here for longer and wondered how I'd manage to. Staying with you will be perfect because I'll be able to experience what it would be like to live in Embo during the winter as well as the summer."

"D'you think you might marry him next door soon, if you don't mind me asking?"

"Well, we have set a provisional date, to be confirmed when we speak to the registrar, but staying here will give us time and space not to rush." I give her a hug. "I'm so grateful to you. Thank you."

"Not at all, lass, it's me should be thanking you."

My temporary housemate

A few days after the girls went home last week, I followed them down to Edinburgh to see if there was anything else I needed to bring up for the winter, along with anything I was going to want to keep from the house in Edinburgh. Also to consult with them about making arrangements for the house itself.

Everything I need from the Edinburgh house has been gathered, collected and transported into my new home. The Edinburgh house we intend to let out furnished on a six-month lease, with Abbie as its factor. We decided not to sell it because, looking long-term at it, we realise it could be converted into a music, drama and keep-fit studio when the three girls are ready to embark on such a joint venture.

The things I have up here have been packed and unpacked into their temporary home in Nan's cottage. All that's left are my few overnight things from last night, which I've popped into the small rucksack I've slung over my shoulder. My car is already parked in the lane behind Nan's house.

There is nothing left for me to do but close up the caravan and take a walk on the beach, my last time as a holiday resident. I look around the caravan that has been my home for several months now. It has served me well. I've loved staying here, though as winter sets in, I have to admit I'll be happy to have a well-built stone cottage round me and a strong roof over my head.

So I lock the caravan door and hand the key in up at reception, before I walk down to the beach.

There is a chill wind today, and a drizzle of rain, so I have the beach to myself, something I'm well used to these past weeks of autumn into winter.

At the bottom of the steps, I take several long, deep breaths, put up the hood of my anorak and head towards the anchor, where this fantastic adventure all started.

However, I don't get far before the rain becomes a bit of a torrent and I head back towards the stairs and up through the caravans to Nan's.

"I'm afraid I'm soaked through," I tell her. "I hope you don't mind."

"Put your coat over this chair, here." She takes the coat from me and puts it over the back of a kitchen chair, which she then draws to the fire. "Eh, we'll get a nice wee steaming from this till it dries." She laughs. "Fair reminds me of when Gerry was still working on the fishing boats."

"Oh, I didn't realise he was a fisherman."

"Yes, we bought this cottage when first we were married just after the war. The fishing didn't last long here after then, though, so I didn't have that many days of stinking, wet clothes." She laughs again. "At least yours'll smell sweeter as the steam rises. But you must be hungry for your breakfast, lass. I doubt you stopped to have some in the caravan today."

"No, I didn't."

"Right, well I've got some mending to do for Gerry, so in you go and make yourself well acquainted with the kitchen while you fix yourself something to eat." She picks up some clothes. "He picks, picks, picks at the hems of his jumpers when he's sitting up, you see." She holds one up for me to inspect. Sure enough the hem at the front has been picked at until it's unravelled at the bottom. "Aye, well, I doubt I'll be mending for him much longer. He rarely sits up by his bed these days." She shakes her head. "Or even on the bed. But, on you go, lass, don't wait for me to stop blethering or you'll starve."

As I walk into the kitchen, she shouts after me, “I’ll take a wee cup o’ tea while you’re making one.”

I smile, realising how fond I’ve already become of this lovely housemate of mine.

Eilidh's wedding

On a cold, wet, January day, my wedding day, I decide to take one last walk on the beach after breakfast, before I am a wife instead of a widow.

Mrs Eilidh MacRae.

I thrill at the thought.

My girls and their husbands and children will be already ensconced in Dornoch Castle Hotel: Abbie no doubt checking everything is ready for the marriage ceremony this afternoon and the family meal afterwards; Emily having a last violin practice of the tune she plans to play for my grand entrance on Abbie's arm, and Donna dancing and singing about the place, because there is no way her rising excitement will allow her to be still. Hopefully Owen can manage to stop her taking off into the stratosphere, and Bryan and Trevor can similarly keep rein on the children's excitement.

I'll join the girls soon, to share a light lunch with them before we all go to Abbie and Trevor's room – the three husbands hiding elsewhere, probably in Bryan's room with all four children.

Our wedding clothes will be laid out on Abbie's bed, waiting for us to get ready, including the beautiful soft, cream suit the three of them helped me choose on our shopping trip in Edinburgh just after I moved in with Nan. The skirt, a floaty chiffon that skims my knees, because the girls tell me I still have 'fantastic legs' and should let them be seen for a change instead of encasing them in old jogging trousers or long floaty summer dresses. I have to say, it feels wonderful when I walk across a room and it brushes my legs. The jacket is a beautiful matching cream silk, as is the camisole underneath. Cream silk low-heeled shoes complete the outfit. I don't think I've ever worn anything so glamorous before.

Neither have I ever before enjoyed a shopping trip with all three of my girls which centred solely on me. They made sure of that by having shopped for their outfits the week before. I was very moved when Emily explained they thought it was high time it was about me, after all the exhausting shopping trips I'd had to endure over the years when the trip was all about one or other, or all three of them.

Ruairidh and I had driven down together and he did his shopping while I did mine. He already had a kilt, but decided he must have a new one to mark the occasion. He suits a kilt and I am looking forward so much to seeing him in this new one, which is one of the Ancient Hunting tartans and mostly blues and greens. The girls tell me they have seen it and matched their outfits to blend well with it, and they have tied a ribbon of the same tartan around my small bouquet of red roses.

He and Nan will arrive at the hotel later, in time, of course for the ceremony, which the registrar is happy to conduct in a beautifully prepared room in the hotel, but also in time for Nan to check in to the room we have booked for her for the night. She was so thrilled to be invited to our small family wedding, and thrilled again to learn we had booked her a room. Like the girls, it had been her desire for a long time to have the luxury of staying there.

I'm guessing Fingal and Bonnie will have booked in yesterday and be enjoying their few nights of luxury too.

Bonnie told me she baked us a wedding cake which I'm dying to see, knowing there will need to be plenty of photographs of it because I'm looking forward just as much to eating it. She has already shown herself to be one of the best bakers I have ever encountered, thanks, she assures me, to the fact she uses so many home-grown ingredients. She'll have milked her own cows 'round the back', churned it to the butter she used, and skimmed off the cream she used.

I can't help wondering if she'll be able to entrust it to the kitchen staff at the hotel, or if she'll proudly produce it when we gather for the meal.

Ruairidh's great niece, Jenna, her husband and her mum will be there too for the ceremony and the meal – her mum promising to look after wee Angus if the evening proves too much for him.

All of this I go through in my mind as I sit sipping my morning coffee in Nan's kitchen, hardly believing this day has finally come. I chuckle to myself because I don't suppose anyone else would think 'finally' a fitting adverb for a six-month courtship, from first meeting to wedding day, but it feels a long time to me because I knew as soon as I set eyes on Ruairidh, he was someone I wanted to stay close to and keep in my life.

Anchored in Embo

After finishing my last breakfast as a widow, I head for the beach. As I walk past the caravan I have not occupied for a while now, I give it a gentle tap on the side. A 'thank you' tap. It served me well as a harbour from which to set sail for new adventures. I pause for a moment at the fence in front of it, as I have any time the weather has permitted me to enjoy a walk these past couple of winter months, to remind myself of its view of the beach.

It's too far towards Golspie to have a good view of the anchor, which worked to my advantage when I was getting to know Ruairidh the first week I was here with the family. It became so much more than an old anchor sunk into the sand, it became our usual meeting place.

On the way towards it today, I relive in my mind the numerous happy times I've walked this beach, danced on this beach, swum in the North Sea and run up this beach to get warm again, knowing I'll be able to repeat all these wonderful adventures time and again, because I'm now a resident in the village of Embo, hardly a stone's throw away.

Already on half-decent early mornings, we dress warmly, wrap ourselves in cosy rugs to sit on our folding chairs on the beach, sipping coffee from the flask Ruairidh makes up and from our favourite mugs, watching the sun rise majestically over the water.

Ruairidh and I plan not only to take regular beach walks but also regular swims. We also have some cycle rides planned – something I look forward to with slight apprehension, since I was decidedly wobbly and a bit cautious the last time, much to the girls' amusement. Before that, I hadn't cycled since I was a wee girl. But I know there is a saying that 'it's as easy as riding a bike', so how hard can it be to retrieve that skill too, just as I've retrieved so many others since I've been here?

When I think of my bulging sketch pads and the tiny painting studio Ruairidh has set up just off the kitchen, where he used to store all sorts of things that are now in the garden hut, I want to dance along the beach, rain or not.

So I do.

I skip and dance, with no need for music because there is so much in my heart.

It's been a fabulous six months, crammed with so much fun and laughter, learning and discovery. Much, much more than the three stagnant years before.

The grief had been severe for too long. It's true it had softened a little over time, but the outpouring of it on this beach showed it was not properly healed. Now it is. Now, when I think of Bill, it is with fondness and gratefulness, never with sadness.

When I reach the anchor, I stand to share my thoughts with it. I stand because it's now raining fairly steadily and the rocks I used to sit on are soaking wet, while I'm hoping my anorak is keeping my bottom dry.

It's been a while since I first sat here, feeling all adrift, lost at sea. I laugh at the memory of my desperate attempts at what Bill called, 'blue sky thinking', as I tried to see a future, any kind of future that was going to be worth living for. Not that I planned not to live, but there is 'living' and 'living', one of them being more like 'existing', the other being what I found here, a future to look forward to with happy anticipation. Staring at the anchor helped ground me then, and it does again.

I'm well aware that Bill is asleep in death, 'conscious of nothing at all' according to the scriptures, so he can't see me, hear me, or know what is happening in my life, something else I find very comforting. What a tortuous thing it would have been for him to watch the depth of my grief and despair for three long, bleak years. I shudder at the thought, imagining how terrible it would have been if he'd been able to watch, helpless to comfort me, and I thank God, no one has to go through that.

But I like to think Bill always wanted and worked for my happiness, so I feel no guilt at reaching out for great happiness again.

Although there is no one to say goodbye to, I feel the need to close the one chapter of my life, before embarking on the next one, and that's why I've come back to stand and look at the anchor, to remember the past, be thankful I had forty years of happy marriage to look back on, and prepare my mind and heart to move into the future that awaits me.

I smile again, remembering that it was Ruairidh who found me, and rescued me from shipwreck. When I was awash with tears and sinking under overwhelming waves of grief and pain, he looked after me, led me to a safe harbour, here in Embo.

I laugh at my allegory. It's true, he did lead me to a safe harbour, but it's funny too, because Embo, in reality, has no proper harbour. It was a fishing village with no harbour at all for a long time. Now what there is of a pier and harbour is old and broken down with not much left of it to shelter any vessel.

But I found my safe harbour, and here he is, with impeccable timing, walking out of the rain and mist towards me, carrying a huge umbrella to hold over me.

I remember being impressed by his gentlemanliness the first time he helped me to my feet. No need for that help today, because I didn't sit down, so instead he takes me in his arms, where I stay for a long time, sheltered from the worst of the rain.

"I thought I'd find you here. Good morning, love," he says, smiling. And there it is, that smile. Such a warm, caring smile. The first thing that made an impact on me when I met him.

I remember other things from those early days too. Things that thrilled me at the time. I smile. "I was just remembering how you sang the song with the same name as mine. You sang it to me back then in Gaelic when we introduced ourselves to one another the first time we sort of met properly."

"I remember."

"You never did sing it to me in English, you know. And you said you wouldn't until you knew me much, much better."

"I remember."

"Will you sing it for me now?"

He looks at me, as we stand there, getting wetter by the minute, the rain fair bouncing off the umbrella. "Really?"

"Really."

"One verse, okay?"

"Only if you promise to sing the whole song to me in Gaelic and then English some other, more clement time."

"Soon. I promise."

He hands the umbrella to me and stands back a little to sing to me, right there, on Embo beach, in the pouring rain.

"The way is long to island glen and shieling
The climb is steep o'er heather, crag and moor
But soft the tear of longing, Eilidh darling
For mem'ry's kiss in Laggan by the shore.
Your hand in mine and promise to be waiting
In sea-girt isle where living vows were made
Your heart will ever guide my spirit sailing
To Tir-nan-og where love can never fade."

"Oh, it's beautiful, Ruairidh. Thank you." I kiss him tenderly and he kisses me back. We stand, clinging together as though we are drowning in the rain.

When I share that thought with him, Ruairidh tells me, "No, my dear one, not drowning. We are saving one another."

Saving. Yes.

These past months have taken me from despair to hope. From shipwreck to safe harbour.

And now I'm anchored here in Embo.

I smile at the thought.

'Anchored in Embo.'

The End

Just a Note

If you have enjoyed reading Anchored in Embo, it would be great if you could tell others about it and/or leave a review of this or any other of my books on either

Amazon kindle: http://author.to/ChristineCampbell

Or if you prefer paperback books:

FeedaRead: https://feedaread.com/profiles/786

Recommendations and honest reviews of my books are the most powerful tools to help bring them to the attention of other readers, so I'd be very grateful if you could spare a few minutes to leave one. It can be as short as you like.

And if you have any questions about the inspiration for this, or any of my other books, or about my writing in general, please don't hesitate to get in touch.

You'll find me here:

Facebook Group

Lifting The Lid Off Christine's Kist Of Stories:

https://www.facebook.com/groups/199853890760414

blog: https://cicampbellblog.wordpress.com/

Pinterest business account:
https://www.pinterest.co.uk/ChristineCampbellAuthor/

Thank you so much.

Published in 2024 by FeedARead.com Publishing

First Edition

A CIP catalogue record for this title is available from the British Library.

Printed in Great Britain
by Amazon

61203733R00211